WHISTLEBLOWER

INSPECTOR WEST

PETER MULRANEY

This is a work of fiction. All characters and events, other than those clearly in the public domain, are the products of the author's imagination, and any resemblance to actual people, living or dead, is coincidental.

Copyright © 2017 Peter Mulraney

Cover image: Drew Hays on Unsplash

ISBN 13: 978-0-6481046-9-8

This edition published 2018.

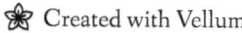 Created with Vellum

To those brave souls that risk all to expose wrongdoing -
Whistleblowers.

MAJOR CRIMES TEAM

DCI Rankin (Chief)
DI West (Carl)
DS Fuller (Harry)
DC Beard (Nigel)
DC Paterson (Wayne)
DC Templar (Lisa)

SUPPORTING OFFICERS

Dr Jonas (Mike) Pathologist
Sgt Lang (Dean) Forensics
SC Head (Charlie) Uniform
PC Chan (Lily) Uniform
PC Monks (Adam) Uniform
PC Priest (Jane) Uniform
PC HighlandCommunity Liaison

CHAPTER 1

On the Tuesday before Christmas, the board members of the Walker Group gathered for their final meeting of the year. As chairman, Peter Walker sat at the head of the table in the boardroom on the top floor of the group's head office on East Terrace.

Seventy-year old Peter Walker, with thirty percent of the group's shares, was the majority shareholder. He'd started the company in his early twenties, building sheds and warehouses, and had grown it into one of the most successful property developers in the country.

The board usually followed his advice on which projects to pursue, given his track record, and the fact that his connections still held enough shares to represent the majority in any vote, especially when his ex-wives followed their usual practice and voted with him.

To Peter's right sat Mario Imbroglio. Mario had a twenty percent holding in the group, acquired as part of the finance package he had brought to the table when the group was facing insolvency at the height of the global financial crisis, when the banks had stopped lending.

Next to Mario sat Warren Hunter, who owned a fifteen percent interest. Warren had been with the company from the start as its accountant. He'd found ways to finance Peter's dreams and had been rewarded with a significant stake in the company.

Opposite Mario, with his back to the window that opened on to a vista of the hills that stood on the eastern rim of the city, sat Dustin Walker, Peter's grandson. Twenty-five year old Dustin had inherited a ten percent interest in the group following his father's death in a skiing accident the previous year. Dustin did what his grandfather told him to do when they met for lunch before each board meeting started.

Next to Dustin sat Monica Webb and Rachel Foley, Peter's first two wives, who held twenty-five percent of the group's shares between them, thanks to their divorce settlements.

Peter shuffled the papers in front of him and took off his glasses, before placing them on the table. He looked across the table at his ex-wives. 'I've decided to retire.'

'As chairman?' said Monica.

'No, Monica. I mean retire as in stop work. I've been doing this for almost fifty years. I want to enjoy myself for a bit before it's too late.'

'You're not thinking of asking Dustin to take over the business, are you? He's only a boy,' said Rachel.

'Dustin and I have had a long chat. He's not ready to take on that sort of responsibility.' Peter looked down at his hands. 'Things would be different if James was still alive. I'd planned on handing things over to him when I was ready to retire but, well, you know why that won't be happening. So, I've had to make other arrangements.'

'What other arrangements?' said Rachel.

'I'm selling to Mario.'

Peter watched the color drain from the faces of Monica and Rachel as they realised the impact of what he had said. He enjoyed witnessing their consternation bubble to the surface and repaint their faces with the red of anger. He hoped Mario would screw them like the bastard had screwed him. 'We wouldn't be here if it wasn't for Mario's intervention when the banks wouldn't help us. I've given him first option, and he's made an offer I'm prepared to accept.'

'That would give Mario fifty percent,' said Monica.

'Sixty, actually,' said Dustin.

His grandmother and her successor turned to face him.

'You don't have to sell just because your grandfather tells you to,' said Monica. 'I don't think your father would be pleased with that decision.'

'My father's not here, Grandma, and there are other things I can do with the money.'

'When is this happening?' said Monica.

'As we speak. The papers were signed yesterday. I'd like to congratulate Mario on becoming the chairman of the Walker Group.' Peter stood and offered his seat to Mario.

'No need to be that formal, Peter, but thank you anyway.' Mario faced Monica and Rachel. 'I'd be happy to make you the same offer I made Peter and Dustin.'

'What about you, Warren?' said Monica.

'I've accepted Mario's offer,' said Warren, without looking up.

'And, what is your offer, Mario?' said Rachel.

Mario opened the folder on the table in front of him and slid a sheet of paper across the table to her, and then slid one to Monica. 'I think it would be best if you signed before you leave. That offer will not be on the table after today.'

———

Mario Imbroglio moved into what had been Peter Walker's office during the first week of January. He'd been a board member of the Walker Group for six years, ever since the opportunity to insert himself into the business had presented itself during the global financial crisis, when he'd introduced himself to James Walker after receiving a tip-off that the group was in financial trouble.

The big banks had withdrawn from the financial facility backing one of Walker's multi-million dollar projects when the group's cash flow had suffered a sharp downturn. Mario had also been aware that James' father, who controlled the group, had been living beyond his means for several years. The man's ego was insufferable but Mario had been trained to manipulate the egos of powerful men.

After constructing a financial package with his backers, who were keen to find legitimate businesses for their money laundering purposes, Mario had persuaded James Walker to introduce him to his father as the group's saviour, as the one who could pull them back from the brink of bankruptcy. His price had been a twenty percent stake in the business.

The old man had called him every name under the sun. He'd even threatened to disinherit James for bringing someone like Mario into the boardroom. But, in the end, he'd signed. His ego couldn't face the prospect of bankruptcy and the exposure of his personal failings as a businessman.

Mario had joined the board and studied the way Peter Walker did things. He didn't like the old man but he admired his way of doing business. Walker seemed to be able to create money out of thin air, provided he had the backing of someone's money to finance his dreams. Mario was particularly amused when he learnt that one strategy the Walker Group used was to build office towers for gold-plated government tenants, sign contracts with the tenants to clean their offices, and then sell the buildings to superannuation funds, who liked the regular income government tenants provided. The group would then build another office tower in another city and repeat the process.

Over the years, Mario had developed a successful working

relationship with James Walker, who had been slated to take over the business when Peter retired. But the Walker world had changed when James met with an accident during a skiing trip to Austria. The old man hadn't been the same after his son's death. He'd lost interest and within a year had offered the business to Mario and his backers.

He'd told Mario he didn't have the time or patience to school Dustin, so that he could take over the business, and confided that it was probably just as well, since it was always the third generation, the grandchildren, that squandered a family's fortune. Mario had reflected on that comment in light of what he knew, and concluded that Peter Walker was blind to his own failings and the cost of his extravagant lifestyle.

Mario's backers were delighted. They liked the diversity of the group's interests, which included ownership of two shopping malls, that would provide them with numerous opportunities for laundering their black market money.

By the time Mario had taken control of the group, several of his lieutenants, including Trevor Hunter, were already holding positions of influence within the group. He knew he'd have to keep the core group of executives in the property development division in place, the people who knew how to turn Peter Walker's dreams into reality, but there was plenty of scope for expanding into operations that Peter Walker would never have considered, not even in his wildest dreams.

Peter Walker's last useful role, prior to his retirement, had been to introduce Mario to his friend Richard Nelson, the Minister for Recreation and Sport. Nelson was another man with a big ego, which Mario planned to massage during negotiations to build and operate the city's second casino.

Mario looked at the final plans for Long Street on the desk in front of him, and decided it was time to start working on the Minister.

CHAPTER 2

ON THE LAST Friday in April, John Drake sat at his desk in The Office of State Supply reading the agency's whistleblowing guidelines, for what must have been the fifteenth time, waiting for four o'clock. John was convinced he was doing the right thing but he was also aware of what often happened to whistleblowers, despite all the words in the Act.

He also knew it was too late to regret looking at things he hadn't been asked to investigate, even though he wished he hadn't let his curiosity get the better of him during the slow period around Easter, when he'd started opening folders on the share drive and reading the contracts behind the payments he administered.

Initially, he'd thought it would be interesting to know the specific terms and conditions in the individual contracts. Then he'd decided it would be useful to understand the agency's procurement policies and guidelines, since the agency was charged with getting the best value for the government's dollars when buying products and services.

When he'd noticed that some of the more expensive cleaning contracts hadn't been awarded to the companies that had submitted the most competitive tenders during the last round of contract reviews, he'd looked into the companies those contracts had gone to, and found a pattern of common ownership.

Aware that contract reviews were conducted by a three person committee of senior officers, that included Sonya Curtis, the head of the agency, he knew there was no way he would be confronting any of them directly. He was intimidated by every one of them, especially Sonya Curtis, who was known among officers at John's level as 'The Bitch'.

John knew he had to tell someone or he wouldn't be living up to his obligations as a public servant. After a week of anxious deliberation, he'd decided to escalate his concerns to the Auditor General, which was one of the options available to him in the whistleblowing guidelines. But, because he would be reporting senior officers, he'd decided it would be prudent to discuss his concerns with Pam Watson, his immediate supervisor, just to be sure he hadn't misunderstood something.

At four o'clock, he put two copies of the document he'd compiled into his bag, picked up the third copy he'd printed for Pam, and walked over to her office.

Pam smiled as he sat down with the document in his lap. 'So, what's on your mind, John?'

'I'm not sure how to say this, but it looks like we might not have done the right thing when awarding some of the big dollar cleaning contracts.'

'Oh? What makes you think that?'

John shifted in his seat. 'Well, I thought I'd read some of the contracts I administer, so I had a look on the share drive. I ended up reading some of the tender documents, you know, to see how the whole process works.' John could feel beads of perspiration forming on his brow. 'Anyway, I reviewed the documents associated with the cleaning contracts I administer, and it looks like several of those contracts went to companies belonging to the Walker Group, even when they weren't the most competitive tender.' John looked up. 'We're supposed to accept the most competitive tender, aren't we?'

Pam leant back into her chair. 'Do you realise what you're suggesting?'

'Yeah, that's the scary bit. If I'm right, it looks like we have a problem at the top. You know who's on the contracts committee, don't you?'

'That's a pretty serious allegation to make, John. And, it's not like you're experienced in these matters, is it? You've only been here a few months.'

Those words hit John like a backhander across the face. He stared at Pam. She didn't intimidate him like the others.

'I've been working in contracts administration for at least ten years, Pam. It's what I was doing at Transport before I came here. I think I know what the rules are and I've studied the guidelines we're supposed to be following, so I think I know what I'm talking about.' John paused to regain his composure. He didn't want to start an argument. 'Sometimes a fresh set of eyes sees things that others have missed, but,' he held his hands up in front of him, 'I could be wrong. That's why I thought I'd better discuss it with you before taking my concerns any further.'

'Wise decision, John. So, what have you got there?'

'It's all in here.' John passed her his document and watched the color drain from her face as she scanned its contents.

'I don't have time to study this now but I'll read it and get back to you as soon as I can. In the meantime, I want you to keep this to yourself. If you've read the whistleblower guidelines, which I hope you have, you'll know they offer you no protection if you leak anything to the media, even if you're right.'

'I intend to stick with the guidelines. Wouldn't look too good if I didn't, would it?'

'If I agree with your findings, this will have to be escalated to the Auditor General. On the other hand, though, John,' Pam flashed him a smile, 'if I don't agree with your interpretation of the data, I'll be advising you to drop this. I'd hate to see you make a career ending mistake simply because you misinterpreted something outside your area of responsibility.'

John felt the wind being sucked from his sails. The tone in her words, along with her body language, told him he wouldn't be getting any support from her.

'Look, you've done the right thing bringing this to my attention.' She looked at her watch. 'I'll catch up with you on Monday, after I've had a chance to study this.'

John returned to his desk and decided that talking to Pam hadn't been the mistake he'd thought it might be. She obviously didn't want him to take his concerns any further, despite her words of support, but the look on her face when she'd scanned the report had told him what he'd wanted to know.

While he packed up his workstation, he decided to post a copy of his report to the Auditor General on the way home, and live with the consequences.

―――――――

Pam slipped John's document into her briefcase and watched him pack up his workstation and leave for the weekend. She admired him for wanting to know about the contracts he was administering. That was more than any of his predecessors had done. But, she wished he hadn't been so inquisitive. Now they had a problem they would have to deal with before he did anything. She hoped to God he'd do as she'd asked him and wait for her to get back to him.

As John walked past her office on his way to the elevator lobby, Pam picked up her personal smartphone.

'Sonya, we have a problem.'

CHAPTER 3

ON THE FIRST Monday in May, DI Carl West was in his third floor office scrolling through the emails in his inbox. There was nothing terribly exciting: a reminder from DC Lisa Templar that she was on the pursuit drivers course this week, another from DC Wayne Paterson about being in court, and one from DCI Rankin, officially allocating DC Wayne Paterson and DC Nigel Beard to his team following DI Reid's early retirement.

Carl smiled when he read the chief's email and thought of his wife, DS Nina Strong, the other member of DI Reid's team, at home on maternity leave, expecting their first child in about six weeks, if their dates were right.

He gazed out of his office window across the rooftops of the southern side of the city and wondered how she'd managed to talk him into becoming a father. His own father had been killed in Vietnam before he'd been born, so he'd had no modelling of what a father was supposed to be like. He'd been reluctant to take on the role, not sure that he would make a good father but, somehow, she'd persuaded him that he'd be good at it, pointing out how he'd mentored Harry and Peter James before him, and how his cousin's children thought the world of him.

His thoughts turned to his maternal grandfather, who'd been

like a father to him after his mother had taken ill and they'd moved in with her parents when Carl was in his early teens, and was the main reason Carl had become a policeman. Carl knew his grandfather would have encouraged him if he'd still been alive; he'd believed in him.

His attention settled on Peter James. He thought of Peter every day. He'd been standing next to Peter the day he'd been shot and killed when they'd gone to interview a suspect in a rape case. He hoped his child would not have to face what Peter's children were living with.

He took a deep breath. He knew he couldn't change history but that didn't mean that history didn't exist. He pushed down the reminder that was always just below his conscious awareness whenever he thought of Peter, that he'd also killed a man that day, and turned his attention to the overnight incident log. It was filled with the usual fights and disorderly behaviour stories. Some idiot had set fire to three bins outside the railway station, and a young man had been knifed in a drunken brawl in front of the Merlin on North Terrace. He thought there was nothing out of the ordinary until he noticed that another homeless man had been found dead inside 7 Long Street. That was the second one in a week.

The phone on Carl's desk rang.

'Got a minute, Carl?' said Mike Jonas, the police pathologist.

'What's up?'

'I've just finished the post mortem of the homeless guy they brought in from Long Street last night.'

'Another overdose?'

'That's my problem, Carl. I don't think these guys are druggies. I know the lab report says the body we picked up last week was full of high grade heroin and alcohol, and I suspect this one might very well be the same, but there's only one needle mark on his body. If he was a user, he'd be marked up like a pin cushion.'

Carl got the feeling he wasn't going to like where this was going. 'What are you trying to tell me, Mike?'

'I double checked my notes from the autopsy of the one they brought in last week. There was only one needle mark on his body as well.'

'Do you think they could be first time users?' said Carl.

'I guess that's possible, but it's also possible someone injected these guys while they were comatose, given the amount of alcohol in the bloodstream of the first guy.'

'Better send me your reports when you're done, Mike.'

Carl called Forensics and asked for whatever they had collected from Long Street when the bodies had been picked up and taken to the morgue. If they'd followed protocol, Forensics would have at least photographed the bodies and the location, even if there had been no apparent signs of foul play.

He dialled DCI Rankin's number.

'Chief, I've just been talking with Mike Jonas. He doesn't have a good feeling about these homeless men from Long Street. We might have a killer on our hands.'

'What makes him think that, Carl?'

'Mikes reckons they're full of heroin and booze but he can only find one needle mark on their bodies. If they'd been injecting the stuff on a regular basis there should be a lot more puncture marks.'

'First time users?'

'Maybe, but they'd have to be bloody unlucky. The lab report is showing high grade heroin, not shit stuff. We need to consider the possibility someone's knocking them off in their sleep.'

'Look into it, Carl, but see if you can keep a lid on it. I don't want the media knowing anything about Mike's theory until we've got something a little more conclusive. There'll be a shit storm if it gets out someone is knocking them off.'

Carl wondered just how many people would really care if

someone was knocking off homeless men. Then he thought of Bishop Kerry. He knew the bishop would enjoy sticking one up the Commissioner, especially after the Church's embarrassment over the Skinner case, and the Church was the major supplier of services to the homeless in the city.

When the evidence packages arrived from Forensics, Carl called DS Harry Fuller and DC Nigel Beard into the Incident Room.

'What's up, Boss' said Harry, as he and Nigel took a seat in front of the whiteboard.

'We need to take a look into the deaths of a couple of homeless guys Uniform have picked up in Long Street over the last week. Dr Jonas is not convinced they're accidental overdoses. He thinks someone may have injected them with heroin while they were asleep.'

'What makes him think that?' said Harry.

'There's only one needle mark on their bodies.'

'Perhaps they were unlucky first time users,' said Nigel.

'That's a possibility, Nigel, but according to the lab report on Mark Tidler,' Carl pointed to a photograph taken at the scene of Tidler's death on the whiteboard, 'it's pretty high grade heroin. Not sure he'd have the money for that sort of stuff.'

'See what you mean,' said Harry, 'unless there's some new kid selling the stuff to these guys. You know, someone who doesn't realise he's supposed to cut the stuff.'

'Either way, we need to find out what's going on. Go and spend some time with the guys that hang around in Long Street. See what you can find out.'

'Do we have a name for the second one, Boss?'

'Richard Wentworth.'

7 Long Street was one of three derelict buildings on the block at the intersection of William and Long Streets in the south-western corner of the central business district. Everyone had been waiting for someone to redevelop the site ever since the collapse of the Nash Group in 2004. The papers had been full of proposed projects over the years but none of them had come to anything.

At some point, someone had smashed in the door to 7 Long Street and it had become a place of refuge for homeless men seeking shelter from the weather, and a place where the desperate came to trade their cash for a chemically induced high. The building was regularly visited by the police, who were only interested in interrupting the business of the drug dealers, not the squatting activities of the homeless.

The drug dealing happened on the ground floor, which provided the dealers with multiple exit points. Their lookouts stood in doorways on the opposite side of the street and around in William Street, from where they could communicate with their colleagues inside the building whenever a police patrol turned into the street. The homeless squatters preferred the third floor, away from the drug crowd and above the level of the street lights.

Harry parked their unmarked silver Ford in the car park of the men's shelter at the western end of Long Street, where the homeless squatters came to shower and eat.

It was lunch time. The crowd sitting at the tables in the dining room on the ground floor, eating soup and bread rolls, was mostly older men dressed in ill-fitting, smelly clothes.

'What do you fuckers want?' said the man nearest the door when Harry and Nigel walked in.

Harry smiled. He knew they stood out like sore thumbs in their clean suits. He walked over to the elderly nun supervising the team of young people serving the meal. 'Hello, Sister.'

'What brings you here, Harry? Have they stopped feeding you down at the station?' She beamed a smile at him. 'Who's your friend?'

'Sister Clare, this is Nigel Beard. He works with me.'

'Well, I didn't think he'd be your boyfriend, Harry. You've both got policeman written all over you, even if you're not wearing uniforms. What brings you here today?'

Harry opened his iPad and showed her the photographs Forensics had given them. 'Trying to find out what happened to these guys. We're not so sure their deaths were from natural causes or accidental overdoses.'

'Took your time working that out, didn't you?' said the old man standing next to Sister Clare.

'Did you know them?' said Harry.

The man looked over his shoulder at the men sitting at the table behind him. 'Yeah, I knew them. They was in here all the time.'

'Were they squatting up the street at number seven?'

The man didn't say anything.

'We're not here to evict anybody. Just trying to find out what happened to them.'

'There's a few of us here that squat there. Not enough beds here and, besides,' he winked at Sister Clare, 'she won't let us drink in here.'

'That's only because you don't know when to stop, Gary.'

His smile revealed a set of nicotine stained teeth. 'I always stop when I hit the floor, Sister.'

Sister Clare rolled her eyes. Harry wanted to laugh. He could see the smirk on Nigel's face.

'Do you think you could introduce us to the group that uses number seven?' said Harry.

The man looked around the room. 'I'll ask if the boys want to talk to you.'

'Thanks, Gary,' said Harry. 'Why don't you enjoy your lunch while I talk to Sister? We can talk when you're finished.'

The man grunted and shuffled away with his lunch. He sat down at the table behind them with his bowl of soup and buttered roll, and immediately engaged the other men sitting at the table in conversation. It wasn't hard for Harry to work out who might be in the group.

'What can you tell me about Mark and Richard, Sister? Were they into drugs?'

'They were alcoholics, like Gary and his friends over there. We never saw them after lunch, just like we won't see that lot until break-fast tomorrow. But I don't think any of the older men are what you'd call drug users. They have to pester people on the streets to get the money to buy their booze, except for pension day. They don't even turn up here on pension day. Sometimes we don't see them for days.'

'Were Mark and Richard regulars?' said Harry.

'They'd been coming in here for as long as I can remember, Harry, and I've been here since your father was a young consta-ble. By the way, how is your father? I haven't seen him for a while.'

'He's good. Taken up golf. Reckons he's practising for his retirement.'

Sister Clare laughed. 'I hear you've taken up with Max Walsh's girl. She should keep you on the straight and narrow.'

The twinkle in her eye told Harry she knew a thing or two about Jessika, who often looked after Sister Clare's men in court.

'What's your mother think about your girlfriend?'

'Keeps telling me to marry her before she changes her mind.'

'I wouldn't wait too long, Harry.'

Gary and two of his mates invited Harry to join them in the car park after lunch. Nigel got the message that the invitation didn't include him and went to introduce himself to a couple of younger men sitting in a corner of the room playing cards.

Harry pulled a packet of cigarettes out of his coat pocket and passed it to Gary. His father had told him about cigarettes being the currency required to extract information from homeless men. He waited while the three men divided up the packet and then lit up.

'Why are you here, mate?' said the man Gary had introduced as Stan.

'We think someone may have murdered your friends,' said Harry.

'How?' said Stan. 'I found Tids. There wasn't a mark on him. Looked like he'd just died in his sleep.'

'Yeah, same with Dicko,' said the man Gary had introduced as Vince. 'I found him when I got back last night.' He held up his mobile phone. 'I called it in. I've even got a picture of him laying there dead.'

'Tids was full of heroin,' said Harry. 'He's got a needle mark in his arm, here.' Harry pointed to the inside of his elbow.

'Bullshit! Tids didn't do no drugs,' said Stan.

'I'm not saying he did but Dicko's got a needle mark in his arm, in the same place.'

'He wasn't into that shit,' said Vince. 'Shiraz was Dicko's poison of choice but he'd drink anything. Never seen him do heroin or any of that shit, and we've been mates for years.'

'Have you seen anybody new hanging about the place?'

'You know what it's like downstairs. New idiots there every night,' said Gary.

'Anybody that's come upstairs to where you guys sleep?'

The three men looked at each other, as if they were uncertain how much they could divulge about what went on downstairs.

'The Westies control downstairs,' said Vince, 'and there's one big guy that makes sure we keep out of their space. Reckons we scare the patrons.' Vince laughed. 'But he always makes sure we get upstairs if we get back late.'

'What time do you boys usually bed down for the night?'

'Hard to say, mate. We're usually tanked by then but we like to get in before dark. There's no bloody lights in that place.'

'Where do you sleep?'

'On the third floor. There's a room up there where we can lock the door.'

'What happens on the second floor?' said Harry.

'That's where the shit-heads shoot up. We don't go there.'

'Where does this big guy leave you if he has to help you up the stairs?'

'On the third floor landing. He props us up in a corner.'

'Isn't that where Dicko was found?' said Gary.

'Tids too,' said Stan. 'I went looking for him when he wasn't back when I woke up. Thought he must have passed out on the stairs.'

'Are you the only guys squatting down there?'

'Nah, there's a few others. They just don't like talking to coppers,' said Gary.

Harry keyed his number into Vince's mobile phone. 'If you remember anything else or see something you think I should know, or if you feel threatened by anyone, call me. If I can't come myself, I'll send help.'

'Shit! You're serious, aren't you, mate? No copper's ever given me his number before,' said Vince.

'I don't want to see you on a slab in the morgue, Vince. Not you; not any of your friends. Maybe you should find somewhere else to sleep.'

'There ain't anywhere else, mate.'

Harry waited for Nigel to slip into the car and buckle up. 'Find out anything?'

'Got an earful on how useless we are at protecting them from gangs like the Westies. Seems they control access to that building in Long Street.'

Harry started the car and eased it out into the traffic in Long Street. 'Yeah, the guys said the Westies are running the drug exchange on the ground floor but they claim there's one gang member that makes sure they don't interfere with the punters. Apparently, he even helps them upstairs when they're drunk.'

'Did they know anything, Sarge?'

'They're the guys who found the bodies. Thought their friends had simply died in their sleep.'

'So, Uniform might have statements from them.'

'Only if they'd hung around to be interviewed. Besides, doesn't sound like they saw anything. They were probably all out to it when it happened.'

'The guys I was talking to told me about ten or twelve of them sleep in or around that building. Not everybody goes inside if it's not raining, and they're not all drunks,' said Nigel.

'Did they see anything?'

'No, but they said they'd ask around and meet up with me if I came back in a couple of days.'

'Make sure you bring some cigarettes.'

'Cigarettes?'

'Secret my Dad told me. If you want information from these

guys you'll need to pay them, and the currency is cigarettes. Even if they don't smoke they can always use cigarettes or, if you're really feeling generous, buy them some metro tickets. Just don't give them cash.'

'Do you think the inspector will want us to talk to the Westies, Sarge?'

'I'm sure he will. Thing is though, will they want to talk to us? We might have to raid the place and pull some of them off the street. Perhaps we should take a look at Long Street.' Harry pulled into a parking space in front of the building, behind a white delivery van.

They were about to enter the building when a uniformed officer stepped out of the gloom and motioned them over. 'Sorry, gents, mind telling me why you're coming in here?'

Harry showed him his badge. 'What's going on?'

'Sergeant Lang's upstairs, Sergeant. They're doing a discreet recheck of the stairwell and the landing where the bodies were found, in case they missed anything, seeing this is now a suspected crime scene.'

Harry decided he could catch up with Dean back at Police Headquarters. 'Okay, we can come back later if we need to.'

CHAPTER 4

BLACK WAS his color of choice. He'd learnt a long time ago that nobody really noticed you when you wore black; you became an amorphous memory without detail. He pulled the hood of his jacket down over his eyes and slowly walked across the street, and into the building. A dark shape materialised in front of him as he entered. He knew what was about to happen. He'd had the same role himself in a similar place, in another city, at an earlier time in his life, and he'd studied the way this guy operated over the last few nights.

He let himself be patted down. He wasn't carrying anything the door guard wouldn't be expecting to find on someone coming to buy what his mates were selling.

The room off the entrance foyer, in which the Westies conducted their business, was dimly lit by the street light immediately outside its boarded-up windows. Transactions took place in the far corner of the room, illuminated by candle light and away from the wind that blew in through the open doorway.

As he approached the dealers, he noticed the door in the wall immediately behind the pile of boxes that served as the trading table. He knew that door would be unlocked and that there would be someone standing on the other side of it with a weapon.

Every place like this that he'd worked in had an exit that the dealers, and their security detail, could use at short notice.

The dealers were a couple of skinny teenage kids. Expendables, like their mates on the doors and the lookouts outside in the street. That didn't mean they wouldn't be armed and dangerous, and full of a bravado that would get them into more trouble than they could imagine if they challenged him. He knew the real power players didn't work on the streets selling the shit these kids were pedalling.

'What will it be, mate?' said the kid working the table.

'Looking for some ice.' He looked around him as if he was nervous.

'Starts at twenty bucks.'

He pulled out his wallet and passed over a hundred dollar bill. The boy slipped the bill into his pocket and pushed five small packets across the table towards him.

'Upstairs if you want a hit before you go home, mate.' The kid pointed to the entrance. 'Back that way and up one.'

He picked up his packets and dropped them into the pocket of his coat. Then he walked back to the entrance foyer and made his way up the stairs. Three doors opened off the first landing he came to. There were several people slumped in various poses on the floor in the room closest to the street, which was illuminated by the street lights below. The other two rooms were in darkness, and empty as far as he could tell. He walked over to the nearest stoned body, a girl with long black hair and tattoos on her arms. She looked like she could use a decent meal. He slipped the packets of ice he'd purchased downstairs into the front of her bra. She didn't notice.

He made his way up to the third level, where the homeless squatters spent the night. He'd spent the last three nights watching them stagger into the building. They usually arrived before the Westies, but sometimes there was a straggler or two that the guy on the door shepherded up the stairs.

The place smelt like a refuse dump. One of the three doors off the landing was locked. He listened silently at that door. He could hear the sound of snoring coming from the room behind it. The odour emanating from the room immediately next to their sleeping quarters strongly suggested to him that the squatters were using it as their latrine. The third room off the landing appeared to be their rubbish tip. He could see broken bottles spilling out of its doorway onto the landing.

He realised it was going to be relatively easy to fulfil the mission he had chosen for himself. All he would have to do was wait for one of them to come home late. He knew the kid on the door would shepherd him upstairs away from the customers, where he would be locked out on the landing by the others, and probably as drunk as a skunk to boot, going on what he'd seen over the last few nights.

He went downstairs and walked back out into the shadows, and waited until the Westies shut up shop. It looked like 3 am was closing time.

He went back to the building around four on Sunday afternoon. It was raining, so he settled into the doorway of the building diagonally opposite the entrance used by the homeless guys. On the previous three times he'd watched them shuffle or stagger along Long Street, he'd counted ten of them. By the time it was dark, he'd counted only eight. He felt a twinge of anticipation.

The rain stopped around eight o'clock, shortly before one of the stragglers made his unsteady way down from William Street and disappeared into number seven. He took out his thermos flask and poured himself a cup of coffee. When he'd finished his coffee, he moved further down the street away from the entrance to another doorway, from where he could still observe the footpath in front of the building while staying out of sight of the lookout when he arrived.

At nine, a grey van pulled up outside the building and six boys, each carrying a sports bag much like the one at his feet, climbed out before it moved away into the night. The Westies had arrived. He smiled to himself. They were a bunch of shopkeepers with fixed hours of business, with no apparent awareness of how obvious their movements were.

He noticed that a different guy was doing guard duty on the main entrance to the building, and that one of the lookouts had taken up position in the doorway he had abandoned shortly after eight, while his mate had disappeared around the corner into William Street.

He wondered if the police ever managed to catch anyone if they raided the place, and decided they probably didn't care enough to worry about it. He certainly hadn't seen any sign of them on the nights he'd watched the place.

He did some exercises on the spot, using the side of the doorway as a wall to support his body while he did his stretches.

The rain started again at ten. It was heavier than what it had been all day. It didn't look like the Westies would be doing much business that night. At ten-thirty the grey van pulled up, and the boys called it a night.

He was almost ready to call it a night himself, when he noticed the last of the homeless guys slowly making his way down from William Street towards the entrance to number seven. The guy was using the building to keep himself upright.

He picked up his bag, ran across the street, and slipped inside the entrance. When the homeless guy staggered in he stepped out of the shadows, like he'd seen the door guard do it, and helped the old guy upstairs to the landing on the third floor. He let him slump to the floor. He stank of wet clothes permeated with urine. He pulled the old guy's coat off him and placed it under his head as a pillow. The old guy was snoring within minutes.

He went downstairs and retrieved his bag. It was time to get down to business. He unzipped the bag, pulled out a short piece of rubber tubing and a screw driver, a syringe, a tablespoon, a small packet of off-white powder, a small bottle of water, and a pair of latex gloves. He placed his mobile phone on the floor and activated the torch. The landing filled with light.

He pulled on the gloves, tipped the powder into the table-spoon, added a couple of drops from the water bottle and then took out his cigarette lighter, and applied heat to the bottom of the tablespoon. When the mixture had liquified he placed the spoon on the floor, inserted the needle into the liquid and drew it into the syringe.

Then he undid the button on one of the old guy's shirt sleeves and pulled the sleeve up to expose the lower part of the old man's arm. Carefully, he slipped the piece of rubber tubing around the upper part of the old man's arm, inserted the screw-driver and twisted it to apply pressure.

When the veins in the old man's lower arm stood up, engorged with blood, he jammed the screwdriver into the old man's armpit, picked up the syringe, inserted the needle into the vein inside the crook of the old man's elbow, and emptied its contents into his bloodstream. He slowly released the pressure in the tourniquet. The old man stopped snoring.

He withdrew the needle and placed the syringe back into the plastic container lined with cotton wool that he used for carrying it. He removed the rubber tubing and placed it into his bag along with the screwdriver and the tablespoon. He checked that he'd put his lighter back in his pocket and picked up his phone.

He looked at the old man stretched out on the floor at his feet. He poked him in the leg with his foot. No response.

'I hope you make some better choices next time, mate. You sure fucked up this life. Look at you. Pissed out of your brain, wearing stinking clothes and living in a hole full of shit. There's no room here for idiots like you.'

He squatted beside the old man and placed two latex covered fingers on the carotid artery running through his neck. There was no pulse. He switched off the torch in his phone, pulled off the gloves and stuffed them into his bag.

He picked up his bag and went downstairs, where he used the exit into the laneway behind the building that the dealers used whenever they were forced to flee. It was still raining. He didn't care. He'd started, and it felt good to be doing the work he knew had to be done.

He looked around him. The lane was deserted. He hadn't expected to see anyone but old habits die hard. He shrugged off the memory that wanted to surface, and started walking to where he'd parked the Toyota earlier in the afternoon.

CHAPTER 5

CARL WAS CHATTING with DC Paterson about his morning in court when Harry and Nigel got back to Police Headquarters. He listened as Harry briefed them on their visit to the men's shelter. What he heard reinforced his suspicion that Mike Jonas was right, but it also made him wonder why the Westies were looking out for the homeless men using the building. That was something he hadn't expected to hear.

'You know, Inspector,' said DC Paterson, 'something's not stacking up for me here. I've been on the streets for around thirty years. I've seen a lot of druggies in that time and I've met a lot of homeless guys. Most of the homeless guys don't do hard drugs, especially not the old guys. They spend their money on booze. It gives them an escape every day, and they only need a few bucks to slip into oblivion.'

Carl pictured the homeless men he saw about the city sitting in doorways or on park benches, or lying on footpaths and squares of council maintained lawn, oblivious to the world moving around them. Wayne was right. If they weren't pestering passers-by for cash, the homeless were often drunk, which was why the State had changed the law and stopped processing them through the courts.

'You may be right, Wayne, in which case we could have a serial killer on our hands. I think we need to talk to the gang running the drug exchange,' said Carl. 'They're probably the most reliable witnesses to whatever is going on in that building.'

'Do you think the chief would authorise a raid, Boss?' said Harry.

'We'll have to coordinate that with the Drug Squad,' said Carl, 'otherwise they'll be complaining that I'm working in their patch, and you know what the chief's like when that happens.'

'We could get them to raid the place and then talk to whoever they bring in,' said Nigel.

'That might work,' said Carl. 'Let me talk to the chief. By the way, Harry, can you catch up with Dean Lang when he gets back from Long Street? I asked him to treat the landing where the last body was found as a crime scene.'

'We nearly walked in on him. I wanted to have a look at the place but he's doing one of his discreet jobs, so I decided we'd take a look some other time.'

'Yeah, well, going by the photos they took when they picked up the bodies, I'm not hopeful he'll find anything. Place looks like a tip.'

The Drug Squad's Tuesday night raid of the Long Street drug exchange netted five members of the Westies gang. Carl sent Harry back to the men's shelter with photographs of the five, and decided to start by interviewing Gavin Potts, who Gary and his mates had identified as the one that made sure they got upstairs safely.

Carl studied Gavin Potts through the two-way mirror as he sat waiting in the interview room with his escort. He was a big boy with bulging muscles, which suggested he spent time working out. He'd been inside twice in the last ten years. Both times for dealing. Carl thought he looked as if he didn't have a care in the world, and wondered whether that was a mask or if Potts had found that centre he'd been reading about in Nina's books on meditation.

As he entered the interview room with DC Wayne Paterson, Carl wondered if someone like Gavin Potts would care about what had happened to two homeless men.

'Hello, Potts,' said Wayne.

A grin spread across Gavins' face as he stood and offered his hand to Wayne. 'G'day, Wayne. Who's your mate?'

'This is my new boss, Inspector West.'

Gavin sat and crossed his arms over his chest. 'Aren't you one of those detectives I see on the TV when some poor bastard's been killed?'

'Yes. I'm from Major Crimes,' said Carl.

Gavin looked at DC Paterson. 'Moving up in the world, Wayne?'

'You could say that. What about you? Still doing the same shit?'

'It's a living.' He looked at Carl. 'I haven't killed anyone, so why do you want to talk to me?'

'We're looking into the deaths of a couple of homeless men.'

'Tids and Dicko, I suppose,' said Gavin. 'Vince said some of your boys had been around asking questions. From what I'd heard I thought they'd just died. God knows they drank enough. Can't remember the number of times I've helped them up the stairs.'

'Did you help them up the night they died?' said Carl.

'I don't work Sundays.'

'Anybody else take care of them like you do?'

'I don't think so. The arrangement we have with the old farts is that they go up before dark and they leave the punters alone.'

'How come you look after them when they get home late?' said Wayne.

Gavin uncrossed his arms. 'Gary's my grandfather.'

Carl didn't know what to say, so he said nothing. He couldn't imagine what it must be like having to cope with that reality.

'What makes you think they were murdered?' said Gavin.

'They were full of heroin, high grade stuff, and there's no evidence they were users, apart from one needle mark in the arm,' said Carl.

'They certainly didn't get any high grade anything from us. The stuff we're selling is cut to shit.'

'Anybody else operating around there?' said Wayne.

'You know the rules, Wayne. There'd be a bloody war going on if there was.'

'When do you guys usually call it a night?' said Carl.

'Most nights we're gone by three. There's not much action after that. Most of the punters are gone by then or they're spaced out upstairs.'

'Know much about those punters, Gavin' said Carl.

'Only that they're losers.'

'Think any of them would be capable of killing a drunk?'

'Who knows, mate? But they certainly didn't do it with anything we sold 'em, if you say it was high grade stuff. Most of them buy a hit and piss off. There's only a few that shoot up on the second, and they're mostly kids with nowhere to go.'

Carl nodded to DC Paterson.

'Thanks, Potts. I'll put in a good word for you,' said Wayne.

'Don't do that, Wayne. Last time you did that I got five years. Just make sure no bastard kills my grandfather while I'm in here.'

After interviewing Gavin Potts, they interviewed the other four gang members. Only one of them, a skinny kid with a shaved head named William Hazel, according to his charge sheet, admitted to working Sundays. He claimed he was a lookout and hadn't seen anything out of the ordinary but he did admit to seeing Dicko stagger into the building around midnight the previous Sunday.

'I wonder what he was doing before then,' said Carl, as he and Wayne made their way back to the Incident Room.

'Probably fell asleep someplace,' said Wayne, 'and only went home after waking up cold and wet. It rained Sunday night. I'm surprised more of them don't die of pneumonia.'

'Are there traffic cameras on that intersection, Wayne?'

'Don't know. I'll ring Traffic, but you know there's more than one way into that building, don't you, Inspector?'

After a lengthy discussion with DCI Rankin, Carl was authorised to appeal to the public for help. Armed with photographs of Mark Tidler and Richard Wentworth, he held a media conference and asked anyone who had been in the vicinity of 7 Long Street on either of the last two Sunday nights or in the early hours of the following Monday mornings, and had seen a person or persons interfering with someone sleeping on the stairwell inside the building, to call Crime Stoppers.

Knowing what people were doing in that location, Carl didn't hold out much hope of anyone coming forward but knew he owed it to the homeless to at least try and stop whoever it was that seemed intent on killing them.

After the media conference, DC Paterson informed him that there were traffic cameras mounted on the lights at every intersection on William Street.

Carl rang the Traffic Control Centre and asked them about the quality of the cameras and whether they could be set to record traffic in Long Street.

'You're in luck, Inspector. The cameras at that intersection are due for a service this week. I'll get them reset for you.'

'What's the quality of their night images like?'

'As long as the vehicle goes through the intersection and moves away from the camera we can get the registration plate.'

'How far down the street will the camera capture at night?'

'Depends on the light and the weather.'

'Do you think you could capture things going on in front of number seven Long Street?'

'Probably, especially with the new cameras.'

'Got anything from last Sunday night, early Monday morning?'

'I'll have a look and let you know, Inspector.'

Carl went to see the chief inspector.

'Chief, I've found a way to get some surveillance on that building in Long Street. There's a traffic camera on the intersection, and the Traffic Centre has agreed to reset one for us to point down Long Street.'

'They got any footage from last weekend?'

'They're having a look.'

CHAPTER 6

Around ten in the morning on Thursday, the fifth of May, PC Lily Chan and her partner, PC Adam Monks, responded to a call about a foul odour coming from a building in Sunshine Street, Bayside. When they arrived at the address, they discovered the building was a derelict warehouse behind the row of trendy shops on Jetty Road.

It didn't take them long to establish the source of the odour: the body of a well-dressed, middle-aged man behind a pile of rubbish on the floor of the warehouse, just inside the door that opened from the laneway that separated the warehouse from the trendy shops.

They secured the scene and called it in to Operations.

Dr Mike Jonas was examining the body when Carl and Harry arrived at the scene just before midday. The place was filthy. Everything except the corpse was covered with a carpet of dust several centimetres deep. There were discarded syringes, crumpled cigarette packets and broken bottles scattered across the floor of the warehouse, and the smell of stale urine and fermenting shit competed with the odours escaping from the slightly bloated body at their feet.

The crime scene investigators had set up a battery powered floodlight to illuminate the area where the body lay, as there was no electricity in the building and very little sunlight reached inside the warehouse through its boarded-up windows.

It certainly doesn't take long for an abandoned building to be taken over by people with base needs, thought Carl, as he surveyed the detritus in front of him.

'Not your usual OD suspect, Carl,' said Mike. 'Check out the suit.'

Carl looked closely at the body. It looked like that of a businessman who'd lost his way and ended up in the wrong place.

'Anything on the body to identify him?'

Dr Jonas slipped his latex covered fingers inside the pockets of the jacket and the trousers. 'Nothing.'

Carl knew it certainly wouldn't be the first time someone had rifled through the pockets of a corpse before reporting it.

'What makes you think he's a possible OD?'

'There's a puncture mark on his left arm, inside the elbow, and that belt.' Dr Jonas pointed to a black leather belt loosely wrapped around the upper portion of the victim's left arm. 'I'd say it was holding up his pants before being used as a tourniquet.'

'Think he might be a first time user?' said Carl.

'I'll have to check in the lab when we've stripped his clothes off him.'

'Any sign of the syringe?'

'No,' said Mike.

'Sounds similar to those two homeless guys,' said Harry. 'They only had one needle mark.'

'I was thinking the same thing,' said Mike, 'but this guy certainly doesn't look like he was homeless, unless he'd taken to the streets this week.'

'How long do you think he's been here?' said Carl.

'Hard to say, probably a few days.'

Carl watched as the crime scene investigators photographed the body and the location. He didn't have much faith that they'd find anything helpful if this turned out not to be another overdose death.

Sgt Dean Lang from Forensics walked in from the laneway.

'Anything useful, Dean?'

'Nothing out there, Inspector. It's been raining off and on for the last few days, and it looks like this door's been open for ages. And, as you can see, everything's covered in dust in here. The one thing I can tell you though, Inspector, is this guy didn't walk in here. Look at the backs of his shoes, and those tracks there.' Dean pointed to two lines that appeared in the dust a short distance in from the doorway. 'Someone dragged him in here and, allowing for the patrol that found the body, I'd say there were enough footprints in the dust when we got here to suggest our friend was dragged in by at least two others.'

'Any clear prints?'

'One of them was wearing size sixteen sneakers, at least. I should be able to give you a brand once I've tested the tread pattern.' He showed Carl the image on his camera. 'Can't tell what the other guy was wearing. Those prints there belong to PC Chan, and that lot that stops just inside the door are PC Monks.'

Carl looked down at the plastic bags on his shoes, and on the shoes of everyone else in the building, and said a silent thank you to PC Chan for knowing her job.

The post mortem started at four fifteen. Carl watched as Dr Jonas examined the naked body of a slightly built, balding, middle-aged man.

'Looks like your victim was forcibly restrained. See that bruising.' Dr Jonas pointed to the upper arms and the abdomen. 'And, there's abrasion to the back of the head, which suggests he may have been held down against his will. This is not looking like a self-administered injection to me, Carl.'

Carl pictured someone holding the victim down on the rubbish strewn cement floor of the warehouse, with a knee in his belly and hands wrapped around his upper arms, and wondered how he'd administered the fatal injection. Then he remembered that Dean Lang had mentioned two sets of footprints, so it was possible that one of his attackers had held him down while the other had pushed the needle into a vein in his left arm.

When Carl refocused, Dr Jonas was examining the body with a magnifying glass, looking closely at all the known spots that people used to inject themselves.

'See any more needle marks, Mike?'

'There's only the one.'

This is looking more like an assassination than an accidental overdose, thought Carl. 'When do you think he died, Mike?'

'Be at least a couple of days ago.'

'Any extraneous biology on the clothing?'

'We've got a couple of drops of blood on the shirt but it's too early to tell if they're extraneous. Could be the victims. I'll let you know.'

Carl watched in silence as Dr Jonas completed the procedure. By the time it was over it was clear that, whoever he was, the victim had been a relatively healthy forty something year old until he'd been injected with whatever it was that had killed him. Any other useful information would be in the toxicology and blood reports, when they came.

'I wonder who he is,' said Mike, as he and Carl made their way to Mike's office.

'Guess I'd better go and find out.'

36

Carl didn't have to wait long to find out whose body they had in the police morgue. The Crime Stoppers Hotline received ten calls identifying him as John Drake, a forty-six year old public servant, within fifteen minutes of the victim's picture appearing on the early edition evening news. One of the callers was his father, Heinrich, who had come in to formally identify the body.

In the quiet of the viewing room in the police morgue, Heinrich Drake confirmed his initial identification of the body.

'Where did you say his body was found, Inspector?'

'In a derelict building off Jetty Road, Bayside.'

'That doesn't make any sense. What was he doing there?'

Carl paused and wondered if there was a way to broach the subject diplomatically, and decided there probably wasn't. 'Did your son have a drug problem, Mr Drake?'

'Why are you asking me that?'

'The building where his body was found is littered with syringes, so it's probably a place used by drug users.'

'I didn't know such places existed, Inspector, but I suppose they must. I'm pretty sure John wasn't a drug user though. But then again, how would I know? It's not something they tell you, is it?'

Carl gave Mr Drake a moment to say his goodbyes and then escorted him to an interview room, where he planned to take advantage of those unguarded moments that usually followed an unexpected encounter with the body of a loved one. Carl knew that parents were particularly vulnerable at that point, and only too willing to help the police catch their child's killer.

'Mr Drake, this is my colleague DS Fuller. We'd like to ask you a few questions before you go.'

Mr Drake looked at Carl. 'Why?'

Carl waited for Mr Drake to sit in the chair he'd offered him. 'We're treating your son's death as murder.'

Mr Drake sprung out of his chair. 'Murder? Why would anybody want to kill him?'

Carl signalled for Mr Drake to resume his seat. 'That's what we're here to find out, Mr Drake,' said Carl, moving his hands in a downward, calming motion. 'When was the last time you saw John alive?'

'Sunday. He always came for dinner on Sunday night.'

'Did he say anything about being in any sort of trouble?'

'Well, he was a bit anxious about something at work. Said he'd found out about something that he felt he had to report to the Auditor General.'

'Did he say what it was?'

'No, but he was worried that if he was wrong about it he'd have to resign. He didn't think he'd have much of a future in the public service if he was wrong, and he wasn't sure he'd have much of a future even if he was right.'

'Whistleblower?' said Harry.

'That's the word he used. I told him to be careful. I know what it's like in the public service. I did forty years in the service myself, in Treasury. Sometimes you get crucified for doing the right thing, especially when you embarrass one of the big boys.' Mr Drake looked at Harry. 'I guess you boys would know what I'm talking about.'

Carl thought of all the times he'd been told to do something to keep the Commissioner happy. 'Yes, I certainly know what you mean.' He exchanged a smile with Mr Drake. 'Do you know if he went ahead with reporting whatever it was?'

'Said he'd posted it to the Auditor General on his way home on Friday.'

'Do you know if he'd told anybody else about it?'

'He didn't say but I got the impression he was keeping it

quiet. He wasn't sure of the office network in State Supply. He'd only been there a few months.'

'State Supply. Is that where he was working?'

'Yes. He'd worked in the Department of Transport for years, ever since he'd joined the service, actually, but he got a promotion at the start of the year and moved to State Supply.'

'Is that where he thought he'd discovered whatever it was that he was reporting to the Auditor General?'

'Yes.'

'Do you know what he did there?'

'He worked in the section that administers what he called big dollar contracts.'

That sounded like the sort of place corrupt officers could be tempted with a bribe to Carl.

'Did you speak to him after Sunday?'

'No. We usually only saw him on Sundays. He was always busy during the week.'

'Doing what?'

'I don't really know to be honest. It's not like he had a wife or kids or anything. He didn't even have a regular girlfriend, as far as I know. At least he never brought one home to meet us.' Mr Drake shrugged his shoulders. 'But he always said he was busy, unless it was a family birthday or something like that.'

'Can you think of anyone who might be able to tell us about what he did outside work?'

'I know this might sound strange, Inspector, but I don't really know all that much about John's private life. When your kids grow up they make their own lives. John didn't talk much about what he did after work, at least not to me. His brother might know. They were pretty close but Martin's at sea. Somewhere in the Persian Gulf, I think. He's a captain in the navy.'

Nothing about family arrangements sounded strange to Carl

anymore. He'd heard them all. 'Perhaps some of his work colleagues will know. Where was your son living?'

'On South Terrace. In that ecological village thing they have there. He owns an apartment there. Number three.'

'Don't suppose you have a key?'

'No. I've only been there a couple of times. Interesting place but John usually came to us.'

'We'll get a locksmith to replace the locks if we have to break in, and we'll send you a key once we're finished.'

'You're going to search his place? What are you looking for?'

'Anything that might tell us why someone wanted to kill him.' Carl handed Mr Drake his card. 'I'm sorry about your son, Mr Drake. I'll do my best to track down his killer. If you think of anything, my number's on this card.'

Auditor General Steven Wilmington agreed to meet with Carl and Harry at ten-thirty on Friday morning, and he didn't keep them waiting.

'Thanks for seeing us at such short notice, Mr Wilmington,' said Carl.

'Happy to help, Inspector.'

'Who received the report from Drake?'

'Chris Richter. He's one of my senior auditors.'

'When did he get it?'

'In Monday's mail but you need to appreciate that we get a number of similar documents every month. Often, they're nothing more than allegations by overzealous public servants who've simply misinterpreted something. People have the best of intentions, Inspector, but they're often misinformed. This is an allegation of mischief by the head of an agency. Who knows what

Drake's motivation was? We often get wild allegations against agency heads based on nothing more than malice.'

'So, what do you do with these allegations?'

'Oh, we're obliged to look into them. Sometimes, they're spot on and we end up saving the government a lot of money or prosecuting people for fraud or corruption, although the corruption work is pursued by the Corruption Commissioner these days.'

'So, has any action been taken on Drake's allegations?'

'I believe Chris has discussed the matter with Elena Standish. She's the audit lead for the State Supply audit, and instructed her to undertake extra testing on the cleaning contract approval process. That's the process that Drake alleges is being abused.' The Auditor General opened his hands in a sweeping gesture. 'I trust, Inspector, that you appreciate that it's impossible to verify every transaction an agency enters into and that we only review a sample of transactions when we audit.'

'I'll leave the auditing side to you, Mr Wilmington.' Carl smiled at the Auditor General. He had no real idea what auditors did, apart from ask a lot of inconvenient questions. 'What exactly is the nature of Drake's allegations?'

'Basically, he's alleging that the committee responsible for deciding which contracts, particularly cleaning contracts, the agency signs is favouring certain companies in contravention of government policy. I can give you a copy of the document, Inspector, if you like?'

'Thanks. That would be helpful.' Carl waited while the Auditor General asked his personal assistant to make a copy of the document. 'What implications do you read into it if his allegations are correct?'

'Some of the contracts administered by State Supply involve millions of dollars, Inspector. If what Drake alleges is correct, it could be that someone on that committee, or maybe everyone on that committee, is receiving some sort of kickback.'

Carl wondered just how far up the chain the corruption might go.

'Who's on that committee?'

'The agency head, Sonya Curtis, and two of her senior officers. So, I'd say these are fairly serious allegations, and they'll be damaging if they're true.'

'I understand that Drake had only been there a few months. How much weight are you giving to his allegations? I mean, would he have been in a position to know what was going on?'

'Good question, Inspector, but we'll only know if we take a look. I've checked his record. He worked in a similar position in Transport, so we can't discount his allegations solely on the grounds that he didn't know what he was talking about.'

'What's Sonya Curtis like?'

'Honest and hard-working, as far as I know, Inspector. She was appointed to lead State Supply about five years ago. I meet with her, as I do with the other agency heads, two or three times a year.'

Carl winked at Harry.

'Tell me, Mr Wilmington, does the same auditor do the State Supply audit each year?' said Harry.

The Auditor General stroked his chin and paused before answering. 'Each agency has a lead auditor, who generally oversees the audit for several years, but the people doing the audit testing change from year to year. That's how we build our expertise, Sergeant.'

'And, who signs off on the audit?' said Harry.

'Ultimately, that's my responsibility but, given the number of agencies, I delegate that task to my senior auditors and we prepare the final reports for Parliament, the ones that I sign, only after they have reviewed all the audits with me.'

'So, if Drake's allegations are correct, your auditors have somehow missed this mischief, possibly for years?' said Carl.

'As I said, Inspector, unless we detect signs of fraud, our audits are based on the testing of samples in accordance with the auditing standards. Given the number of transactions conducted by State Supply, it's quite possible we simply haven't sampled the relevant transactions.'

'What about the contract approval process itself?'

'Yes, that's reviewed every year but, as I said, we only check a sample of contracts to confirm that they're following the process.'

Carl nodded to signal that he understood but wondered whether that was true or if the audits could have been structured to make sure those transactions were never examined.

'Can't say I'm looking forward to this, Inspector. If Drake's allegations are correct, this is going to be somewhat embarrassing for me and my office.'

'I'd appreciate the names of the people on that committee, Mr Wilmington. I may need to speak to them.'

'You'll find them in Drake's report. He named them.'

'I might also want to speak to the officer that leads the State Supply audit.'

'Elena Standish. She's not in today. She doesn't work Fridays.'

'Do you have her contact details?' Carl waited while the Auditor General asked his personal assistant to get Elena's contact details.

'Is there anything else I can do for you, gentlemen?'

'Did Drake make contact with your office at any time?'

'Not that I'm aware of, Inspector. Let me ask Chris.' The Auditor general stepped out of his office and returned a few moments later with a tall young man dressed in a dark suit, who he introduced as Chris Richter.

'Mr Drake attended a workshop I presented late last year, when he was still with Transport. I handed out my business card to participants in case they had follow up questions. I guess that's why he sent his allegations to me.'

'So, you have had no contact with him, then?'

'I tried to ring him on his mobile on Tuesday to let him know I had received his package but he didn't answer my call.'

'Did you leave him a message?'

'I left my number and asked him to call.'

'So, what you're telling me is that no-one here knew anything about his allegations until they arrived in the mail on Monday?'

'I think that's correct, Inspector,' said Chris Richter.

'And, it's only you, Mr Wilmington here, and Elena Standish that knew anything about them until this morning?'

'That's right, as far as I know, Inspector. I haven't discussed the matter with anybody else.' Chris Richter looked at his boss.

'And, I certainly haven't discussed it with anybody, Inspector, until you called,' said the Auditor General. 'Our protocol is to test the allegations as part of our annual audit process to see if there is any substance to them, before alerting anyone in the agency, especially when the allegations concern the agency head.'

Carl handed the Auditor General his card. 'I appreciate your assistance, Mr Wilmington, but I think we have all we need for now. If you think of anything, you can get me on this number.'

Carl sat in DCI Rankin's office and waited for the chief to finish his telephone conversation.

The chief inspector returned the receiver to its cradle and made a note in the pad on his desk. 'So, what's the story, Carl?'

'Appears Drake was whistleblowing on some mischief involving the head of State Supply, someone called Sonya Curtis. According to his father, he'd sent some kind of report alleging misconduct to the Auditor General last Friday.' Carl leant back into his chair. 'I've just come from a meeting with the Auditor General. He's confirmed his office got Drake's document on Monday.'

DCI Rankin rested his elbows on his desk and joined his fingers together. 'When does Mike think he was killed?'

'Probably sometime Tuesday morning, or possibly as early as Monday night.'

'Who knew about his allegations?'

'The Auditor General and at least two of his officers. A young guy called Chris Richter, who's responsible for the State Supply audit, and a woman called Elena Standish, who leads the hands-on audit team. We haven't spoken with her yet. She doesn't work Fridays and she's not answering her phone.'

'Do we know where she lives?'

'Yes, but it appears she's away for the weekend.'

DCI Rankin looked across the plaza to the State Administration Building, located opposite Police Headquarters. 'So, it's possible no-one at State Supply knows anything about Drake making these allegations.'

'We'd have to ask to be sure, but I'd say there's a fair chance that's the case.'

'If that's the case, Carl, what's our motive?'

'Good question, Chief.'

'I wonder what else Drake was mixed up in that might explain why he got himself killed.'

'And, then there's the question of how he was killed. It's pretty much the same MO used on those homeless guys in Long Street.'

'Then you'd better get out there and earn your money, Inspector, before the media get wind of that and start running serial killer stories.'

DI West's team of detectives stood around drinking coffee and waiting for him to emerge from his meeting with DCI Rankin to start the briefing. DC Lisa Templar was showing the others her pursuit driver certificate, and graciously taking the ribbing they were giving her about her driving.

'You can drive me anytime, Lisa' said Carl, as he joined them. 'I've had enough of Harry trying to kill me every time we leave the office, and I've seen Wayne's file.' He smiled in DC Paterson's direction. 'He holds the force record for the number of single vehicle incidents.'

Wayne bowed and they applauded his accomplishment.

'And we all know Nigel's driving is so bad that he's had to get personal coaching from a particular hot shot pursuit driver in Uniform.'

The room erupted in laughter. DC Nigel Beard's courting of PC Lily Chan was the team's favourite amusement, especially since he went bright red anytime she was mentioned.

Carl stood in front of the whiteboard adorned with John Drake's photograph, and several other images taken at the crime scene and the post mortem.

'Okay folks. Let's get started.' He waited for them to settle.

'This is what we know. Uniform found the body of our victim, John Drake, Thursday morning, on the floor of an abandoned warehouse in Sunshine Street, Bayside, in response to a call from a member of the public complaining about the stink.'

Not wanting to prompt another round of snide remarks at Nigel's expense, Carl restrained himself from mentioning that PC Chan had found the body.

'This bruising on the upper body,' he pointed to the photograph labelled A, 'suggests that someone forcibly held the victim down, while either that person or an accomplice administered a lethal dose of what Dr Jonas suspects was heroin into his system. I'd say if our killer was acting alone, he probably sat on the victim and pinned his arms down with his legs to get the needle in.' Carl mimed the actions he imagined the perpetrator had taken.

'I guess he could have had help,' said DS Fuller.

'He probably did, Harry. At least Sgt Lang from Forensics thinks there were two of them based on the footprints found at the scene.' Carl pointed to the image of the sneaker track. 'And, one of them has big feet going by that print. Now, where was I?' Carl looked at his notes. 'There's only one needle mark on the body, so I think it's safe to say Drake was not a long-term user.'

Carl noted the thoughtful expression on DC Beard's face. 'That suggest something to you, Nigel?'

'We've had two other ODs with a similar MO this month,

Inspector. Both homeless guys. Do you think there might be a connection?'

'Too early to tell, Nigel, but we need to keep that in mind as a possibility,' said Carl, writing a note on the whiteboard. 'The estimated time of death is early Tuesday morning, possibly late Monday night.'

Carl watched as they all noted that detail.

'Our victim worked at The Office of State Supply and, according to his father, he posted a report detailing some sort of misconduct in that agency to the Auditor General's office last Friday.'

Carl looked at Harry. 'DS Fuller and I spoke with the Auditor General this morning. Drake's made some fairly serious allegations of corruption against the agency head, a woman named Sonya Curtis. This is a copy of Drake's report.' Carl pulled the report out of his folder and placed it on the table in front of the whiteboard. 'Wayne, I want you to take a look at this and see what you can find out about the other parties linked to whatever Drake claimed he'd uncovered.'

'How many people in the Auditor General's office know about these allegations, Inspector?' asked DC Paterson.

'Three, as far as we know. The Auditor General himself, Chris Richter who's responsible for State Supply, and Elena Standish, who actually does the audit of State Supply. We've spoken to Richter but we haven't been able to speak with Standish yet.'

'What about at State Supply?'

'Good question, Wayne. We don't know.'

'When was the last time anybody saw him alive, Inspector?' said DC Templar.

Carl looked at his notes. 'His father said he'd last seen him on Sunday evening. We'll have to follow up with his work colleagues to trace his movements on Monday. Richter told us he tried to call him on his mobile on Tuesday without any luck. Of course, he was probably already dead by then.'

'Was there a phone with the body, Boss?' said DS Fuller.

'No, and no wallet or keys either. I guess someone helped themselves, considering where the body was found,' said Carl.

'That someone could have been his killer,' said DC Paterson.

'But I guess we're ruling out robbery as the motive then, Inspector, given the way he was killed?' said DC Beard.

'I'd say robbery was highly unlikely, Nigel, especially if the lab confirms he was pumped full of high grade heroin.' Carl looked at his notes again. 'DS Fuller and I are meeting with Drake's manager at State Supply this afternoon. I've got a team from Forensics searching Drake's apartment and Uniform are taking statements from his neighbours and interviewing people in the vicinity of the crime scene. Nigel, I want you and Lisa to interview Drake's work colleagues from the Department of Transport. We need to find out as much as we can about what he did after hours, okay?'

CHAPTER 8

HE PREFERRED READING the paper to watching the TV news. He didn't like the way they sensationalised everything on television, and he was sick of seeing all those pictures of Syrians killing each other with crude barrel bombs dropped from helicopters.

He turned the page and scanned the stories on page five. There it was. Four lines neatly advising readers of the discovery of the body of Mark Tidler, described as a homeless squatter and known alcoholic, in a building in Long Street. There was no photograph. There was no mention of any police investigation. He shook his head. Four lines summarising a complete life. The very brevity of it confirming his belief that he was doing the world a favour by ending failed human experiments that nobody cared about.

He put down the paper and poured himself a drink from the Johnny Walker bottle on the table, and took a measured sip as he contemplated his next visit to Long Street.

He had more than enough heroin to dispose of the entire tribe of incompetent, failed specimens living in the building in one evening, if he wanted to. All he'd have to do is disable the mechanism they used for locking the door to their sleeping quarters. He guessed there'd be a sliding bolt on the inside that someone had installed during a lucid moment, and wondered how they'd react to finding their precious bolt removed or if they'd even notice. Someone would, he thought. Someone had to be sober enough each night to remember to lock the door that left the late comers stranded on the landing.

He decided it would be more fun picking them off one by one, and watching to see if any one of them would actually change his behaviour in an attempt to prolong his miserable, misspent life. At the very least, by a process of elimination, he'd find out which member of their tribe was the guardian of that door on the third floor.

He drained his whisky and checked his phone for messages.

He slipped into the building, through the entrance that was always open to Long Street, a little after three-thirty in the morning and shook the water from his jacket. The ground floor was deserted.

He was in no hurry to complete his mission. If he found a sleeping straggler locked out on the landing, he'd dispatch him. If not, he'd come back again, when he had another sleepless night to fill.

When he reached the second floor he glanced into the shooting room. No-one in the room seemed to notice him standing in the shadows as he surveyed its floor, lit by the lights in the street below. There were three stoned users sprawled on the floor. He was tempted to take one of them out, but decided they were still young enough to salvage their lives, if they wanted to. He turned away and made his way silently up to the third floor landing.

It was dark on the landing, darker than he remembered from the previous week. The stench was almost unbearable. He switched to breathing through his mouth and let his eyes adjust to the darkness.

After a few minutes, he could see into the gloom, and the form of one of his targets, propped up in the corner of the landing away from the stairs, materialised in his field of vision.

He took out his mobile phone, activated the torch and placed it facing the wall next to the right arm of the man on the floor. There was enough light for him to see what he needed to see to do what he'd come to do. He pulled the guy's arm out of his coat. The old man didn't move. He checked to confirm that he was still alive, and then got out his equipment.

It was all over in less than ten minutes, and two minutes after he'd confirmed his victim no longer had a pulse, he walked into the lane through the drug dealers' escape hatch and headed for the street where he'd left the Toyota, wondering how many lines the paper would use to sum up this one's life story.

CHAPTER 9

CARL AND HARRY walked to the State Administration Building across the plaza from Police Headquarters and took the elevator to the Office of State Supply, which was located on the fifteenth floor. They had to wait to speak to Pam Watson, who was still in a meeting when they arrived.

'I suppose you want to talk about John,' said Pam, when they were seated in her office.

'We're trying to establish Mr Drake's movements in the days before his death,' said Carl. 'When was the last time you saw him?'

'Last Friday, just before I left the office.'

'He didn't come into work on Monday?'

'I believe he was here but I wasn't in Monday, and he hasn't been in since. I mean, he didn't come in after Monday.'

'Is there anyone who can confirm that he was here Monday?'

'Pat was in Monday. He sits next to John. Would you like to speak to Pat?'

'Yes, but before we do that, perhaps you could tell me where you were on Monday, Ms Watson?'

'I was at home. My son wasn't well. I had to keep him home from school.'

Carl glanced at Harry. He was taking notes. 'How would you describe Mr Drake? What sort of person was he?'

'He'd only been with us for a few months, so I can't say I knew him all that well. I didn't mix with him socially, but as far as work goes, he did what I asked him to do. I'd say he was competent and he was pleasant enough.'

'Do you know if he was prone to depression or anxiety?'

'Not that I am aware of, Inspector. From his leave records, I'd say John was one of those guys who never got sick. He's certainly never used any sick leave since joining us.'

'Did he apply for any leave on Monday?'

'To be honest, I haven't looked. I assumed he'd applied through my manager when he didn't come in. That's the standard protocol and John knew all the protocols. He was a stickler for the rules.'

They watched as she opened an application on her computer and checked.

'Oh, there's nothing here, which suggests he must have intended to come in on Tuesday.'

'How did he seem to you last Friday?'

'Same as always.'

'He didn't look as if he had something on his mind? Something bothering him?'

'I only spoke with him briefly, Inspector. As you can imagine, my days are full of meetings, and last Friday was no different.'

Carl noted that she wasn't looking directly at him, and that beads of perspiration were glistening along her upper lip.

'Did he get on with his colleagues?'

'I think so. I haven't had any complaints or heard any rumours to the contrary.'

'Do you have any idea what he did after hours?'

'As I said, Inspector, I really didn't have anything to do with him outside of work and he hadn't been here long enough for me to get to know him all that well.'

'Perhaps you could show us where he worked and introduce us to Pat before we go, Ms Watson,' said Carl.

'Okay, we can do that now. Pat's just outside.'

They left her office and walked to a workstation, that Carl realised was within line of sight from Pam's desk, where she introduced them to Pat Williams, who confirmed that Drake had been in the office on Monday.

'Didn't seem any different to me, Inspector.'

'What was he like to work with?'

'Kept to himself most of the time.'

'Any idea what he did after work?'

'Not really. We only talked about work stuff and things like the footy most of the time. Perhaps if he'd been here a bit longer he might have told me more about himself.' He pointed to a photograph of a warship on the wall of John's workstation. 'The only thing he ever mentioned about his family was that his brother was the captain of a warship in the Persian Gulf. Seemed pretty proud about that.'

Carl looked at the photograph and thought anyone would be proud of a brother commanding one of those ships.

'When did he leave for the day?'

'Usual time. Four-thirty. He liked to catch the tram before the five o'clock crowd.'

'What did you make of that, Harry?' said Carl, as they stepped out of the elevator into the lobby of the State Administration Building.

'Sounds like he didn't tell them anything about his suspicions.'

'You'd think he'd tell his manager, wouldn't you? I mean he'd only been in the place five minutes.'

'Maybe he thought she was in on it,' said Harry.

'You could be right. I'm not sure she was being one hundred percent honest with us when I asked her about how Drake appeared to be last Friday.'

'Yeah, I got that feeling as well.'

They walked out into the weak autumn sunshine and headed across the plaza towards Police Headquarters.

'What if Drake was just one of those delusional trouble-makers the Auditor General was talking about? You know, someone who thought he had discovered something when really there was nothing there?'

'If that's the case, Harry, why is he dead?'

At the end of the day the team gathered in the Incident Room to debrief.

'It appears Drake was at work on Monday until he left to catch the tram home around four-thirty. No-one there seems to know much about his life outside of work, and there was no mention of him raising any concerns with his manager. Sounds like he was a bit of a secret squirrel. Any luck at Transport?' said Carl.

'We interviewed eight people from the section he worked in, including his former manager,' said DC Templar. 'None of them knew anything about what he did outside of work either. The manager said he regarded him as a competent worker and a reliable team member but said he'd been surprised when Drake had applied for the position at State Supply.' DC Templar referred to her notes. 'There was one young lad though, a lad named Malcolm Reid, who'd only joined Transport a few weeks before

Drake moved to State Supply. He told us he'd seen Drake hanging out with young girls in some of the student nightspots around town.'

'Bit of a cradle-snatcher, then,' said DC Paterson.

'Perhaps we have an angry drug dealing father on our hands, Boss,' said DS Fuller.

'Thanks, Lisa. That gives us another line of inquiry to investigate besides suspecting someone in the Auditor General's office.'

'Why do you suspect someone there?' said DC Beard.

'Think about it, Nigel. Who else could have tipped off the parties that their little arrangement with State Supply was up?'

'What if there was no little arrangement, Inspector?'

'Why would you think that, Wayne?'

'Because according to Drake, the arrangement would have to be with the Walker Group. That's who he's named in this document. Apparently, they own the companies that have the contracts for cleaning Police Headquarters and City Hospital. He reckons those contracts are overpriced by at least fifteen percent, and claims they were renewed last year without a proper review. You know who the Walker Group is, don't you, Inspector? Peter Walker.'

Carl took a moment to review what he knew about Peter Walker, the chairman of the Walker Group, which was one of the city's most successful property developers. Walker was a friend of several ministers of the State Government. 'You could be right, Wayne. I can't see Walker bribing a couple of public servants to get a cleaning contract signed.'

'It may not be Walker himself that's involved, though. It could be one of his managers making sure he looks good to his boss,' said Harry.

'Guess that's possible,' said DC Paterson. 'I'll see if I can find out who's running the cleaning companies Drake named.'

'Okay, we know Drake was still alive late Monday afternoon.

Think we need to focus on finding out what he did and where he went after he left work. DCI Rankin made a public appeal for help in that regard during today's media conference. That should air in tonight's news and tomorrow morning's paper. Let's see what response we've had when we meet in the morning.'

Carl left the office and drove home. He wasn't sure what to expect when he got there. Nina seemed to be in a different mood every night now that her pregnancy was approaching full term.

In recent days, she'd even given him a hard time about the hours he was keeping, which had surprised Carl. He'd assumed she'd be more understanding in that regard, until he'd thought about it. That's when he'd realised how frustrating it must be for her to be home alone and constrained by a swollen body.

On the way home, he stopped at a florist's and bought her a bunch of flowers, and then called to say he would be home in ten minutes.

When he arrived home she was in the kitchen, with one arm under her swollen belly, cooking. The flowers got him a kiss and an eyelash flutter backed by a cheeky grin.

Over dinner Nina quizzed him about his casework. She might be on leave but she liked to keep her hand in and Carl found talking with her often helped clarify his thinking.

'Sounds like the only people that knew about his allegations are in the Auditor General's office,' said Carl.

'I suppose it's possible someone there could be colluding with the people in State Supply. Perhaps the person that does the audit.'

'We haven't been able to interview her yet.'

Nina collected the empty plates and took them over to the kitchen bench.

'What about the deaths of those homeless men? Making any progress with that?'

'We haven't got much to go on. No witnesses. Dean's even been back and taken another look at the landing where the bodies were found. Interesting thing, though, is they were killed the same way as this Drake guy. Not exactly the same MO but close enough.'

'Wonder what the connection is there. Do you want coffee?'

'I'll make it.' Carl went into the kitchen and made himself an espresso. Coffee was something else Nina had given up for the duration of her pregnancy. As he made his coffee, he wondered if there was a connection between the cases as well but couldn't see it.

'What do you think a guy who lives on South Terrace was doing in Bayside late at night, Carl? It's not like Jetty Road is a red-light district.'

'Maybe he didn't go there voluntarily. Dean reckons he was dragged into the warehouse. We're only assuming he was killed there. It's possible the body may only have been dumped there.'

'I'm sure you'll work it out. You always do. Can you massage my shoulders?'

CHAPTER 10

Sgt Dean Lang from Forensics appeared in the doorway of Carl's office. 'Got a moment, Inspector?'

Carl beckoned him in. 'What's up?'

Sgt Lang handed him his preliminary report on the forensic examination of John Drake's apartment.

'That apartment's had the once over, Inspector. As soon as we opened the door it was pretty obvious someone had been through its contents before we got there. And, the thing is, whoever it was didn't break in. I'd say they had a key.'

'Any prints?'

'Mostly Drake's. A couple of others but I'd say our intruder was wearing gloves. Probably thought that was all he'd need to do to remain invisible.'

'And, was he successful?'

'You know how it is, Inspector. People think if they wear gloves they won't leave any identifiable trace of having been there.'

From long experience of working with Dean Lang, Carl knew he was about to hear something of value to his investigation.

'We picked up quite a bit of hair from the carpet, and not all of it from the same head. And, we've got a collection of pubic hairs from the sheets on the bed. At a guess, I'd say the victim had shared his bed with someone since the last time he'd changed his sheets.'

'So our intruder might be a girlfriend?'

'Who knows? But you'd have to wonder what she was looking for and why she was looking for anything at all, don't you think, Inspector?'

'More likely to be his killer, I'd say. At least now we know what might have happened to his keys.'

'Guess so.'

'Find any matches in the DNA database?'

'We're working on that. I'll let you know if we get a hit.'

'Anything else?'

'Only this.' Dean handed him a photograph of a black, dust covered briefcase with an evidence tag on it inside a large plastic bag. 'There's thirty thousand dollars in cash in that briefcase. Found it in the ceiling.'

'Funny place to keep your savings.'

'Might not exactly be savings, Inspector. I'll test the notes. If he was in the trade there'll be telltale traces of drugs on the notes. The stuff comes out through your pores. It's bloody hard to wash off.'

'Hadn't picked Drake as a dealer.'

'Having smelly bank notes doesn't make him a dealer, Inspector, but it does make you wonder where he got the money, and why it was in his ceiling and not in the bank.'

'Did Drake have a computer?'

'We didn't find one in the apartment but there was a wireless gateway modem. Maybe that was one of the things our intruder was after.'

Carl's picture of his victim as a lonely, middle-aged, law abiding public servant was morphing into he didn't quite know what, and he was beginning to suspect that his death might not be connected to his allegations of corruption within State Supply.

He hoped somebody had seen Drake in or around either Jetty Road or Sunshine Street. He knew there was a string of nightspots in among all the trendy shops on Jetty Road, and the number of syringes in the warehouse suggested it got regular use as a shooting gallery, so there was a possibility people had been about even if he'd been killed in the early hours of Tuesday morning.

Carl looked at the pictures on the whiteboard in the Incident Room and wondered whether he should merge Drake's murder with the investigation into the deaths of the homeless men, but he still couldn't see the connection between them, apart from the mode of execution. Drake had been killed in the same way but he certainly hadn't been homeless.

'Wayne, I want you and Nigel to visit the homeless shelter in Long Street again. See if anybody remembers seeing anything. We need to let them know we're doing something.'

By Tuesday morning, Carl was beginning to doubt whether they'd get any sightings of Drake from the public. There had been no calls to the Crime Stoppers Hotline since their public appeal for assistance.

'Excuse me, Inspector. Thought you'd like to know I've just taken a call from a woman who remembers Drake being on the tram.'

Carl looked up from his screen at DC Paterson. 'And?'

'She told me she remembered him because he was having a loud, heated argument with someone on his mobile phone,' said DC Paterson.

'Did she remember any of the conversation?'

'Only that he was very apologetic when people on the tram glared at him.'

'Did she remember where he got off?'

'Said he was still on the tram when she got off at South Terrace.'

'That's interesting. Drake's apartment is on South Terrace.'

'Must have been going someplace else, Inspector.'

'We need to find out who he was talking to and where he went. Let's see if DS Fuller's had any luck with Telstra.'

They walked over to DS Fuller's desk. 'Got Drake's phone records yet, Harry?'

'About half an hour ago.'

'Who was he talking to around 16:45 on the Monday? Sounds like he was having an argument with someone.'

DS Fuller opened the email he'd received from Telstra and clicked on the attachment. 'Here we go, Boss.' He scanned the spreadsheet. 'Looks like he made quite a few calls to that number.'

'Find out whose number it is.'

It took DS Fuller fifteen minutes to get that information from Telstra and report back to Carl. 'The number belongs to a George Brock. Got an address here for an apartment in Bayside.'

'Okay, I'll take Wayne and go and have a chat with Mr Brock.'

CHAPTER 11

SONYA CURTIS and the members of the contracts approval committee sat around the table in their preferred meeting room, which was located next to Sonya's office. On Sonya's left, sat Pam Watson who provided secretarial services to the committee. To her right, sat the two other active members of the committee: Mary Grant and Helen Stein.

The four women had known each other all of their lives. They had grown up within similar working class families living in the same depressing suburb and had attended the same schools. Sonya had been their leader ever since their first encounter in kindergarten.

Pam, who had fallen pregnant during year twelve, had been the only one of the four not to go to university straight from school. While her friends had studied commerce and worked part-time, she'd become a single mother and lived on the supporting mothers pension. She'd resumed her studies when her daughter had started high school, and that's when she'd met Trevor Hunter, a charming mature-aged student who, like Pam, had been completing a commerce degree to get on in the world. That encounter had led to Trevor fathering Pam's son but he had refused to leave his wife for her.

When her son had started school, Pam's friends had persuaded her to join them in the public service and had helped her find a position in State Supply. As it turned out, she had been the spearhead and when they'd realised what they could do there, Sonya had set the plan in place that resulted in them becoming the contracts approval committee.

Coincidently, in the years since he'd fathered Pam's second child, Trevor Hunter had risen to become the chief executive officer of the cleaning division in the Walker Group; an outcome which had given the contracts approval committee an opportunity to strike a mutually beneficial arrangement with him, thanks to his relationship with Pam.

On the table in front of each committee member lay a copy of the document John Drake had given to Pam. In the corner behind Pam's chair sat the dull grey paper shredder that had become a permanent fixture of the meeting room used by the committee.

'Does anyone disagree with Pam's initial assessment of the document?' asked Sonya.

'He certainly didn't do a very good job of backing up his allegations with any concrete evidence,' said Mary.

Sonya turned her gaze to Helen Stein.

'I agree. There's nothing here that can't be explained by a reference to an appropriate policy or government directive,' said Helen.

'There will no doubt be a thorough audit of our processes,' said Sonya, 'as I have it from a reliable source that he sent a copy of this report to the Auditor General.'

'Shit!' said Pam.

The committee members looked at her.

'That means John was killed for nothing, doesn't it?' said Pam.

'You mean he was killed because of this?' said Mary, holding up her copy of the document. 'How did anyone else know about it?'

'I thought it was only prudent to alert them,' said Sonya, 'and how were we to know John had already sent his report to the Auditor General?'

'What did you think they'd do?' said Mary.

'Destroy any evidence their end,' said Sonya. 'I had no idea they'd have him killed.'

The committee members stared at each other.

'With the police sniffing around, who knows what they'll uncover?' said Pam.

'There's no way they can trace his death back to us. We didn't kill him,' said Sonya, ' and we didn't ask for him to be killed either.'

'We tipped them off, for Christ's sake!' said Mary.

'How are the police going to know that?' said Sonya.

'Don't they trace phone records?' said Mary.

'I didn't use my phone,' said Pam. 'I told Trevor when he came to see Brian on the weekend.'

'Are you sure you know who Trevor's working for? I can't imagine Peter Walker arranging for someone to be killed,' said Mary.

'He works for someone called Imbroglio now that Walker has retired,' said Pam.

'With a name like that he's probably in the mafia. No wonder they had John killed.'

'We could be jumping to conclusions,' said Helen. 'Anyone could have killed him. It could even have been accidental, when you consider where his body was found. He could have committed suicide, for all we know.'

'Do we know if the police have access to the report he sent to the Auditor General?' asked Mary.

Sonya twisted her hands together. 'I believe they do.'

'So, what are we going to do?' asked Mary.

'We tell the police we don't know anything about Drake's allegations.' Sonya turned to Pam. 'Shred all these copies, Pam. I'd ask you to delete his personal files but I think that would be a mistake if the police come looking for them, and besides, I don't think we can make them disappear in any case.' Turning back to the others, she continued, 'and we maintain that we have awarded all contracts in accordance with government policy, and open our records to the Auditor General when he asks. And,' she paused, 'no-one is to do anything out of the ordinary.'

'Do you think we're in any danger?' asked Mary.

'What do you mean?' asked Sonya.

'We know the facts. John only thought he knew what was going on, and God only knows how far they'll go to make sure we keep quiet once they find out the Auditor General has a copy of his allegations.'

'It's our job to make sure they remain nothing but allegations,' said Sonya, 'and, remember, it cuts both ways. They have more to lose than we do now if they killed John.'

Shortly after the contracts approval committee meeting ended, Sonya Curtis received a call from Steven Wilmington.

'Coffee in ten,' said Steven.

Sonya looked at her diary. 'I can make it in twenty.'

'I'll be waiting.'

When Sonya arrived in the coffee shop in the lobby of the State Administration Building, Steven was seated at their usual table in the back corner. It was both public and private enough at the same time.

They held hands under the table.

'You realise I'm going to have to authorise a thorough audit of your contract approval process. Is that going to cause you a problem?'

'Will Elena be leading the audit as usual?'

'No. I've got the Corruption Commissioner breathing down my neck on this one, seeing that the police are claiming our informant has been murdered. In fact, I've just had a very uncomfortable meeting with him. I'll be sending in a completely fresh team to dispel any perception of corruption in my office.'

'Do you have that many people, Steve?'

Steven smiled. 'I've got enough. I'll be allocating the audit to the Transport team. They have the required contract experience. You should be hearing from them within the next week or so.'

'That shouldn't be a problem. I'm sure everything is properly documented and we always follow the appropriate guidelines, but thanks for the heads up,' said Sonya.

They waited in silence while the waitress delivered their coffees.

'How did the police find out that he had made these outrageous allegations? You didn't call them, did you?'

Steven looked across the coffee shop before answering. 'I generally keep this sort of thing strictly in-house until we've had time to investigate. You have no idea how many of these we get, and most of them are based on a complete lack of understanding of events. Some are pure malice.' He smiled and squeezed her hand. 'But we can't have the public thinking we're all corrupt just because someone thinks he's found something. So, no, I didn't call the police, they called me. Appears Drake told his father that he'd posted a document to my office. They wanted to know what was in it.'

'I wonder what Drake's motivation was for making these allegations. He didn't strike me as someone who'd be driven by malice or ambition.'

'Maybe you or someone else in your office did something that pissed him off. We get allegations from disgruntled employees all the time.'

'I didn't think he'd been with us long enough for anyone to piss him off, Steve. He was one of those guys that kept to himself and was so shy he never looked you in the eye when he was talking to you. Pam tells me she doesn't think he even had a girlfriend. Although, I think a boyfriend would have been more likely myself.' She drained the last of her flat white. 'He must have been up to something outside the office, though, don't you think?'

Steven shrugged his shoulders. 'Who knows? Let's wait for the police to sort it out. Isn't that what we pay them for?'

George Brock's apartment was not located in the upmarket section of Bayside. When they arrived at the address Telstra had provided, they discovered that the apartment was one of ten in a rundown building on Seaview Street that had once provided budget accommodation to families enjoying a seaside holiday. Carl thought the building looked like it was waiting for someone to knock it down.

The building had two levels. The only access to the apartments on the upper level was by an external staircase that opened onto a balcony exposed to the elements. DC Paterson knocked on the door of number five on the upper level, while Carl enjoyed the ocean view visible through the trees that had begun to shed their leaves in preparation for the coming winter. There was no response.

'Try the place next door,' said Carl.

DC Paterson banged on the screen door of number six. A dog barked from somewhere behind the door.

'Shut up, Freddie! Stop it!' The door of the apartment cracked open behind the locked screen door. 'Who's there?'

'We're the police, sir. Can we have a word?' said Carl.

There was a click, and the screen door opened to reveal an

elderly man, and a very excited fox-terrier, which scooted out of the apartment and sniffed around Carl's shoes, before cocking its leg and peeing on the wall.

'Inside, Freddie!'

The dog ran back into the apartment and started barking.

'Thought I told you to shut up!'

The dog put its tail between its legs and dropped to the floor.

'Stay there!'

The old man stepped out onto the balcony and closed the screen door. The dog peered at them through the screen, tongue out and tail wagging.

Carl showed the old man his badge. 'We're looking for George Brock.'

'Who's he?'

'We understand he lives in number five.'

'Oh, him. Is that what his name is?'

'Any idea when he might be home?'

The old man screwed up his face. 'Haven't seen him for a few days.'

Carl wondered whether Brock had already done a runner.

'When was the last time you saw him?'

The old man scratched the back of his head. 'Be nearly a week now, I reckon. Can't say for sure.'

Carl pulled out his iPhone and found his image of John Drake. 'Do you know this man?'

The old man squinted and peered at the image. 'Can't say that I know him, but I know who he is. He comes to see the boy next door.'

'Boy?'

'That's right. Be lucky if he was twenty.'

Carl looked at DC Paterson, who shrugged his shoulders.

'Do you know if he works?'

The old man laughed. 'Works? You've got to be joking. He's

nothing but a layabout. Don't know where he gets his money from, unless it's from idiots like that guy in the photo.'

Carl wondered whether Brock was a rent boy. 'When was the last time you saw this man here?'

'He was here one night, last week. I think it was Monday. Yes, Monday. They had one hell of an argument over something. Even Freddie hadn't heard swearing like they were carrying on.'

'Did you see him leave?'

'They left together, around seven thirty. Seemed to have sorted out whatever their problem was.'

'Oh, how could you tell?'

'They were holding hands, like lovers.' The old man screwed up his face as if he'd just bitten into a lemon. 'Bloody, gays. We used to bash 'em back in my day.'

Carl smiled, and wondered whether that's what he had on his hands. 'Did you see either of them return?'

'Can't say that I did. It's not like I spend my life watching their comings and goings. I do go to bed, and when I do, Inspector, I sleep like a log unless Freddie goes troppo.'

'Does Mr Brock have any other visitors?'

'There's another young fellow that comes around but only during the day. He's here every week. Sometimes three or four times. But the boy goes out a lot, and he seems to have plenty of money. Always got new clothes, and he did up the apartment a few months back after he moved in.' The old man twisted his lips. 'Must have paid for it himself. I can't get the bloody landlord to do anything in my place.'

'Do you have a contact number for your landlord, sir?'

The old man went inside to locate his landlord's telephone number. Freddie went troppo and barked at Carl and Wayne through the screen door, until he was hit with a slipper.

When Freddie stopped barking, Carl asked Wayne to try

Brock's number. The call went through to voice mail but they could hear a phone ringing inside apartment five.

The apartments were managed by the Bayside office of Ellis Real Estate. A young woman answered when Carl called the number the old man gave him.

'We don't have a George Brock at that address, Inspector.'

'Who is apartment five leased to, then?'

'To a John Drake.'

'Do you have a photograph of him on your file?'

'Oh, yes, we have a photographic record of all our tenants, Inspector. Makes it a lot easier if we have any problems.'

Carl left DC Paterson at the scene with Brock's elderly neighbour and went to speak to the property manager. He showed her the photograph of John Drake on his iPhone. It matched the one she had in her file.

'We picked up Mr Drake's body from a building in Sunshine Street last Thursday.'

'You mean he's dead?'

'I'm afraid so.'

'Then who's this George Brock you asked about? I'd never heard of him before you called.'

'I haven't met him yet but, according to Telstra, he gave them apartment five as his home address. I'm trying to locate him in relation to Mr Drake's death.'

'Well, I'm not sure how I can help you, Inspector.'

'I think it might be a good idea if we took a look inside that apartment. I have some concerns for Mr Brock's safety.' Sensing she was not quite sure of her position, Carl pushed on. 'His neighbour told me he hadn't seen Mr Brock for nearly a week, and we can hear his phone ringing from inside the apartment.'

'Don't you need a search warrant or something to do that?'

'Not if you agree to open the door, and it will save us all the trouble of having to get the door replaced if I don't have to knock it down.'

The property manager opened the top drawer of her desk and took out a key, which she used to open the key safe on the wall behind her.

'This is the key to number five. I'm on my own here today, so I'd appreciate it if you'd return it when you're finished.'

Carl issued her a regulation receipt for the key and gave her his card. 'I'll drop it back shortly, if it's all clear, otherwise I'll call you if I need to hold on to it.'

'We're open until six, Inspector.'

'One more thing, if I may? How did Mr Drake pay his rent?'

'We do everything by direct debit these days, Inspector.'

DC Paterson was scratching Freddie's belly when Carl got back to the apartment block. Freddie was lapping up the attention, while his owner leant over the rail with a cigarette and told DC Paterson about all the tenants that had lived in number five over the twenty years he had lived in number six.

'Okay, Freddie, we'd better go in so these policemen can do their job.'

Carl inserted the key and opened the door to apartment five. The odour of stale air trapped indoors for a week or more greeted them. The interior was nothing like the outside of the building or the interior of number six. The floor was covered with deep-pile black carpet, which filled the apartment with a smell that betrayed its recent installation. The black and chrome furniture in the main area of the apartment looked new, as did the chrome kitchen appliances. An iPhone 6 was plugged into a charger on the bench.

A roughly made double bed stood in the main bedroom. The second bedroom contained a black wooden desk with a laptop on it and a black filing cabinet, which was locked.

The white tiles on the floor of the bathroom gleamed in the late afternoon sunlight streaming in through the clear glass window, when DC Paterson opened the door.

'Oh shit! Inspector, you'd better take a look in here.'

DC Paterson backed out of the bathroom. 'Don't go past the doorway, Inspector. We'll have to secure the scene.'

Carl looked into the bathroom. The black, full length bath along the white tiled wall of the small room held a partially clad body, tightly wrapped in clear, bloodstained plastic.

They retraced their steps to the door and stepped outside.

'I guess that's George Brock,' said Carl.

'Nice of them to gift wrap him for us.'

It was dark outside by the time Dr Jonas and the crime scene investigators from Forensics arrived. Dr Jonas took one look at the body in the bath and decided his best course of action would be to transfer it as it was to the morgue.

The bathroom looked spotless. In fact, the crime scene investigators found no sign of a struggle in the apartment until they pulled back the duvet on the bed. The white sheets were stained with dark marks that looked like dried blood. Once they realised the victim had been killed in the bedroom, they looked more closely at the black carpet and spotted a trail of dried bloody footprints leading from the bedroom to the bathroom, and another trail that went towards the front door.

A search of the desk drawers unearthed the key to the locked filing cabinet.

'Interesting collection in here, Inspector,' said the constable examining the drawers of the filing cabinet.

'What have you got?' said Carl.

The constable held up a carton of syringes. 'Unless your victim is a type one diabetic, I'd say he might have a drug problem.'

'Any sign of drugs?'

The constable removed more boxes from the filing cabinet. 'Got some bagged up white powder here, Inspector.'

Carl looked at the small pile of clear plastic bags of white powder, neatly stacked inside the box in the constable's hand, and wondered if Brock was a dealer.

'Fair bit of cash in here, Inspector.'

Robbery, thought Carl, obviously wasn't the motive for whoever had killed Brock, assuming the plastic wrapped body was Brock.

'Got a driver's licence here, Inspector,' said DC Paterson, from the bedroom where he was going through the pockets of the clothes hanging in the wardrobe.

'What's the name?'

'Georgina Brock and, Inspector, there's a hell of a lot of women's underwear in these drawers and some pretty dresses hanging in here.'

CHAPTER 13

DC Templar asked for a moment of Carl's time as he walked past her desk on his way back from lunch on Wednesday.

'What's on your mind, Lisa?'

'I've been running some background checks on the people on that committee at State Supply. They appear to have a long history.'

'Oh, how long?'

'Right back to their days at City Girls High.'

'Intriguing, but not all that surprising given the size of this town.'

'Yes, that was my initial thinking as well, but then I discovered that most of them had joined State Supply around the same time, and that prompted me to consider if there was some other connection.'

Carl wondered where Lisa was going with this. 'And, is there another connection?'

'I checked their employment histories with the public service. It looks like three of them have moved around from agency to agency as a group for the last twenty-five years. First, Sonya Curtis moves to an agency and then the other two follow, within a few months. The odd one out is Watson. She didn't join the public service until ten years ago, and she's been at State Supply all that time.'

'Sounds like Sonya Curtis moves around with her own support group.'

Lisa sank back into her chair. 'I thought public service jobs were supposed to be awarded on merit.'

'They probably are, officially, but sometimes it's who you know that makes the difference. The way life is I'm afraid.'

'Does that mean I can rely on you to put in a good word for me when I'm ready to apply for sergeant?' Lisa's face lit up with a grin.

'Only if you deserve it.' He winked at her.

'Is this something I need to write up, then?'

'Make a note of it. If anything, it will serve to warn us to be on guard if we need to have further dealings with them, but unless we can establish a connection between their activities and Drake's death, that's the sort of information that could be of use to the Auditor General if he suspects corruption, and I'm sure he has access to it already.'

Carl looked at his watch. He still had a few minutes before he'd have to leave for Brock's autopsy at one thirty. 'Found out anything else about our Mr Drake from your interviews?'

'I had an interesting chat with his sister-in-law this morning. I met her for coffee at the airport. She's in security down there. She was a bit reluctant to talk at first, but then she told me she thought Drake had been leading a double life, presenting the good boy image to his parents but doing other stuff she wasn't clear about. Said her husband had warned her to be wary of him, and not to leave their daughters alone with him before he left on his last deployment to the Gulf.'

Carl stood with DS Fuller and waited for the pathologist to conduct his autopsy of the body found wrapped in plastic in George Brock's apartment. Attending autopsies was one part of the job Carl never enjoyed but he always marvelled at the way Mike Jonas went about it in a calm, relaxed manner, as if he was examining the most precious thing on earth.

Dr Jonas cut the plastic wrap and started to peel it from the body.

'God, he must have used a whole bloody box of this stuff!' said Mike.

It wasn't long before it became obvious that the driver's licence found in the apartment belonged to the deceased.

Beneath the bloodstained plastic wrap was the body of a young woman, with short dark hair, dressed in a bloodstained T-shirt that had once been white. The body had three deep stab wounds, just below the breast line, and a slash across the throat that, in Dr Jonas's opinion, had been inflicted post mortem as if her killer had wanted to make sure she was dead.'

Dr Jonas slowly examined the exterior of the body looking for other signs of injury.

'Looks like she had sex with someone before she was killed.'

'Did he leave his card?' said Carl.

'I'll take a swab, but we won't know until we get it tested.'

'When do you think she was killed, Mike?' Carl watched as Dr Jonas weighed his options.

'Hard to be exact. This plastic would have sealed the body from the air. That would slow decomposition. I don't know. Possibly, a week. Could be longer.'

'Did they find a weapon?' said DS Fuller.

'Forensics have a carving knife from the kitchen that's tested positive for blood. We'll know for sure when we cross check the blood with the victim's, but the wounds look like they could have been inflicted with that sort of knife,' said Mike.

Carl wondered what he and Nina were doing, bringing another person into a world where people killed beautiful young girls in the prime of life and helpless old men who couldn't defend themselves.

'You okay, Boss?'

'Think I need a holiday, Harry, or a change of job.'

'I'd buy you drink, except Nina would kill both of us if she found out.'

CHAPTER 14

Twenty-year old Georgina Brock's driver's licence listed her address as being in the leafy eastern suburbs. The address of her parents, according to Motor Registrations. Carl went to the address with PC Highland, a community liaison officer, who would handle arrangements once he had broken the news to Georgina's parents.

When Carl knocked on the door of the large stone house, set back from the road behind a manicured cypress hedge and a lawn large enough to play bowls on, it was opened by a middle-aged woman with a head of bleached blonde hair, dressed in jeans and an off-white silk blouse that did little to conceal her feminine assets.

'Mrs Brock?' asked Carl.

'Depends who wants to know, Luv.' She grinned at him but did not come out on to the porch.

Carl smiled, and thought he could see where Georgina had gotten her looks, as he took out his badge. 'Inspector West, City Police.'

'Ooh, an inspector.' She flashed him a smile, then crossed her arms over her breasts, as if she'd finally remembered she wasn't wearing a bra. 'What do you want?'

Carl heard the snap of her defensive shield sliding into place and wondered why she was wary of him.

'I need to talk to you about your daughter Georgina.'

'She doesn't live here anymore. Kicked the little bitch out months ago. She was nothing but trouble.' Mrs Brock started to close the door.

Carl stepped forward and stopped her from shutting the door. 'Do you mind if we come in?'

'Why don't you go away?'

Carl wondered what sort of girl Georgina Brock had been if her mother didn't want to talk about her. 'I can't, Mrs Brock. I'm afraid I have bad news.'

Mrs Brock released her hold on the door and turned her head into the house. 'George! The police are here about Georgina.'

A man, who looked considerably older than Mrs Brock to Carl, joined her at the door. 'Who are you?'

'I'm Inspector West, from City Police, Mr Brock.' Carl held out his badge. 'I'm sorry, but we're here to inform you that Georgina has been killed.'

'Noooo!' Mrs Brock raised her hand to her mouth and fell against her husband.

Mr Brock wrapped his arms around his wife to support her and looked at Carl.

'What? In some sort of accident?'

'I'm afraid she's been murdered.'

'Murdered?'

Carl nodded, and stepped into the hallway to help Mr Brock carry his wife into the front room.

While Mr Brock tended to his distraught wife, PC Highland found her way into the kitchen, where she put the kettle on and made a pot of tea.

Carl waited while the Brocks sat in the soft-leather chairs of their lounge room, drinking sweet tea. Mrs Brock sat in silence, holding a cup of tea in her lap, her forgotten breasts pushing against the sheer material of her off-white blouse, which now matched the color of her face.

'Are you sure it's Georgina?' said Mr Brock.

Carl handed him the clear plastic bag containing Georgina's driver's licence. 'This was in the apartment where her body was found.'

Mr Brock looked at the driver's licence and handed it to his wife. 'We haven't seen her for months.'

'Your wife said you'd thrown her out.'

Mr Brock looked at his wife. She nodded her head. 'I guess there's no need to deny it any longer, Inspector. She got mixed up with the drugs crowd at university. She wouldn't listen to us. God, we tried everything but I didn't expect this to happen,' said Mr Brock.

'No-one ever does, Mr Brock. Did you know where she was living?'

Carl waited as Mr Brock took several deep breaths and blew his nose loudly in a tissue.

'We didn't exactly part on good terms, Inspector. She's only called once since she left and that wasn't very pleasant.'

Mrs Brock handed the driver's licence back to Carl. 'What happens now?'

Carl noticed there was no longer a tone of defiance in her voice. 'We'll need someone to formally identify the body and claim it for burial. Constable Highland will organise that with you, when you're ready.'

'Anything else?' said Mrs Brock.

Carl found the photograph of John Drake on his iPhone. 'Do either of you recognise this man?'

'Isn't that the guy that was found dead the other day? I saw his picture on the TV,' said Mr Brock.

'Yes, his name was John Drake. Does that ring any bells?'

'Can't say it does,' said Mr Brock, looking at his wife.

She shook her head. 'Doesn't mean anything to me. Why are you asking?'

'He was paying the rent for the apartment Georgina was living in.'

Carl took their blank stares to mean they had no idea what their daughter's living arrangements had been. 'Any idea why she was going by the name of George and dressing as a man?'

'She's been known as George to her friends since school, Inspector, and she's never been into girls' clothes. I had a hell of a time getting her to wear her school uniform when she was at high school,' said Mrs Brock.

'Did she have a boyfriend?'

'That was the bloody problem, Inspector. She did anything and everything Ryan said,' said Mr Brock.

The tone in his voice, and the infusion of some color back into his face, suggested to Carl that there was probably a fair amount of animosity between Mr Brock and this Ryan.

'Ryan who?'

'Ryan Whitaker. Georgina met him on campus last year. She was hard enough to live with before she met Ryan but she was bloody impossible to live with after she'd met him.'

Carl let him catch his breath.

'Is he the drugs connection?'

Mr Brock swept his right arm around him, pointing at the furnishings. 'It's not like we're short of a dollar, Inspector. She always had whatever it was she wanted but Ryan filled her head with wild ideas of riches. They were selling drugs to others, not using them.'

'You didn't think to report them?'

'It's not like you want to get your own child into trouble, is it? Besides, we were hoping she'd eventually come to her senses. She was a bright girl.'

Obviously, not as bright as her parents had hoped, thought Carl.

'Do you know where we can find this Ryan Whitaker?'

'I wish I did, Inspector. I'd kill the bastard myself if I could.'

Carl gathered the team together for an end of day briefing.

'I've spoken with Brock's parents. She was studying civil engineering at City University and, according to her father, dealing drugs to other students along with her boyfriend, Ryan Whitaker.' Carl wrote Ryan Whitaker on the whiteboard beneath the photograph of Georgina Brock. 'I've asked Harry to track him down.' He looked at his detectives. 'The question that's bothering me, is why was Drake paying her rent?'

'I wonder if it's linked to what that young lad told us about seeing Drake hanging about in student nightspots,' said DC Templar.

'I'd like you and Nigel to visit a few and find out.' Carl turned to DC Paterson. 'Do we have any more sightings of Drake, Wayne?'

'We've had a couple of calls from people saying they'd seen him with a young woman in a restaurant on Jetty Road on the Monday night, and a couple of others that tally with what that lad told Lisa.'

'Perhaps you'd better tell the team what Brock's neighbour told you.'

Wayne scratched his head. 'He was convinced Brock was a boy, so I'm not sure how reliable his observations are. Anyway, he told me there had been four or five different young people living in the apartment over the last five or six years. All young women until Brock, and that our mate Drake had been a regular visitor since the first girl moved in. He also told me that

Brock had another frequent visitor, a young man that visited four or five times a week but only during the day as far as he knew.'

'I wonder if that was Ryan Whitaker,' said Carl. 'Making any progress with City University, Harry?'

'They want to see a search warrant. Something about privacy issues. Anyway, I've got it in hand. Should know all about Whitaker this time tomorrow,' said DS Fuller.

'What did you find out at the bank, Nigel?'

'That was pretty weird, Inspector. Drake only has the one account with a credit card attached to it. The only regular withdrawals are the rent payment for the Bayside apartment, and payments for utilities at both his South Terrace and the Bayside apartment, and for his mobile phone. There are a few other credit card transactions that look like online purchases, but not many. But there are two types of deposits. His public service pay and monthly cash deposits ranging from one to five thousand dollars. The account's got a current balance close to three hundred thousand.'

'He must have been meeting most of his living expenses from another source, like the cash in his ceiling,' said Carl. 'Question is, what's that source?'

'Do you think Brock's murder is linked to Drake's, Inspector?' said DC Templar.

'Who knows? What we do know is that whoever killed Brock used a knife on her while she was on the bed, and then wrapped her body in a mile of plastic wrap, the sort you use in your kitchen. That's definitely a different MO.'

'Maybe we have a jealous boyfriend, Inspector?' said DS Fuller. 'Perhaps he found out that she'd been having sex with Drake.'

'Well, Harry, you'd better ask young Ryan when you find him.'

'Be interested to know what Dr Jonas' swab turns up, especially if it's a match with Drake,' said DS Fuller.

'Speaking of MOs, Inspector, don't you think it's more likely that whoever knocked off Drake might also be knocking off the homeless guys in Long Street?' said DC Paterson.

'I've discussed that with the chief, Wayne. He agrees there's a pattern with the homeless deaths but he's not convinced Drake's part of the pattern. The way Drake was forcibly injected suggests he was executed, while the others look like they were killed by someone taking advantage of the fact they were already pissed out of their minds. We need to find whoever it is, though, before every homeless bloke in the city wants to be locked up for his own protection.'

'How are we going to do that?'

'The Chief's persuaded Uniform to up their presence in Long Street and to engage with every homeless person on the street. We have to hope someone saw something and is prepared to trust us or is scared enough to talk to us.'

'Have you read these statements from Drake's neighbours, Inspector?' said DC Templar.

'Not yet.'

'Well, there's one here from the woman that lives in number one that's interesting. Looks like Drake had a visitor early Sunday evening, a guy that looked like a rugby player in a suit and dark glasses, is how she described him. Said he got into one of those big black Toyota things, and was only there for a couple of minutes because Drake wasn't home. She heard him knock and watched him leave, but she didn't think anything of it at the time.'

'Might be worth seeing if you can find anything from the traffic cameras in the area,' said Carl.

While Lisa made a note, Carl glanced at his watch. He'd promised Nina he'd be home before six. 'Okay, folks. I've got to go. I'll catch you in the morning.'

The apartment was in darkness when Carl got home. Nina was asleep on their bed, propped up by a sea of pillows, with the embroidered quilt her mother had made for her the year she'd left home to attend City University on the bed beside her, as if she'd discarded it during her sleep.

Carl hadn't seen that quilt for weeks. It was a sure sign Nina had been thinking about her parents, who had been killed in the car crash that had nearly taken her away from him only months before they'd been married. Seeing the quilt reminded him that their daughter would have no grandparents to fuss over her, and Nina would have no mother to support her in those early days of motherhood. He hoped they had made the right decision having a child and that somehow he'd be able to support her, despite the crazy hours he sometimes worked.

As he stood in the doorway of their bedroom, Nina opened her eyes and smiled weakly at him.

'I thought I heard you come in.'

Carl walked over and stood by the bed. 'Are you okay?'

'I'm feeling really tired. Do you mind making yourself something to eat?'

'What about you? Do you want me to get you anything?'

'I just want to sleep.'

Carl bent down and kissed her on the forehead. 'Are you sure you're okay? You feel really hot.'

'Just having a flush. They come and go.'

'Anything else going on?'

'Only the usual football match.' She placed a hand on her swollen belly and Carl watched it move as his daughter changed her position within her uterine home.

'Isn't she supposed to have her feet up the other end by now?'

'Dr Merry said we'd only need to worry about that if she

doesn't turn in the next couple of weeks. Apparently, they do it all in their own good time, if they're going to do it.'

'Do you want me to bring in the fan?'

'That would be nice.'

Carl retrieved the fan from the bench in the kitchen and set it on the chair in the corner of the bedroom, so that he could direct a stream of moving air over Nina as she lay in the bed. As he gazed at her, he guessed he'd be sleeping in the second bedroom, surrounded by all the baby stuff they'd purchased for their daughter.

CHAPTER 15

THERE WAS no sign of Ryan Whitaker at the address City University had given to Harry.

'Check his letter box, Nigel.'

DC Beard walked across the litter strewn yard to the bank of letter boxes in the wall that stood between the building and the street. The letter box for number six was stuffed full of junk mail and a couple of utility bills with week old postmarks.

'Looks like he hasn't cleared it for about a week, Sarge.'

Harry tried the mobile number the university had given him. It went through to voice mail. He knocked on the door of number five. A young woman holding a small boy on her hip partially opened the door. Harry could see the chain lock.

'Police,' said Harry, holding his badge out for her to read. 'I'm looking for Ryan. Have you seen him?'

She released the chain lock and opened the door. The boy buried his head into his mother's shoulder.

'Haven't seen him for a few days.' She pointed to the parking area with her free arm. 'His car's not back. He doesn't go anywhere on foot.'

'What does he drive?' said Harry.

The boy snuck a quick look at Harry, before hiding his face in his mother's shoulder again.

'He's got one of those black Toyota SUVs. Mad having one of them in the city if you ask me, but, hey, it takes all kinds.' She adjusted the boy's position on her hip.

Harry opened his iPad and showed her the photograph of Georgina Brock he'd extracted from her driver's licence record at Motor Registrations. 'Recognise this girl?'

The boy reached out to touch the iPad. His mother turned her body to place it out of his reach.

'Yeah, that's Ryan's girlfriend, George. She's around here all the time.'

Harry showed her the head and shoulders photograph of Ryan the university had supplied. 'Is this Ryan?'

'Yeah, that's him. He's hard to miss. Built like a brick shit-house.'

'Ryan,' said the boy, pointing at the iPad.

Harry smiled at him but he ducked his head into his mother's neck.

Harry handed the woman his card. 'Do you mind giving me your name?'

'Susan,' she said.

'When Ryan comes home, Susan, can you please call me on this number? It's important. George has been murdered.'

'Oh shit! You don't think Ryan did it, do you?'

'Mummy, you said a naughty word.'

'Shush, Jamie! I'm talking to the policeman.'

'Why would I think Ryan killed her?' said Harry.

'They had a doozy of a fight last time she was here.'

'Oh, when was that?' said Harry.

'A couple of weeks ago.'

The wail of a baby in distress erupted from within Susan's apartment. 'Sorry, gotta go.'

When they got back to the car, Nigel ran a query on Ryan Whitaker for the address they had with Motor Registrations. 'Do you have his date of birth, Sarge?'

Harry handed him the sheet of paper from City University.

'2014 Toyota RAV4, color black, registration RYAN-001.'

'Get an APB on it.'

Harry called DI West. 'Boss, Whitaker hasn't been home for at least a week. Apparently, he had a fight with Brock the last time she was here, and get this. According to his neighbour, he's built like a brick shit-house and drives a black RAV4. I've got an APB on it.'

'Did City give you any next of kin info?'

'I've got a Morton Sands address. We're going there now.'

When Harry and Nigel arrived at Ryan's parents' house in Morton Sands, the first thing they noticed was a black Toyota RAV4 parked under the carport. Nigel snapped a series of photographs of the car before they knocked on the door.

A tall woman with shoulder-length dark hair, dressed in a black woollen dress, opened the door to them.

'If you're selling something or want to talk about the Book of Mormon, I'm not interested.'

'We're the police, Mrs Whitaker. I'm Detective Sergeant Fuller,' said Harry, holding out his badge.

Mrs Whitaker smiled at him. 'The police? How can I help you?'

'We'd like to speak to Ryan.'

'Ryan's in Bali, Sergeant. He went with his girlfriend last week. They won't be back for a couple of weeks.'

'Do you have his flight details, Mrs Whitaker?'

Mrs Whitaker retrieved the paper with Ryan's itinerary from

the door of the fridge in the kitchen, where Ryan had stuck it with a magnet. 'He left last Wednesday. I drove him to the airport.'

'Do you mind if I make a copy of that?' said Harry.

Mrs Whitaker handed him the sheet of paper, which he photographed with his iPad.

'Do you mind telling me what this is all about, Sergeant?' said Mrs Whitaker, when Harry handed back the itinerary.

Harry showed her Georgina's photograph. 'Is this his girlfriend?'

'She was his girlfriend for a while last year but he's gone to Bali with his new girlfriend, Samantha.'

Harry wondered how new this new girlfriend was, given what Ryan's next door neighbour had told him.

'I take it you've met Georgina, Mrs Whitaker?'

'She calls herself George. Bit too headstrong for Ryan, if you ask me. It would never have worked out.'

'I'm afraid she's been murdered.'

Mrs Whitaker gasped and placed a hand over her mouth. It was several seconds before she said, 'And, you think Ryan had something to do with it?'

'We don't know who killed her, Mrs Whitaker. We're trying to work out why she was killed. We're here because we were told she was Ryan's girlfriend, which is why we'd like to talk to him. He might be able to help us find whoever killed her.'

The color returned to her cheeks as Mrs Whitaker took several deep breaths.

'He told me he hadn't seen her for months, so I'm not so sure he'll be able to help you, Sergeant.'

'Are you sure that's right, Mrs Whitaker? We've just come from speaking with one of Ryan's neighbours, who told us Georgina had been with Ryan only a couple of weeks ago.'

Mrs Whitaker shrugged her shoulders. 'Well, that's what he told me.'

Harry wondered if Ryan was one of those boys that told his mother whatever he wanted her to know, especially when the truth wasn't so convenient. He knew he'd spun a few yarns with his own mother on occasions, when he hadn't wanted her to know something.

'When was the last time you saw Georgina?'

Mrs Whitaker looked up to the right, as if she was reading through her memory files. 'The last time I saw her would have been Christmas. She was here for Christmas dinner.' She looked at Harry. 'They were still madly in love at that point. I haven't seen her since then.'

Harry showed her a photograph of John Drake. 'Do you know this man by any chance?'

Mrs Whitaker studied the photograph for several moments. 'That's John. I met him at a function at the university. One of those student dinner things they have at the start of the year. He was there with one of Ryan's friends, Helen, I think her name is. He's too old for her, in my opinion, but she was all over him.' She screwed up her face. 'Disgusting little man. Gave me the creeps.'

'His name was John Drake. He was paying the rent for the apartment Georgina was living in.'

'Don't tell me she took up with him after Ryan dumped her? I didn't think she'd be that stupid.'

'That's one of the things we're trying to work out.'

'Why don't you ask him, instead of bothering Ryan?'

'Because he's dead, Mrs Whitaker.'

She looked at Harry and then at Nigel, who was standing quietly behind Harry on the porch. 'You sure are a bearer of good news, Sergeant.'

'You wouldn't happen to know this Helen's last name by any chance?'

Mrs Whitaker shook her head, and then her eyes lit up. 'Let me get Ryan's year books. She went to school with him. Come in and have a coffee while I find them.'

Harry and Nigel sat in the front room with Mrs Whitaker, drinking coffee while she flicked through her son's year books, which she had retrieved from his room.

'Here she is. Helen Daniels. I remember now, her father owns the bakery down on the Esplanade. It's called The Hot Sands Bakery.'

The Hot Sands Bakery occupied the lower floor of a two storey bluestone building on the Esplanade at Morton Sands. The upper floor of the building had a glass enclosed balcony with a commanding view of the waves washing onto the beach across the road. It appeared to be a residence. The coffee shop attached to the bakery had a large plate glass window offering a view of the ocean. It was full of customers enjoying coffee and cake when Harry and Nigel arrived.

Reg Daniels, a tall, broad-shouldered, middle-aged man wearing a striped apron over his clothes, ushered them into a backroom away from the crowd as soon as Harry introduced himself.

'How can I help you, boys?'

Harry showed him his photograph of John Drake. 'Do you know this man, Mr Daniels?'

'I saw his picture on the TV. Why are you asking me about him?'

Harry noted the look of concern on the baker's face. 'We've been told he was a friend of your daughter Helen.'

'Friend isn't a word I'd use.'

'What word would you use, Mr Daniels?'

The baker pulled a chair out from under the table and sat down. 'Sit down, boys, this could take a while.'

Harry and Nigel followed the example of the baker. Nigel opened his notebook and placed it on the table in front of him.

'Helen met this Drake fellow when she started university. That was the year before last. At first, I thought he was one of those mature-aged students but then I found out he wasn't even a student.' The baker studied the back of his hands before looking directly at Harry. 'He's one of those bastards that prey on young girls, splashing money around for sex. She wouldn't listen to us. We were old fuddy-duddies with yesterday's values. John was wonderful. They were in love. I ask you, when was the last time you saw an eighteen-year old in love with a man old enough to be her father?'

'That must have been difficult,' said Harry

'It gets worse. Half way through her first year at uni she left home and moved in with him. That nearly killed her mother. Then he set her up in her own apartment down at Bayside. She stopped coming to see us after that.'

'Do you have her address?'

'She was living in an apartment in Seaview Street but I think she's moved back into the city. Let me ask my wife.'

'That address in Seaview Street wouldn't be apartment five, fifteen Seaview Street, would it?'

'How did you know that?'

Harry showed him his photograph of Georgina Brock. 'Do you know this girl?'

Mr Daniels shook his head. 'Who is she?'

'Her name was Georgina Brock, but her friends called her George.'

'Helen talked about a George when she first went to the university. I thought he was a boy.'

'She's dead. Her body was found in that apartment on Seaview Street.'

'Was she connected to Drake as well?'

'He was paying the rent.'

'God, this is worse than I thought.'

Harry looked at Nigel, who shrugged his shoulders. 'What do you mean, Mr Daniels?'

'A friend told us that Helen was working for an escort agency, you know, as a high society prostitute. I didn't want to believe it but he showed us a website. Helen's picture is on it, and so is that girl's I think.'

'Do you have that website's address?'

'It's on my computer upstairs.'

Mr Daniels opened the email he had received from his friend and clicked on the link. It opened a webpage filled with photographs of scantily clad young women in suggestive poses.

'That's our daughter there,' said Mr Daniels, pointing to an image of a blonde girl in transparent pink lingerie, 'and, there's that girl you showed me the picture of.'

Harry wrote down the web address and noticed that Nigel was doing the same. He looked at the picture of Georgina Brock and decided there was no way anybody could have mistaken her for a boy.

'Have you spoken to your daughter about what she's doing?'

'She won't listen to me. Says I don't understand the industry. Says all she does is go out to dinner with visiting businessmen who want someone to talk to, and that it's good money. Claims she's making more than enough to pay her uni fees. I don't believe her, of course. If it's only about companionship, why are they dressed like that? It's money for sex or I'm the bloody Pope.'

'We need to talk to her. Can you give me her contact details?' said Harry.

'Come downstairs. My wife will have her current address and phone number.'

Helen Daniels was dressed modestly in jeans and a light pink sweatshirt when she opened the door of her city apartment to Harry and Nigel. She didn't look anything like the picture they had seen on her father's computer screen. Harry wondered how much Photoshopping had gone into her internet image.

Helen escorted them into her sitting room where they sat on soft, black leather sofas. Harry noted her apartment was more spacious than the one he shared with Jessika, and decided that her father was probably right about the amount of money she was earning.

Harry showed her the photograph of John Drake. 'Is this the man you knew as John Drake?'

Helen nodded her head. 'I can't believe he's dead.'

'Do you mind telling me the nature of your relationship with him?'

'He was someone that gave me a job.'

'That's not the story your father gave us.'

Helen slumped back into the sofa and wrapped her arms around her knees. 'My father sees everything in black and white, besides, he didn't like John and he doesn't like it that I'm making my own money.'

Harry decided talking about her father wasn't such a good idea. 'When was the last time you saw John?'

'I haven't seen him since I moved in here.'

'When was that?'

'First of December, last year.'

'Who pays your rent?'

Helen smiled. 'Me.'

'I understand you lived in an apartment in Bayside before moving here, is that correct?'

'Yeah. I stayed in a place in Seaview Street for a few months. It's much better here.'

'I understand John paid the rent for that apartment.'

'That was only while I established myself with the agency.'

'What was in it for John?'

Helen looked at Harry. A broad grin spread across her face. 'You guys really are clueless, aren't you? John was one of the owners of the agency. I had to earn that rent.'

Harry now understood what it was that Drake was doing after hours.

'You're right, we know very little about John, which is why I appreciate your frankness, Miss Daniels.' Harry returned her smile. 'How did you meet him in the first place?'

'Ryan introduced me to him at the Merlin. He knew I was looking for a part-time job so I could get away from home and John was always looking for girls like me.'

'Ryan Whitaker?'

'Yeah. We've been friends since high school. Someone else my father doesn't approve of.'

Harry showed her his photograph of Georgina Brock. 'Do you know this girl?'

'Yeah, that's Ryan's girlfriend, George.'

'When was the last time you saw her?'

'Be at least a week ago, before they went to Bali.'

'How well do you know her?'

'She's a friend.'

'I'm sorry to be the bearer of bad news, but Georgina didn't go to Bali. She's dead.'

Helen's eyes widened. She sat up and gripped the edge of the sofa. 'What?'

'We found her body in that apartment you lived in at Bayside.' Harry thought she was going to scream before she sank back into the sofa.

'How did she die?'

'We're treating her death as murder.'

'Murder? Who would want to murder someone like George?'

Harry looked at Nigel. 'She was doing the same kind of work as you, wasn't she?'

Helen nodded.

'I guess you know there are some risks involved in doing what you do, don't you?'

'But we don't bring clients home, we always go to the client's hotel, and we have a driver that picks us up.'

'Was Georgina into anything else apart from working at the agency?'

'Not that I'm aware of. You'll have to ask Ryan. He might know.'

'I'll do that when he gets back from Bali. By the way, his mother told us he'd gone to Bali with a girl called Samantha. Do you know who she is?'

'There was a Samantha at school with us but if she's with Ryan, that's news to me.'

Harry could almost see the cogs turning inside her head.

'Does that surprise you?'

'Well, yes. George was the one that told me they were going to Bali.'

'Ryan's neighbour told us they'd had an argument the last time she'd visited Ryan at his place. Was that something you'd expect?'

'Well, she's pretty feisty and Ryan does like to stir her up, so that wouldn't be out of the ordinary. Would be just like her to change her mind and tell him she wasn't going. Maybe Ryan took this Samantha to get back at her.'

Harry knew he'd have to wait until he could speak to Ryan before he'd really know what had gone on between them, so he decided to change subject.

'I don't know much about this agency work you're doing, do you mind telling me how you get your assignments?'

'I get a text message.'

'Who sends it to you?'

'Someone at the agency I suppose.' Helen shrugged her shoulders. 'I don't know who precisely.'

Harry thought that would be right. 'Who do you call if you need to talk to someone, like if you're sick and can't work?'

'I used to call John. I was one of his girls.'

'Who do you call now?'

'They told me to call Todd.'

'Does this Todd have a last name?'

'I only know him as Todd. I can give you his number if that will help.'

'Does the agency have a street address?'

Helen shrugged her shoulders. 'We always meet in a room at the Hilton International. I don't know where the office is.'

'How do you get paid?'

'The client pays me cash. I take my fee and give the rest to my driver.'

'And, who is your driver?'

'I call him Henry but I don't know if that's his real name.'

'And, how do you get in contact with this Henry?'

'I send him a text. I can give you his number too, if you want.'

'That might be a good idea, Miss Daniels.'

When they returned to Police Headquarters, Harry worked his telephone company connections to get names and addresses to go with the numbers Helen Daniels had given him. Nigel went to visit Georgina Brock's neighbour to ask him if he recognised Ryan Whitaker as her day time visitor.

CHAPTER 16

HE PUT DOWN THE PAPER. The article on page three, which described the police raid on the drug exchange in a derelict building on Long Street, did not mention any connection between the drug dealers arrested and the deaths of homeless men in the building.

He poured himself a whisky and wondered what the police were thinking, if they thought at all. He picked up the paper and read the article again. He was intrigued by the very fact of the raid as, according to the journalist, the Westies had been operating their drug exchange in the building for more than twelve months without any effective police interference. He smiled at the self-serving sanctimonious tone of the journalist, who had taken the police to task for their failure to shut the place down sooner. He knew from his own experience how easy it was to elude the police if you had effective lookouts and good communications.

He wondered if the police had jammed the mobile phone frequency around the building before storming in or if they'd caught the lookouts napping. He knew it was easy to doze off in a doorway after several hours of standing around waiting for something to happen, especially when nothing did.

He assumed the police had cased the place before the raid and knew about the escape route through the laneway. Besides, it wasn't as if the Westies, who operated like a bunch of shop-keepers in his opinion, had been making any effort to hide their activities. He knew from his own observation of their comings and goings, that any casual observer in the area would have known where their lookouts were. He also knew that the police didn't always wear uniforms and could have taken out the look-outs before sending in their raiding party. He'd been caught in a raid when they'd done just that.

He downed the whisky. That was a memory he didn't want to contemplate. He had not enjoyed his time in prison.

He knew he should be grateful to the police for clearing the building, as it meant he'd have unfettered access while the West-ies' foot soldiers were on remand, unless someone came up with the bail money required to get them back on the street. He knew from personal experience that was highly unlikely to happen. The power players didn't waste money on expendables.

He poured himself another shot and wondered which home-less failure he'd get to save next.

He slowed the Toyota as he drove past the building. It looked deserted. He checked the doorway where he knew the Long Street lookout stood. There was no-one there.

His was the only vehicle on the street. This part of town was dead after dark. He looked at the dash display. It was almost half-past two in the morning. He turned into the laneway that ran alongside the building and couldn't believe his luck, when his headlights picked up the prone form of one of the building's squatters propped up against the wall of the building.

It looked like the old man he'd seen talking to the door guard the first night he'd visited the place. He killed the lights on the Toyota, grabbed his bag and stepped out into the night. Even if someone walked past the end of the laneway they wouldn't see him kneeling over the body in front of the Toyota.

He checked the old man for a pulse. There was no point in killing one that was already dead. There was a pulse; he was definitely alive even if he'd drunk himself into oblivion. The old man stirred as he undid the buttons on his coat and turned him on his side. He waited for him to settle, then eased his victim's arm out of the coat and undid the button on his shirt sleeve.

He slipped the rubber tubing around the old man's upper arm and pushed his sleeve up past his elbow to expose his veins. He heated the heroin with a few drops of water in the tablespoon using his lighter, then took the syringe out of its container and removed the safety cap from the end of the needle. When he'd filled the syringe, he twisted the screw driver around in the rubber tubing to engorge the old man's veins with blood. He jammed the end of the screw driver into the old man's armpit, picked up the syringe and inserted the needle into a vein, and slowly pushed in the plunger. He released the pressure in the rubber tubing and then withdrew the needle. He held his latex covered finger over the injection point, as he'd watched Red Cross nurses do whenever he'd donated blood, and waited while the heroin was propelled towards his victim's brain by the pumping of his heart.

The old man stopped breathing.

'Better luck next trip, mate!'

He packed up his equipment and checked for a pulse. Satisfied, he climbed into the Toyota and slowly drove down the lane and turned on to South Terrace.

CHAPTER 17

TODD HENDRI HAD FIRST MET John Drake at City University when they were part-time, mature-aged students. John had been working on a degree in public administration. Todd on updating his accounting qualifications so that he could take over his ailing father's practice. Their friendship had grown out of a mutual interest in young women, sex, and making money.

Late one night, after another alcohol fuelled discussion in the bar of the Student Club, where they went to mingle with the local talent, they'd decided to conduct an experiment to test John's hypothesis that young female students would have sex with older men in exchange for an all expenses paid night out on the town. They'd agreed on a plan, and given themselves a semester to test the concept.

During that semester of testing they'd spent a considerable sum of money, and enjoyed frequent sex with their target audience. By the end of their little experiment they had identified six girls who were happy to fuck them in exchange for a good time any time they asked.

With their proof of concept in the bag they'd shifted focus, with the intention of transforming their knowledge and new contacts into a money making business. After they'd discussed the prospect of making money working as escorts with their girls, and shown them how they could make more money in a night than they could working all week in a shop or restaurant, their six girls came on board.

Todd set up a company: Discreet City Escorts. Then he created a website, with appropriately suggestive photographs of their initial stable of girls. By the end of that semester, Discreet City Escorts had moved all the way from concept to operational reality.

Todd had realised that businessmen away from home, looking for a night out with side benefits, wouldn't want a transaction on their credit card statement that they might have to explain to a spouse in another city. So, from its beginning, the business had operated on a cash only basis, with a sliding scale of fees and services, some of which were not openly advertised but only implicitly suggested by the way the girls were presented on the website.

Within six months, John's crazy idea had grown into a successful small business offering beautiful escorts, who could provide companionship and intelligent conversation, and other unspecified services as required.

Todd and John had laughed like madmen when they'd realised that ever increasing university fees would provide them with a fresh group of girls to refresh their stable every year, as their older escorts graduated and moved on to other careers. They'd drawn up a ten year business development plan and dreamed of selling their business for millions, convinced they'd cornered a specialised niche in the market.

In the early years, they had encountered a couple of teething problems: clients not paying and parents objecting to what their daughters were doing. They'd overcome the first problem by requiring the client to provide his credit card details when he made a booking, and informing him that they would charge his card with an entry clearly marked as an escort agency if he failed to pay. The Seaview Street apartment had solved the parental interference problem.

Todd ran the business from his office. Most of it happened automatically online. Each girl managed her own availability and the system sent her a text message whenever a client confirmed a booking. She then liaised with the driver that delivered her to the client and picked her up when her assignment concluded. If Todd needed to meet with any of the girls to iron out issues, he met them somewhere in the city.

Everybody got paid in cash. The client handed the cash to the escort. She took her share, determined by the level of service she had provided, and handed the rest to the driver, who took his fee and delivered the rest to Todd.

Todd settled accounts with John at the end of the month. He kept complete records but not in the same file he used for recording income for tax purposes.

John recruited girls to replenish their stable each year, using the techniques they had tested during their initial experiment. Todd recruited the drivers from his client base of taxi drivers, and participated in the agency's training program designed to help the girls become relaxed about going out with older men and providing sex services.

The business had grown every year for five years without a serious hitch. They'd made a stack of money and were on track to meet their forecasts so that they could sell up within five years and retire. Now the shit had hit the fan.

Todd sat in his office with his head in his hands, contemplating what to do now that John was dead and Georgina had been murdered in the Seaview Street apartment.

He wasn't sure what was going on. In the last year, they'd received a couple of approaches from parties that were interested in buying the business, which Todd had turned down. He didn't think they'd get the money he wanted at their current earnings. He'd discussed it with John, and they'd decided to stick with their ten year plan. Now he wasn't so sure he wanted to keep going on his own.

He searched through his phone and found the numbers of the callers who had expressed an interest in the business and wrote them down. He decided he'd think about it, and then thought about the girls, considering whether he'd need to talk to them about additional security measures. He'd told them not to take clients home.

He wondered if Georgina had been freelancing on the side. She was the sort to do her own thing. Pity, he'd liked her. She'd given him one of the best blow jobs he'd ever had.

The telephone on his desk interrupted his thoughts of the evening she'd spent with him. He didn't recognise the number. He was tempted to let it go through to voice mail but, thinking it could be a new client for his accounting practice, he answered the call.

'Hendri Accounting Services, how can I help you?'

Todd listened to a male voice telling him that he'd taken care of Drake, and that he was coming for him next, if he didn't shut Discreet City Escorts and stop taking advantage of innocent young women.

The caller hung up before Todd could respond. There was something familiar about the voice but he couldn't put a name to it. He imagined the caller had probably tried to disguise his voice, seeing as he was making a death threat.

He'd received a lot of threats over the years from disgruntled clients but no-one had ever threatened to kill him before. He didn't know whether to take the call seriously or treat it as a joke. In the end, he decided it was probably one of his competitors taking advantage of the situation to rattle his cage. He knew that there were some unsavoury characters operating in the industry, and some that would be happy to see him put out of business.

Todd gazed at the photograph of his father on the wall of the office the old man had once occupied, and wondered what advice his father would give him, if he'd still been around to give it, and decided it certainly wouldn't have been to call the police. His father had firmly believed that getting the police involved in anything only meant further trouble.

CHAPTER 18

REG DANIELS SAT in his van in Seaview Street and waited. He'd followed Drake and the girl when they'd left the apartment at seven thirty, and watched them enjoy a meal together across the restaurant from the table where he'd eaten alone. Drake and the girl had walked back to the apartment in Seaview Street at nine fifteen. Reg had walked along behind them and climbed back into his van to wait for Drake to come out and make his way home. It was now almost eleven o'clock.

There was no sign of Drake's car, so Reg assumed Drake had come down from the city on the tram, which suited him just fine. It meant he could intercept him in the darkness of the street and not have to jump him in the car park outside the apartments.

Reg drummed his fingers on the steering wheel. If Drake didn't come out soon he'd lose tonight's opportunity and have to come back another time. He'd promised his wife he'd be home from the card game around midnight. That was as late as he dared stay out, given that he had to be up at the crack of dawn to have the baking done in time for the breakfast trade.

The door of the apartment opened and Drake came out. He walked along the balcony towards the stairs. He appeared a little unsteady on his feet as he slowly made his way down the stairs. Reg smiled. It looked like what he had in mind for Drake was going to be easier than he had imagined.

Drake didn't seem to notice the van when he went past on his way towards the tram stop at the end of the street. Reg let Drake walk along the footpath on his journey towards the tram stop. It was much darker a little way down the street, away from the street light that illuminated the entrance of the car park that serviced the apartment block. Reg got out of his van and followed Drake, twisting the length of green nylon rope he'd selected for the task in his hands, and slowly closed the gap between them. He concentrated on keeping his breathing under control and his steps silent. His heart was pounding. He'd never killed a man before.

He stopped next to a street tree and took several deep breaths. He pulled the rope tight between his hands and prepared himself to launch the attack that would end the scumbag's life. But, before he'd mustered the courage to take those last few steps and slip the rope around Drake's neck, a black SUV without lights slid past him in the darkness and stopped alongside Drake. The passenger side rear door opened. Reg stood still. A shadow emerged from the car and dragged Drake into the dark interior of the vehicle. The door closed and the SUV sped off into the night, in the direction of the tram stop. The whole operation had taken no more than five seconds.

'Fuck!' Reg swore into the night. Someone had abducted his target right in front of him. He hadn't even been able to get the registration number. He hoped they hadn't seen him, as he slipped the piece of rope into his coat pocket and retraced his steps back to the van.

Reg sat for several minutes trying to comprehend what he had just witnessed. He'd spent a small fortune on private investigators tracking down Drake and his partner, and now it looked like he wasn't the only one after them. He wondered who else Drake had pissed off and whether it would be safe to continue with his plan.

He decided he'd wait and see what happened, before going after Hendri.

Reg was furious when he heard the news that John Drake had been murdered. He was angry that someone else had killed the bastard and denied him the satisfaction of exacting revenge for the humiliation he felt for what Drake had done to his daughter.

After a few days of swearing and distracted baking, that nearly cost him several trays of sourdough bread, he decided he was up against professionals, people who knew how to kill, and that scared him. He prayed they hadn't seen him or his van in the street.

One morning, as he was taking a tray of yeast buns out of the oven, it dawned on him that at least Drake was dead. Someone had made the bastard pay, which was what he wanted, and thanks to whoever it was, he wouldn't be facing a murder charge. As he placed the tray of fresh buns onto the bench to cool, he realised there were other ways to hurt people, to make them suffer. Psychological torture was something he knew about, thanks to Drake and Hendri, so it was time to give Hendri some of his own medicine.

He'd heard how the police used phone records to track people down, so he knew he couldn't use his own telephone. Besides, he didn't want his wife to know what he was doing, so later that day, when he went to the Post Office to collect the mail from their post box, he used the public telephone in the post box foyer of the Post Office to call Hendri and threaten to kill him.

He felt better after that, but the euphoria came to an end

after a few days when the police came and told him about Georgina Brock, and started asking questions. Now he was worried about Helen's safety, and more determined than ever to shut the agency down for good.

CHAPTER 19

THE WEEKEND DELIVERED the body of a third homeless man from an apparent overdose in the vicinity of Long Street. This time they knew who he was as soon as Harry had seen his photograph: Gary Potts.

Carl thought it was starting to look as if someone was on a mission to rid the city of homeless men but knew he'd have to wait for the full autopsy and toxicology reports to know for sure. He decided it wouldn't hurt for Wayne and Nigel to revisit the homeless shelter in Long Street, just in case someone had seen anything they were prepared to talk about, while he and Harry interviewed Todd Hendri.

Carl scrutinised the building as Harry parked their silver Ford in the car park reserved for clients of Hendri Accounting Services. It looked as if the building had once been a suburban residence, like most of the other business premises they had driven past in the street.

As he got out of the car, Carl glanced around the parking area. There was a black BMW sedan, parked next to the back entrance, and a white Toyota Corolla, parked where it would catch the afternoon shade in summer. Nothing out of the ordinary. Nothing to tell him that this was the home of Discreet City Escorts.

The white haired woman at reception called Mr Hendri as soon as Carl had shown her his badge.

A door opened across from the receptionist's desk, and Todd Hendri invited them into his office.

'How can I help you, gentlemen?'

'Mr Hendri, I understand that, in addition to whatever it is you do in this office, you're also one of the owners of Discreet City Escorts. Is that correct?'

'Yeah, that's right. I run Discreet City Escorts. Is there a problem?'

'We're investigating the murder of this girl, Mr Hendri.' Carl waited while Harry showed Todd a photograph of Georgina Brock. 'I understand she worked for Discreet City Escorts?'

'George,' said Todd, rubbing the sides of his head and leaning back into his chair. 'She'd only been with us for a few months. Tragic. We've never had anything like this happen before. I don't know what to say.'

'Perhaps you can start by telling me when was the last time you saw her?'

'Early April. We had a little show for the girls before Easter. I usually don't have all that much to do with them, that's John's area, or at least it was.'

'That would be John Drake?'

'Yeah, poor bastard.'

'Is this him?' Carl waited for Todd to look at the photograph on Harry's iPad.

'That's him. Still can't see what the girls saw in him. But there you go, he had something.' Todd shrugged his shoulders.

'Mind telling me why you haven't made contact with us about either of these deaths?'

'I don't know anything about them, mate. How could I help you?'

Another self-centred, unthinking idiot or someone with something to hide, thought Carl. 'Has it crossed your mind that you or your girls might be in danger?'

Todd drummed his fingers on the desk. 'Why would I think that?'

Carl wondered if he really was that naive. 'Whoever killed Georgina didn't break into her apartment. He may have used a key taken from John's body.'

'You're not saying someone targeted them because of the business, are you?'

Carl watched as Todd's eyes darted between his and Harry's, and noticed that he was tapping two fingers on each hand onto his thumbs.

'I don't know for sure, Mr Hendri, but it's a possibility we need to keep in mind. Tell me, how many girls do you have on your books?'

'Fifteen.'

Carl didn't know much about escort agencies, as he had never worked in Vice, so he didn't know whether they were dealing with a large or small agency, but he needed to know more about how it worked.

'How would I go about booking an evening with one of your escorts?'

Todd looked at him as if that wasn't a question he'd expected from a senior policeman.

'I want you to explain the process, Mr Hendri, not make a booking.'

'Oh, sorry, you threw me there for a minute.'

Carl and Harry watched as Todd walked them through the booking system on his computer.

'How many booking records do you have for Georgina?'

'As I said, she hadn't been with us very long.' Todd opened her account listing. 'Seven.'

'What details do you capture on your clients?'

'All we ask for is a name, so the girls know who to ask for, and a credit card.'

'I guess they could give you any name. How do you ensure you get a valid credit card number?'

'We don't accept a booking unless the card validates?'

Carl thought that could be a useful security feature for both the firm and the girl, but wondered how that could be done without leaving a record that could be traced, as he was sure most users of escorts would prefer not to have an escort agency entry on their credit card statements.

'How do you do that?'

'Seen those pending transactions for a few dollars on your online account that never end up on your statement?'

Carl nodded. 'Ah, so that's what they are.'

Todd smiled. 'We didn't pick our name by accident, Inspector.'

'Did John have access to this information on his computer?'

'Yeah, he and I were the administrators but I revoked his access as soon as I heard he'd been killed.'

'Wise move. Looks like someone lifted his laptop from his apartment. Probably the same person that killed him.'

'Fuck! That means someone could have accessed this information if they'd been able to log in.'

'Was John strict about keeping his passwords safe?' said Carl.

'I told him to be, but who knows?'

'Have you noticed anything out of the ordinary?'

'No, but this information could be dynamite in the wrong hands.'

Carl watched as a look of despair spread across Todd's face, and decided now was a good time to tell him why they'd really come to see him.

'I'd like the details of Georgina's clients, including their credit card numbers.'

'I'm not sure I can do that, Inspector. Part of our terms of service is keeping that information confidential.'

Carl ignored his objection. 'And, I'd like the names and addresses of your girls and their drivers.'

'That's confidential information as well, Inspector. We don't even use their real names on our site.'

'I don't think you understand, Mr Hendri. I'm not asking.'

Todd stood and pointed his finger at Carl. 'You can't just barge in here and flash your badge and demand names. I've got rights!'

Carl crossed his arms on his chest. 'Do you know what a search warrant is, Mr Hendri?'

Todd sat down. 'I've heard of them.'

'This is what a search warrant looks like.' Carl put his hand inside his coat and extracted a folded piece of paper from an inside pocket, and passed it to Todd.

He waited while Todd read the warrant.

'Let me make it as clear as I can for you, Mr Hendri. Either you give me what I've asked for or I'll call in my search team and take this place apart. And, Mr Hendri, this is a murder investigation, so don't get any ideas about there being any accountants concessions on what I can examine. What will it be?'

Carl waited while Todd weighed his options.

'If it gets out that I've given you my clients' credit card details, I'll be ruined.'

'I'm investigating two murders connected to your business,

Mr Hendri.' Carl paused for effect. 'You may not have a business to be ruined if there are any more.'

Todd collapsed into his chair. 'You really think I'm in danger?'

'I'm not sure I'd like to be in your shoes, Mr Hendri, but I'll do what I can to protect you and your girls if you'll help me.'

'I guess that means the guy threatening to kill me if I don't shut up shop, probably isn't joking.'

'Perhaps you'd better tell us about that.'

When they arrived back at Police Headquarters, Harry rang his contact at Telstra and explained he was dealing with a death threat, and asked her for a log of the calls to Hendri Accounting Services for the previous Monday, the ninth of May. Then, with the required paperwork in hand, he walked across the plaza to talk to his contact in B&A Bank's Head Office about getting the account holder details that went with the credit card numbers Todd Hendri had given them.

His contact at the bank told him it might take a few days to get the details to him, but his Telstra contact had a list of the numbers that had called Hendri Accounting Services on the ninth of May in his inbox within an hour.

Harry identified the number that matched the time Todd had told them that his death threat had been received. He called his contact at Telstra, who informed him that it was the number of the public telephone in front of the Morton Sands Post Office. She gave him the number for the Post Office.

Harry called the manager of the Morton Sands Post Office to ask if they had a CCTV camera covering the area where their public telephone was located, only to discover that the CCTV camera covering the area had been vandalised several weeks ago, and that she was still waiting for their maintenance people to replace it.

He hung up and let DI West know that he'd hit a wall on the death threat.

'Send Nigel and Lisa down there to door knock around the Post Office. There might be security cameras in other businesses down there that cover the entrance to the Post Office.'

———

Carl sat in Mike's office, across from the morgue in the basement of Police Headquarters, following the autopsy of Gary Potts. The cluttered interior of the pathologist's office was a stark contrast to the highly organised, stainless steel laboratory where Dr Jonas and his team dissected, measured and analysed the dead.

'I think you have a serial killer on your hands, Carl. This poor bastard definitely was not a user, at least not of narcotics. There's plenty of evidence that he's given his liver a workout with alcohol, and clogged his lungs with cigarettes, but he's like your Mr Drake and the other two when it comes to injecting. No other needle marks.'

'But there's no clear sign he or the others were restrained like Drake.'

Dr Jonas smiled. 'I keep forgetting you don't have teenage kids.'

'I'm working on it, Mike, but what's that got to do with it?'

'How is Nina by the way? Is she ready to kill you yet?'

'I think the only thing stopping her is the thought of you slicing me up after the fact.'

'Tell her I can do her a special price.' Mike laughed. 'Now, getting back to business. The latest bit of advice they're giving kids these days is not to mix alcohol with other drugs, and there's a good reason for that. If your muscles are already relaxed from one drug, taking another one does nothing to guarantee you'll keep breathing, and that's what kills you - forgetting to breathe, especially if the second drug is heroin.'

The picture of the body of a homeless man propped up against a wall, that he'd posted on the whiteboard in the Incident Room, popped into Carl's mind and he saw how it could be done.

'So, if these homeless guys were already under the influence of alcohol, sleeping it off, in fact, what you're saying is they wouldn't need to be restrained, right?'

Dr Jonas opened a file on his computer. 'I got the full toxicology for Richard Wentworth this morning. He's the second of your homeless boys. Not only was he full of high grade heroin, his blood was nine parts alcohol. And, we already know he only had one needle mark, just like Tidler and Drake.'

'And, you reckon Potts' report will be the same?'

'You could smell the alcohol in his stomach contents.'

Carl stood. 'Think I'd better go talk with the Chief.'

CHAPTER 20

Todd's mother, who worked as his receptionist as she had for his father before him, had gone home at four o'clock. At six, Todd decided it was time to call it a day and head down the street to the Bayside Hotel for dinner, before going home to watch TV.

Todd wasn't into cooking. He'd been eating out ever since his wife had divorced him a little over ten years ago, in what he thought of as an acrimonious legal action that had vaporised his wealth to enrich her lawyer.

That outcome had become part of the rationale Todd had constructed to explain to himself why he had agreed to test John's hypothesis and set up the agency. Now, with John and Georgina dead, he wasn't so sure it had been such a wise decision.

The policemen that had visited him earlier in the day had put the wind up him, with their talk of murder and of him being a potential target. He'd been so frightened that he'd handed over confidential client records and told them about the death threat he'd received. He didn't know what they could do about it but they had promised to look into it. After they'd gone, he'd called each of the girls to reassure himself that they were okay and to remind them not to let clients know where they lived.

One reason Todd parked his car close to the back door was he didn't like getting wet when it rained. As he opened the back door of the building and stepped onto the porch, he looked into the darkness and listened. The rain had stopped. He turned, flipped off the light, and locked the door.

When he turned to walk to his car, a large man, holding something in his right hand, materialised out of the gloom that held his car, just as Todd pushed the button on the remote and the indicators flashed to signal that the car doors had unlocked. In that flash of light, he realised the man was holding a pistol.

'Don't do anything silly, Mr Hendri.'

'What do you want? I don't keep cash on the premises,' said Todd.

'My boss wants a word with you.'

The man pointed towards the parking area. Todd saw the outline of a dark colored SUV blocking the exit to the street and wondered what the hell was going on.

'Put your bag down and place your hands on the wall behind you.'

Todd lowered his briefcase and umbrella to the floor of the porch, and turned to face the wall. The man patted him down.

'Okay, let's go.' The man placed a hand on Todd's left arm and guided him to the left side rear door of the SUV. The interior light did not come on when he opened the door. 'Get in.'

Todd did as he was told. The outline of a small man, illuminated by the nearby street light through the vehicle's tinted windows, was visible at the other end of the seat.

'I have a proposition for you, my friend.'

'Who the hell are you?' said Todd.

'Who I am is not important. What's important is what I can do for you, my friend.'

'Oh, and what's that?'

'I can protect you.'

'What makes you think I need protection?' said Todd.

The man placed something heavy in his lap. 'Open it.'

Todd felt the object and realised it was a laptop. He prised open the lid. The screen lit up and illuminated the interior of the SUV. Todd noticed that his companion was wearing dark glasses, even though the sun had set more than half an hour ago. Todd looked at the logon screen of the laptop. He could see two logon choices. One for 'John' and one for 'Guest'.

'John's password is duckie321, with a capital K. Your partner didn't have much imagination when it came to passwords, my friend.'

'This is John's computer? How did you get this?'

'Your partner made a serious mistake, my friend, and he paid the price. I'm here to see that you don't pay that same price.'

Todd felt the butterflies in his stomach breaking formation.

'Why should I trust you if you killed John?'

'Did I say that?'

Todd wondered if the guy was playing mind games with him.

'Then how did you get his laptop?'

'Let's say it came to me in a business transaction.'

Todd wondered what the fuck that meant. 'Why would I want you to protect me?' said Todd. 'I can go to the police if I think I need protection.'

'You could, but it wouldn't do you any good. They don't know who or what you need protection from.'

'And, you do?'

Even in the dark interior of the vehicle, there was enough light for Todd to see that the bastard was smiling at him.

'Protection's my business, my friend, and you need my services, otherwise you won't have a business to sell next week, let alone in five years' time. You've already lost your partner and one of your better assets.'

Todd realised he'd been reading their business plan, and wondered if he'd killed Georgina as well.

'What's this protection going to cost me?'

'John's share of the profits.'

'What? Fifty percent? You're out of your mind.' Todd tried to open the door. It was locked. He realised he might not be getting out of this lightly.

'Think about it, my friend. I'm offering to protect you and your agency for what you would have paid to John. It's costing you nothing.'

Todd could see his logic but that didn't mean he wanted to pay. 'And, if I choose to decline your generous offer?'

'Then I won't be responsible for what happens, and I assure you, Mr Hendri, you will wish you had accepted my offer.'

The tone in his voice sent a shiver through Todd's body. For a moment, he thought he was going to wet himself. He took a deep breath. He wanted to get out of the car but he didn't want to end up as another statistic on the nightly news. And, then he thought about the girls.

'How does this work?'

'We work in the shadows, Mr Hendri, but we're always there. My man will visit when it's time to pay.'

'How will I know you're actually protecting me?'

'You'll be alive.'

Todd ordered a double Scotch, no ice, instead of the usual beer, before going into the dining room.

'Heavy day, Todd?'

'Bloody day from hell, Fred.'

'Yeah, well don't have too many of those, mate. I hear the booze bus will be outside later tonight.'

'Thanks.'

Todd took his whisky and walked through to the dining room, where he sat at his usual table.

'Hello, Mr Hendri. What'll it be tonight?'

'I'll have the fish, Mary.'

'Anyone joining you?'

'No, not tonight.'

'Okay, I'll get that started. Shouldn't be long.'

Todd watched the television on the wall and sipped his whisky, and wondered what in God's name John had gotten them mixed up in. He didn't know whether to call the police inspector who'd visited him or not.

He ate his meal and watched the horse racing on the television, and tried to put his visitors out of his mind. He looked through the glass doors to where a group of excited punters sat next to the betting window at the end of the front bar, and shook his head. He'd never understood why people wasted their money betting on the horses.

He was enjoying a small serve of apple pie and cream when a fire engine, siren blaring and lights flashing, turned into the street outside the dining room window. Everything was bathed in a flash of red and blue light, and the plates on his table rattled, as the truck thundered past into the night.

He wondered where it was going. His office was at the other end of the street that ran past the side of the hotel where he was sitting. Then he remembered that he hadn't set the bloody alarm when he'd locked up. He'd have to do that on his way home.

When he'd finished his meal, he bought a bottle of Jameson, went out into the street and climbed into his car. When he crested the slight rise in the street as he made his way inland, the flashing lights of the fire truck came into view, as did the light created by a fire burning in a building about where his office was located.

The closer he got the more apparent it became that his office was on fire. The fish he'd eaten for dinner turned in his stomach. He slowed to a crawl.

A policeman waving a torch stepped in front of his car and directed him to pull over. When he stopped, the policeman signalled for him to wind down his window.

'You can't get through this way, sir.'

'That's my office.'

Todd stood with the other bystanders and watched as his office building was reduced to a blackened shell, despite the efforts of the fire crew.

When the fire chief stood down his crew, Todd introduced himself and asked him what he'd thought had happened.

'Looks like arson to me, mate. These places don't burn that fast without a bit of help. She was lit up like a roman candle when we got here. Anybody inside?'

'No. There's only two of us. Mum goes home at four. I went down to the pub for dinner around six thirty.'

'What made you come back?'

'Heard you go past the pub. Remembered I hadn't set the alarm.'

'Doubt that would have made much difference, seeing hardly anybody lives around here.'

'Yeah, but they would have called me when it went off.'

'What's their response time? Ten? Fifteen minutes? Whoever started your fire would have been gone by then.'

A police sergeant walked up to them. 'You the owner, sir?'

'Yeah. Todd Hendri.'

'Mind coming with me, sir?'

Todd followed him to his squad car in the street.

'Mind telling me where you were this evening, sir?'

'I was having dinner down at the pub. I go there most nights.'

'What time did you leave your office?'

'Around six thirty.'

'What are you doing here now? I mean, how did you know the place was on fire?'

'I saw the fire truck go past the pub, that's when I realised I hadn't set the alarm.'

'That usual for you, sir, to forget?'

Todd got the feeling he was under suspicion. 'I've had a rough day, Sergeant, and I don't particularly appreciate what you're insinuating. But, before you put you other foot in it, do you know a detective inspector by the name of West?'

'What's that got to do with anything?'

'He's investigating the murder of my business partner and one of my workers. He was here this morning telling me I could be in danger. In fact, he's looking into a death threat I received last week. Why don't you give him a call?'

'What's your business partner's name, Mr Hendri?'

'Drake. John Drake.'

'Stay here.' The sergeant climbed into the squad car.

Todd watched as he used the radio and then eased himself out of the car.

'We'll be sealing this as a crime scene overnight, sir. We'll have a team of investigators here first thing in the morning. The Inspector asked me to take you to the local station. He's on his way there. He wants to talk to you.'

Todd wondered if the poor guy ever got any time off.

'Is that your car?' he pointed to the BMW.

'Yeah.'

'One of my officers will ride with you to the station. Do you know where it is?'

Carl arrived at the Bayside Police Station a little after nine o'clock. Todd Hendri was waiting for him in the interview room on the ground floor.

'Wasn't expecting to see you again today, Inspector,' said Todd, as Carl entered the interview room. 'Don't you have a home?'

'Fortunately, my wife is a fellow officer, though I must admit, it's been a long day.' Carl didn't tell him that he'd already been home and spent a few hours with Nina.

'Too bloody long for me.'

'Anything you need to tell me, Mr Hendri?'

'What do you mean?'

'Any other threats since the one you received last week?'

Todd twisted his hands together.

'I had some visitors after you left. When I was locking up. They said they'd protect me from whoever had killed John and George.'

Carl wondered whether the mob was playing in the escort agency space. He thought traditional prostitution was more their style. 'What were the terms offered?'

'They want John's share of the profits, and they had his laptop.'

'You realise that could mean they're connected to John's death, don't you? How did they explain the laptop?'

'I asked him about that. He denied it of course. Said he got it through some business transaction, but he knew John's password.'

Alarm bells started ringing in Carl's brain.

'What did they look like?'

'One of them was a big guy but I didn't get a good look at him. It was dark, and he was dressed in black. Had one of those hooded jackets on. What I can tell you for certain is he had a gun.'

'What about the others?'

'There was only one other guy. I didn't get a good look at him either. Only briefly when I opened the laptop. Dark hair, skinny, be in his forties I'd say, was wearing sunnies, even though we were sitting in the dark. Nice suit.'

Not a bad description from a brief glance, thought Carl.

'Did they come into the office?'

'No, they were waiting for me outside. Made me get into their car. One of those four-door Toyota SUVs. Latest model I'd say. Still smelt like new inside.'

'Did you accept their offer?'

'Didn't think I had much choice. He said I'd regret it if I didn't.'

Carl leant back in his chair. 'Doesn't look like your arrangement is off to a good start.'

Todd shrugged his shoulders. 'What are we going to do about the girls? I'm scared.'

'Can you still access your website?'

'Yeah. It's on a server somewhere in the States.'

'Might be time to give your girls a holiday.'

Carl could almost see the wheels turning behind Todd's eyes.

'The girls won't have any income if I take down the site. How will they pay their rent?'

Carl thought that maybe he had misjudged Hendri.

'You have any cash reserves?'

'Yeah.'

'I hope you weren't keeping them in your office.'

Todd smiled. 'I'm not that stupid.'

'Your girls might have savings as well but I think paying the rent might be the least of their worries. How long will it take you to take down the site?'

'I can do that as soon as I can get online.'

'What about cancelling appointments?'

'There's no way I can do that online but I guess I could ask the girls to stay home.'

'You might want to tell them that I'm advising them to stay home,' said Carl.

CHAPTER 21

THE FIRST THING Carl did when he arrived in the office on Tuesday morning was check the Discreet City Escorts website. He wanted to see if Hendri had decommissioned it overnight as he had promised. He opened his email and clicked on the link to the site that Harry had sent him. His browser opened a page with a message advising that the site was experiencing technical difficulties and that service would resume as soon as possible.

Satisfied that Hendri had followed through on his promise, Carl joined the team in the Incident Room, where Harry was reading the witness statements collected by Uniform from the residents that lived in the vicinity of Hendri Accounting Services.

'Anything useful, Harry?'

'This one could be. It's from the woman that lives two houses down from Hendri's office on the opposite side of the street. According to her, Hendri left his office around six most nights. Apparently, her kitchen window overlooks the driveway into Hendri's car park, so she sees him drive past on his way to the Bayside Hotel for his evening meal. Said she knew where he was going as her sister works in the dining room at the hotel. She says he was late leaving last night, and that another car, a big black four wheel drive, came out of his driveway about ten minutes before he did. Then she noticed a van of some sort pull into the car park about five minutes after Hendri's BMW had gone up the street. At the time, she thought it was someone looking for Hendri, as a lot of his clients drive vans. Anyway, whoever it was didn't stay very long and drove off towards the hotel, so she assumed the driver knew where to find Hendri if he wasn't in his office at that time of night. She noticed the fire about ten minutes after the van had disappeared. That's when she called the brigade.'

'Did they get any specific details on the other cars?'

'No. She says she could only see shapes and headlights. Apparently, the street lights aren't all that flash around there.'

'See if the Bayside Hotel has any security cameras covering that street. Anything else in those statements?'

'There's only a handful of residents living around there and it looks like no-one else saw anything until after the fire had started.'

'Let me know what Forensics come up with.'

'What are we doing about the women who work for Hendri, Inspector?' said DC Templar. 'Aren't they at risk?'

'Community Liaison are talking with them today, advising them to stick with their studies for the time being and to report any suspicious contacts.'

'What about Hendri, Boss?'

'Well, he told me an interesting story last night, and it sounds like that statement may have verified it. Claims he was late going to the hotel because he had a couple of visitors, who were driving a black Toyota SUV, when he was getting ready to leave at six. They offered to protect him, and they had Drake's laptop.'

'Did he give you a description we could use?'

Carl looked at his notes. 'One of them was a large guy dressed in black, wearing a hooded jacket, and he described the other guy as skinny with dark hair, wearing sunglasses and a nice suit.'

'Could be anybody,' said Harry.

'Rugby player in a suit with dark glasses and driving a black Toyota SUV,' said DC Paterson. 'Sound familiar?'

'I wouldn't have thought of a rugby player as skinny,' said DC Templar.

'What if the big guy doesn't always wear a hoodie?' said DC Paterson, 'and, remember, they had Drake's laptop.'

'You reckon they could be protecting Hendri from themselves?' said Carl.

'Mob 101,' said DC Paterson.

'Why would the mob kill someone like Drake?' said Harry.

'Bloody good question, Harry,' said Carl, turning to DC Paterson.

'Killing Drake would make it a lot easier to intimidate Hendri,' said DC Paterson, 'and, I'd say they were either after his business or out to shut it down.'

'Well, they've achieved one of those things, Wayne, at least for the time being,' said Carl.

'Why would they go to the trouble of making him an offer and then burn his office down? Didn't he accept their offer, Inspector?' said DC Beard.

'He told me he didn't think he had any choice but to accept it,' said Carl.

'So, who torched his office, then?' said DC Beard.

'We need to find out who was driving that van, Nigel, so why don't you call into the Bayside Hotel and check their security footage for last night on your way down to Morton Sands to see if anyone has a camera covering the Post Office?'

DC Beard nodded his head in agreement and started collecting his things.

Carl felt his mobile phone vibrating in his pocket. He looked at the display. Traffic Control. He took the call.

'Inspector, we've got a black Toyota SUV in Long Street on the recording for the early hours of that Sunday morning you asked us to review. It turns into the lane between Long and South, and doesn't emerge onto South Terrace for thirteen minutes.'

'Do you have the registration details?'

'Sending them through to you now, Inspector. Registered owner is one Dario Finestra. He's on the national database.'

'Get an APB out on the vehicle, and remind people he's dangerous.'

Carl ended the call and opened the email app on his phone. Then he opened the email from Traffic Control.

'Looks like we might have someone to talk to about the killings in Long Street. See what the national database has on Dario Finestra, Harry.'

They waited while Harry interrogated the national database.

'Did time for dealing. Released around ten years ago.'

'Do we have a picture?'

'Looks like someone that works out.'

'Or plays rugby,' said DC Paterson, peering over Harry's shoulder.

'According to Traffic his last known address is 35 Hamley Street, Northfield. Get some armed back up, Harry, and go see if he's home.'

JUST AFTER SIX on Tuesday evening, Todd Hendri pulled into the car park of the Bayside Hotel intent on getting himself a meal. As he stepped out of the BMW, a large dark form appeared in front of him and blocked his exit.

'Mr Hendri, we need to talk.'

'What happened to all that protection your boss promised me?' said Todd.

'That's what we need to talk about.'

'I'm listening,' said Todd, 'but it had better be good. I can't say I'm happy with your service after last night.'

The big man leant in close to Todd's face. 'The boss wants you to understand that if there is no business, there's no protection.'

'The police are involved now,' said Todd. 'They told me to shut up shop to protect my girls.'

'Too bad you've taken their advice.'

'It wasn't exactly advice, mate.'

'You're on your own, Hendri.'

The big man turned and walked away into the shadows, heading out of the car park. Todd looked around to see if anyone had noticed, and then walked across the car park and entered the hotel.

'Do you have a security camera on the back car park, Fred?'

'You're the second person to ask me about security cameras today, Todd. Why do you want to know?'

'I've just been accosted by someone out there and wondered if you'd have that on tape.'

'Let's have a look.'

Fred came out from behind the bar and took Todd down the corridor to his office. 'I had the police here this morning wanting to know if any of our security cameras covered Bay Street.'

'And, do they?'

'Yep.'

'What were they looking for?'

'They wanted to see what traffic came up the street around the time your office went up.'

'Did they have any luck?'

'They took away a copy of last night's tape. They weren't all that hopeful, given the poor lighting, but they reckon they have ways of enhancing the images. Now let's see.' Fred sat at his desk and pointed at the bank of screens on his wall. 'That's the back car park, there.' He pointed to the screen in the top left hand corner of the bank of monitors. 'Let me rewind the tape.'

They watched a grainy recording of Todd's BMW pulling into the car park from Bay Street and stopping in a parking bay opposite the entrance to the dining room.

'That's the spot with the best lighting,' said Fred, as a man dressed in black, with a hood over his head, walked into the camera frame from the direction of the back wall of the hotel and stood in front of Todd as he got out of his car.

'Looks like he was waiting for you.'

They watched until the man walked out of view and disappeared into the gloom of the Bay Street exit.

'I'd say he knew where your camera was, Fred. Not one facial shot.'

'Do you want a copy?'

'Yeah, I want to pass it to the police. They might recognise the bastard from behind.'

CHAPTER 23

THE BOSS HAD INSTRUCTED him to extract Hendri's administrator password, which would give them control of Hendri's operation and make Hendri himself expendable. He chuckled to himself as he watched Hendri walk into the hotel with his tail between his legs. He liked playing games with hapless idiots like Hendri. He climbed into the Toyota and headed for Hendri's house, where he intended to welcome him home with a little surprise before persuading him to hand over the password, and sending him on his way to his next reincarnation.

He drove out of Bay Street and turned on to the Esplanade, where the police had set up a random breath testing station. There was no way he could avoid it without attracting attention to himself. He hoped they'd let him pass but the officer standing next to the orange cones on the road waved him in to be tested. He smiled at the officer and guided the Toyota into the testing zone. He knew being tested wouldn't be a problem; he hadn't had a drink since enjoying a glass of red over lunch with the boss, but he hated blowing into their little machines.

His was the first vehicle in the line of cars herded into the testing zone. As he came to a halt he got the feeling something wasn't quite right. The testing officer hadn't approached him. He was listening to someone talking to him on his radio. He checked the rear-view mirror. The officer who had waved him into the line was talking into his radio and walking towards him, with his free hand working on the holster holding his gun.

He took his foot off the brake, pulled the steering wheel hard left as he pushed down on the accelerator, and drove over the cones separating him from the flow of traffic on the Esplanade. There was a blaring of horns and a squealing of tyres as cars braked to avoid colliding with the Toyota as he cut across the line of traffic and sped from the scene.

Within seconds there were red and blue lights flashing and sirens screaming as the police gave chase, but he'd managed to open a gap that had filled with traffic in the time it had taken them to respond. He turned into the next available side street, killed the lights on the Toyota and turned right at the first intersection, and then left at the next without hitting the brakes. The next right turn bought him back onto a main road. He flicked the lights back on and merged into the line of traffic heading towards the city.

When he checked the mirrors, there were no red and blue lights in the traffic behind him. He couldn't believe how easy it had been to lose them. His heart was pounding. He let out a sigh of relief and wondered if he'd overreacted. Perhaps he'd only imagined they were closing in to arrest him but he doubted it. His intuition rarely misinformed him. He knew the boss would not be happy when he found out about the homeless men, because it looked like the police had. He realised he'd have to dump the Toyota and torch it, after he'd taken care of Hendri, and then he'd have to disappear and start over someplace else.

He drove through the next intersection and turned left into the first available side street, intending to slip out of the area as quietly as possible. He was certain the police would be moving to seal off the main roads.

A police car with its lights flashing pulled into the intersection in front of him and blocked his path. He stood on the brakes and prepared to throw the Toyota into reverse. A second police car with flashing lights blocked off his exit to the main road he'd just turned off. He could see a policeman aiming a pistol at him over the roof of the police car behind him. He put the Toyota into drive and aimed it at the front end of the police car blocking the intersection ahead of him.

There was a loud bang and the sound of breaking glass as he rammed the patrol car and pushed it out of the way. A police officer appeared on the roadway in front of him and fired four rounds into the windscreen of the Toyota. The glass shattered. He felt a sharp pain in his neck and then another in his shoulder. He couldn't see where he was going. He couldn't get his left arm to move. He felt his body being thrown into the steering wheel. Its forward motion came to a painful end, arrested by his seatbelt, as the Toyota mounted the kerb and collided with a tree.

The door of the Toyota burst opened and a policeman shone a bright light into his eyes.

'Don't move!'

The desk sergeant beckoned to Carl when he entered the building from the rear car park.

'We picked up your Dario Finestra last night, Inspector. He did a runner from a booze bus down at the Bay and rammed a patrol car when they cornered him. Clown wasn't even over the limit.'

'How did they manage to corner him?'

'They were testing a drone with night vision enhanced cameras above the RBT. Silly bugger didn't have a chance.'

'I didn't know we had a drone.'

'Apparently, we've got a squadron of them, Inspector. There's an article in the latest Force News, you should have a read. Seems they're a damn sight cheaper than a helicopter when you just want to keep an eye on things.'

'Where is Finestra now? Downstairs?'

'He's in City. Gunshot wounds to the neck and shoulder. Not life threatening according to the latest update. You should be able to talk to him later today. They operated on him last night.'

Carl nodded. He was thankful they hadn't killed his suspect before he could interview him. 'Who was the shooter?'

'PC Chan.'

'She's getting herself a bit of a reputation as a shooter. That's the second time she's shot one of my suspects.'

'At least she hasn't killed anybody yet, Inspector. Let's be thankful for that.'

Carl walked over to the elevators and pushed the button for the third. He didn't wish the pain of killing another human being on any officer. Killing someone, even in the line of duty, was not easy to live with and he knew he'd be living with it for the rest of his life. Whenever he thought of it, and that was most days, he wished Dale Reed hadn't been so impulsive. He wished he'd dropped the gun. He wished he hadn't shot Peter James.

He was grateful Lily Chan hadn't killed Dario Finestra, not for Finestra's sake but for hers.

Carl's phone rang as he stepped out of the elevator onto the third floor of Police Headquarters.

'Inspector West? It's Todd, Todd Hendri. Do you have a minute?'

'Sure. What's on your mind?'

'One of those guys, you know, the ones that were supposedly

protecting me, well, one of them accosted me in the car park of the Bayside Hotel last night. Said their protection deal was off.'

'Did he give you a reason?'

'His words were no business no protection.'

'Well, that could be a good thing, Mr Hendri.'

'Not if I decide to continue after you arrest whoever it was that set fire to my office.'

'Well, that would be your call, Mr Hendri.'

'Anyway, I'll worry about that later. What I wanted to tell you is that I've got a copy of the security camera recording of the guy talking to me in the car park from the hotel. It's not very clear but I understand you have tools that can enhance images.'

'Have you viewed the recording?'

'Yeah, but it doesn't show his face, it only shows him from behind.'

Carl thought it might not be of much value but he didn't want to put Hendri offside, in case he needed more information from him. 'Take it to the Bayside Station and ask them to send it through to me. I'll get one of our technicians to see what he can do with it.'

Carl walked into the Incident Room.

'Did you hear they got Finestra last night, Boss,' said Harry.

'Heard downstairs.'

Carl walked over to where DC Beard was standing near the whiteboard and put his hand on his shoulder. 'You seen Lily?'

DC Beard nodded to affirm that he had.

'She okay?'

'She's a bit shaken.' He turned and looked at Carl. 'The bastard tried to run her over. Her sergeant told her to take some time off. She's gone to spend a couple of days with her mother.'

'You okay, Nigel?'

DC Beard nodded his head. 'I'm just thankful she came home alive.'

'Me, too,' said Carl. He turned back to face the rest of the team.

'Okay, people, let's see what we can find out about this Finestra. At the moment, we know his vehicle was in the vicinity of Long Street in the early hours of the morning Gary Potts was found dead in the laneway between Long Street and South Terrace. Traffic have confirmed that his Toyota was recorded entering that laneway and emerging from it onto South Terrace some thirteen minutes later. Sufficient time to despatch Potts if he'd been in the laneway when Finestra entered.'

He looked at the whiteboard with its collection of photographs of dead homeless men. 'I'd say his actions last night speak for themselves but we'll need concrete evidence linking him to the deaths to convince a jury.'

'Do they have any footage from the time of the other two deaths, Inspector?' said DC Templar.

'No, we only have this footage because Traffic agreed to reset their cameras on both intersections bordering that block after Dr Jonas told us he thought the first two had been murdered.'

'Forensics are going over his vehicle and they've got a team searching his apartment,' said Harry, 'and, I've got Telstra working on getting me his phone data, so we'll know where he's been and who he's been talking to.'

'Do we have his DNA profile on the database?'

'No, but I'm sure we'll have his profile sooner rather than later after last night, Boss.'

'While I think of it, Harry, call Bayside and get them to courier in the recording Hendri is dropping in there today. Apparently, he was accosted in the car park of the Bayside Hotel last night, and the hotel has given him a copy from their security camera.'

'Might not be that useful, Inspector,' said DC Beard. 'Sgt

Lang wasn't hopeful they'd be able to get anything useful from the copies we brought back yesterday.'

'How did you get on at Morton Sands?'

'Waste of time. No-one has a camera covering the front of the Post Office.'

CHAPTER 24

WHILE CARL WAITED for City Hospital to confirm that Dario Finestra was well enough to be interviewed, he received an update from Sgt Dean Lang on Forensics' search of Finestra's vehicle and residence.

'Some interesting stuff in a sports bag under the front seat of the Toyota, Inspector. A syringe with a needle attached to it inside a plastic container lined with cotton wool, a length of rubber tubing, a tablespoon, a small bottle of water, a screwdriver, a box of latex gloves and several packets of an off-white powder,' said Sgt Lang.

'Any idea what the powder is?'

'Heroin would be my guess but I'm getting it tested along with the powder we found in his apartment.'

'Anything else?'

'I've got two handguns in addition to the one he had on him, and more than enough material from his bathroom to compile a DNA profile. The boys also collected a few strands of hair from the back seat of the Toyota that appear to come from different heads.'

'Thanks, Dean. Keep me posted.'

Carl had no idea what the hair might tell them but appreciated the fact that Dean's people were always thorough.

———

Late on Wednesday afternoon, Carl looked through the glass panel in the hospital room door at the prisoner in the bed within the room. Dario Finestra looked like he'd seen better days. Several intravenous drips were attached to his body, his face was covered with stitches sealing numerous cuts, and his neck and left shoulder were heavily bandaged. Carl noted that his body filled the bed, and thought of the rugby player image one of Drake's neighbours had used.

'Has he called a lawyer?' Carl asked the sergeant in charge of the guard detail.

'He hasn't said a word to anybody, Inspector, not even to the medical staff.'

Carl looked at Harry. 'This could be interesting.' He pushed the door, and they walked into the room. The man in the bed glared at them and then shut his eyes.

'Mr Finestra, I'm Inspector West from Major Crimes. I'm here to find out why you're actually here.'

'I don't give a shit who you are. Fuck off! I've got nothing to say.'

Carl smiled. He wasn't that easy to deter, and besides, he wanted to see Finestra's reaction to what he had to say.

'What were you doing at Bayside last night, Mr Finestra, and why did you drive off from the Breath Testing Station? I understand you weren't anywhere near the limit.'

Carl waited. No response. Finestra didn't even open his eyes.

'Mind telling me where you were in the early hours of Sunday morning?'

Dario Finestra remained silent but opened his eyes and glared at him.

Carl walked closer to the bed to make sure Finestra could hear him. 'I'll tell you where I think you were, Mr Finestra, and what I think you were doing. Perhaps that might jog your memory for you.' Carl paused to see if he'd blink and say something.

Finestra simply looked at him.

'I think you were in the laneway between Long Street and South Terrace, killing a homeless man by the name of Gary Potts.'

Dario Finestra closed his eyes.

'You better get yourself a lawyer, Mr Finestra, because in addition to the charges you're already facing from last night's incident, I'm charging you with the murder of Gary Potts.'

The big man opened his eyes and glared at Carl, but said nothing.

'There will be a magistrate's hearing tomorrow morning, Mr Finestra, so you might want to get onto that lawyer sooner rather than later.'

They walked into the car park where they'd left the silver Ford. 'Do you think Finestra could be the thug that's been threatening Hendri, Boss?'

'Guess that might explain why he was in Bayside last night.'

'Too bad the footage from the Bayside Hotel is crap.'

Carl stopped walking and leant on the roof of the car. 'Shit! Hendri said they made him sit in the back of a Toyota SUV.' Carl pulled out his mobile phone and called Todd Hendri, and asked him to come in and do a DNA test first thing in the morning.'

'Do you think that will help?' said Harry.

'Dean's got a pile of hairs from the back seat of Finestra's car.'

'That would potentially link him to Drake, wouldn't it? Didn't they have Drake's laptop?'

'Yeah, and his feet are certainly big enough for those size sixteen sneakers, aren't they?'

Carl called Dean Lang and asked him to test Finestra's shoes against the footprint they had from the Drake crime scene. Then he opened the door and slipped into the car.

'Did you know we had drones, Harry?'

'Not until this morning.'

'We need to find out more about them. Sounds like they could be useful surveillance tools, and a lot quieter than the helicopter.'

'Let's hope they come with trained operators, Boss. I'd hate to see what Wayne could do with one, given his driving record.'

They laughed.

'I wonder how long all this DNA profiling will take,' said Carl.

'Probably be the middle of next week at the earliest.'

'Get anything from Telstra?'

'I've got Lisa looking at the data. She should have an update for us tomorrow morning.' Harry turned the car into the traffic flow. 'What did you make of Finestra's refusal to talk to us?'

'Old style mafia, Harry. Code of silence. But he doesn't realise how much he's actually told us by not saying a word.'

'Be interesting to see who his contacts are.'

Carl stood in front of the map of the city that DC Templar had stuck to the whiteboard devoted to the homeless men case. She'd placed a cluster of crosses on 7 Long Street and linked them to a Post-it note listing dates and times. She'd also marked several crosses on the part of the map that took in Bayside and linked them to a second Post-it note. Carl read her notes.

'Looks like Finestra has been a busy boy, Lisa. No sign of him being in Morton Sands near the Post Office?'

'Not that I could find, Inspector. I checked for the day Hendri told us he'd received the death threat.'

Carl looked at the Post-it notes again. 'But he was in Long Street in the wee hours of the morning on each day a body was found there, and he had the equipment required to administer a lethal dose of heroin.' Carl looked at his detectives. 'Why was he killing homeless men? Doesn't make much sense to me if he's a mob hitman.'

'Random acts of kindness,' said DC Paterson, 'you know, ending lives of misery.'

'Who's to know whether their lives were lives of misery, Wayne?' said DC Templar. 'That's a bit of a moral judgment, isn't it?'

Carl glanced at Lisa. If looks could kill, Wayne would be dead. He wondered whether Wayne had said it simply to stir her up, but admired her for her retort.

'Point is, people, if he killed them, we need to nail him for it, and let the justice system sort out the rest. Any news from Forensics on that powder they found, Harry?'

'They've confirmed it's heroin.'

'So, he had all the required ingredients and was in Long Street at the right time for each death. Be pretty hard to convince anyone that was sheer coincidence on all three occasions, I'd think, even if we have no idea why he did it.'

'What about his activity in Bayside, Inspector?' said DC Templar. 'He was there on the Monday night Dr Jonas thinks Drake was killed, in the vicinity of where we found the body and in the area where Brock's apartment is located.'

'We need to place him at the scene. I've asked Forensics to

compare the footprint they photographed in that warehouse with Finestra's shoes. Hopefully, they'll have something for us later today, and Todd Hendri's coming in this morning to give us a buccal smear, so we can see if any of the hairs found in Finestra's car belong to him.'

'Any sign he was actually in Brock's apartment?' said DS Fuller.

'We won't know that until they've run a comparison using his profile but,' Carl pointed to the map, 'it looks like he was in the vicinity of Drake's apartment on the Sunday before he was killed.'

'Think we have our rugby player in dark glasses,' said DC Paterson.

'What about around Hendri's office?' said Carl.

'He was there that night, but he'd been gone for more than half an hour when the fire started,' said DC Templar looking at her notes, 'but he was in the vicinity of the Bayside Hotel on Tuesday night.'

'Things are not looking good for Finestra, Boss, no wonder he didn't want to talk to us.'

'If he didn't set fire to Hendri's office, Inspector, who did?' said DC Beard.

Carl made a note on the whiteboard for the arson case and turned back to Lisa. 'What did you find out about him from his call log?'

'Most of his calls are either to or from the same number. It's registered to a company called Spy and Fry.'

'Who are they?'

'I looked them up. They're a debt collection agency.'

'We might need to pay them a visit. That could be where he works between hits. What about the other numbers?'

'There are only two others, sir, but one of them is Ryan Whitaker's.'

'Maybe that's where Finestra was getting his heroin,' said Harry.

'More likely the other way around,' said Carl, 'if Finestra really is a hitman for the mob.'

'Whose is the other number?'

'Belongs to someone called Samantha Paulus.'

'See what you can find out about her. She could be the girlfriend.'

'Isn't Samantha the name of the girl Whitaker took to Bali?' said DC Beard.

CHAPTER 25

WARREN HUNTER SAT with a glass of whisky in his right hand and wondered what had happened to all the dreams he and Peter Walker had started out with. He was thankful he had enough money to be well off in retirement, but it wasn't quite how he'd imagined his retirement would be.

Mary, his wife of forty years, was dead. She'd fallen to breast cancer five years ago. Probably just as well, he thought. She would never have agreed with what he had done, had she known.

Their son Trevor was mixed up with the mob, thanks to his marriage to Angela Imbroglio, and now the bastards had control of the firm that he and Peter had worked so hard to create.

He took a sip of his whisky and cursed the banks. The very same banks that had made heaps from them over the years, through the exorbitant fees they'd charged to arrange funding facilities, had lost their nerve during the global financial crisis. He still couldn't believe that when they'd needed the banks to stand behind them the bastards had refused to help them. He'd never forgive that betrayal which had thrown them to the wolves. And, the wolves had come, right on cue, dressed in Armani suits.

If Peter hadn't been such a fool with his personal finances, getting himself hopelessly into debt indulging himself with his rich man's toys, he suspected things might have turned out differently. They might have been able to save the firm from the fate that had befallen it. The banks might even have stayed with them. He took another sip of his whisky.

Warren knew he wasn't actually a saint himself, and that it was his own weaknesses that had allowed Mario into his world. He wished he'd never seen the inside of a casino. He knew he'd never be going near one ever again, even if the group got government approval to build one.

He wondered whether James' so called skiing accident had really been an accident or if the mob had removed him so they could complete the purchase. He'd read somewhere that they were long term strategists, unlike Peter who had only lurched from one development to the next.

He regretted his complicity in the final surrender but understood that Trevor's future depended on it. The things you do for your kids, he thought, as he took another sip of his whisky.

Warren wished he'd never met any of the Imbroglios but softened when he thought of his grandchildren. He adored them but dreaded what the future held for them. His son had moved across the line that separated good from evil, and taken his whole family with him, including Warren. He'd been seduced by the money, and that fast-talking Italian. Warren knew there was nothing he could do about it now.

He put down his empty glass and called Peter's number, only to get his voice mail.

CHAPTER 26

CARL'S SMARTPHONE vibrated in his pocket as he made his way around the supermarket, dropping the items on Nina's list into his trolley. He looked at the information displayed on its screen. The caller was DCI Rankin. Something had to have happened for the chief to be calling him on his rostered day off.

'Hi, Chief.'

'Hope I haven't caught you at a bad time, Carl.'

Carl pushed his trolley into a quiet corner, away from other shoppers.

'Just doing the shopping, Chief. What's up?'

'We've got a body on the South Coast, on the beach at Carrick.'

Carl didn't think that was so out of the ordinary. 'Why are we interested? Can't the locals handle it?'

'It's Peter Walker, Carl, and he didn't drown.'

Harry parked the car outside the Tuscan style villa Peter Walker had built on the foreshore at the southern edge of Carrick. The house faced the sea and was surrounded by two acres of gardens.

The property was enclosed within a high stone wall, designed to protect the plants from the prevailing southerly winds. At the ocean end of the garden in front of the house, a wooden gate opened onto a path that led down to a sandy beach, a short walk through the sand dunes between the house and the water.

'Must be nice having the money to build a place like this, far enough out of town to have a private beach on the edge of your front garden,' said Carl, as he took in the scene.

'Not much good to you when you're dead, though, is it?' said Harry.

'Ah, you're always full of good cheer, Harry.'

Carl pressed the doorbell and they waited in silence until a young woman dressed in jeans and a loose white sweatshirt opened the door.

Carl held out his badge. 'Mrs Walker?'

She nodded.

'Inspector West, City Police. This is Sergeant Fuller. May we come in?'

The third Mrs Walker led them into the lounge and they sat in soft leather chairs, positioned to allow users of the room a view of the ocean vista through its floor to ceiling windows.

'When was the last time you saw your husband alive?' said Carl.

'Yesterday. He went for a walk after lunch, about one thirty.' She found a tissue in her pocket and blew her nose.

'Any reason why you didn't go with him?'

'He didn't ask me.'

'Was that unusual?'

'No. He preferred going on his own. It was sort of like a meditation for him, being out there alone with the waves. Sometimes he'd be out there for hours.'

'I understand you found the body. What made you go looking for him?'

'We had a dinner engagement. He said he'd be back by four. I got worried when he wasn't back by half past, so I called him. He didn't answer his phone. He took it everywhere with him.'

'I know you've given a statement to the local police, so I won't go over those details but do you have any idea who might have killed him? Did he have any enemies?'

'I'm sure he did, Inspector. He'd been in business for fifty years, not that he talked about his business deals with me. Part of our pre-nuptial agreement. He didn't want me anywhere near the business, especially after his first two wives managed to get their hands on a share of it. He said my role was to keep him happy in his old age.' She smiled.

Carl could see why Peter Walker had given her that role. He guessed she was in her mid to late thirties, about the same age as Nina.

'If you don't mind me asking, Mrs Walker, what else does your pre-nuptial agreement cover?'

'That's okay, Inspector. It's pretty straight forward, actually. It says I get nothing from Peter, unless I stay married to him for five years. If we get divorced for any reason after that, I get a predetermined amount based on how many years we stayed together.' She smiled. 'Peter had been taken to the cleaners by his first wife. That was before I was born. Then he married Rachel, who was his personal assistant. Apparently, she wouldn't marry him unless she had a pre-nuptial, and she knew what Monica got. That's where Peter got the idea for a pre-nuptial. Guess he was hoping for third time lucky.'

'And, how long have you been married?'

'Nearly two years.'

Carl hoped she hadn't been left out in the cold by that pre-nuptial she'd signed. 'What happens to you now that he's dead?'

'I inherit half the estate. The other half goes to Dustin, that's

Peter's grandson, unless Peter changed his will without telling me.'

Carl made a mental note. She clearly had motive, and although she appeared distressed, she wasn't distraught; but he wondered how distraught a woman in her position was supposed to be.

'Are you here on your own, Mrs Walker?'

'No, my mother is here with me. She came down last night as soon as I told her what had happened.'

Carl looked out onto the beach. 'Have you seen anybody poking about outside or on the beach since you arrived?'

'No. It's pretty quiet out here, Inspector. That's why Peter chose this spot. When he was still working we came here on weekends to get away from things. Since he'd retired, we've practically been living here. He was actually talking about selling the apartment in the city.'

'What did you think about that?'

Carl didn't think she'd be in love with the idea of moving out of the city but hardly thought that would be motive enough for her to kill her husband.

'Oh, I like it better in the city. It's pretty dead down here, especially this time of the year. Not much nightlife, if you know what I mean. No clubs, unless you count the golf club, and that's not quite the same, is it?'

'No, I don't suppose it is,' said Carl.

'Have you been in contact with any members of your husband's family?'

'There's only Dustin and Marion. Marion was married to Peter's son, James. He died in a skiing accident in Austria last year. Dustin's their son. He's overseas, studying something in America. I spoke to Marion last night.'

'What about your husband's former wives?'

Mrs Walker dabbed her eyes with her tissue. 'Monica doesn't

speak to me but I've been in touch with Rachel. She's nice. She's going to help me with the funeral arrangements.'

'Did your husband keep in contact with them?'

'They were both on the board of his business, so he saw them at least every second month, and Rachel lives in Walker Tower. Peter was always going down to see her. I think they were still good friends, despite what happened. She's been with him in one way or another for more than forty years, so I suppose that's not all that surprising.' She looked up and smiled. 'In fact, I often wondered which one of us Peter thought of as his wife.'

Carl nodded as he imagined what that might have meant to her.

'You mentioned that your husband had retired. Was he still involved with his business?'

'No, he sold it when he retired.'

'When did that happen?'

'At the end of last year. He told me he'd lost interest after James was killed. Said he wanted to have some fun before he got too old.' Tears streamed down her face. 'I'm sorry. Is there anything else?'

Carl placed his card on the coffee table. 'If you think of anything, my number is on this card. Will you be staying here, Mrs Walker?'

'We're going back to the city tomorrow. It's too depressing here.'

───────

Carl and Harry walked along the beach to the spot marked as the crime scene. The local constable, who had responded to Mrs Walker's call for help, had told them that she had been struggling to stop the sea from claiming the body when he arrived, and that the incoming tide had washed the beach, obliterating any footprints in the sand except for those left by Mrs Walker. The only things he'd seen that suggested there had been a struggle were the scratches and the bruising on the victim's neck.

A crime scene investigation team had scoured the area without much luck. The strong southerly wind that blew in from Antarctica during the winter months had rolled the sand across the top of the dunes immediately behind the beach before their arrival, leaving them nothing but a trail of blurred footprints that appeared to go nowhere.

'I suppose the killer could have simply walked back along the beach into town,' said Harry.

'Either that or he had a vehicle up there.' Carl pointed to the road beyond the dunes. 'Let's hope someone remembers seeing it.'

'When's the autopsy, Boss?'

'In the morning.' Carl checked the calendar on his phone. 'It's at ten.'

'Who do you think we should talk to next?'

'I'd like to have a chat with the former Mrs Walkers. They might be able to tell us more about him than the current Mrs Walker.'

'You don't think she could have killed him, do you?'

'Who knows, Harry? She wouldn't be the first young wife in a hurry to get her hands on her sugar daddy's money, and you heard what she said about their pre-nuptials and his will.'

'Yes, and she'd no doubt be better off under the terms of the will by the sound of it.'

Dr Jonas was kitted up and waiting for them when Carl and Harry arrived in the morgue below Police Headquarters for Peter Walker's post mortem examination.

'You boys sleep in or something?'

'Sorry, Mike. We were waylaid by the Commissioner. He's got the Honourable Richard bloody Nelson breathing down his neck. Wants this case solved yesterday.'

'Ah, nothing like a bit of political interference to get the Commissioner's attention, hey?'

'Don't know why they think their friends are any more important than anybody else we have down here in the freezers.'

'Ego, Carl. They're important people, otherwise they wouldn't be government ministers, would they? Anyway, take a deep breath and suit up.'

'I'm not taking any deep breaths down here,' said Harry. 'You never know what you might be breathing in.'

Mike Jonas laughed. 'See you boys inside.'

Carl and Harry pulled on the green gowns, slipped on the plastic hats and shoes required for witnessing an autopsy, and went in to watch.

The post mortem revealed that Peter Walker had been suffering from several of the health issues expected of a man of his age, especially one who had enjoyed the excesses of the good life. He was slightly overweight, his lungs were scarred from years of smoking, and his liver looked like it had worked overtime protecting him from himself. The autopsy also revealed damaged muscle tissue in his neck below the surface bruising. Along with the scratch marks in the skin of his neck and the flesh under his fingernails, gouged out as Peter Walker had fought for his life, the tissue damage confirmed that he'd been strangled with a piece of rope.

'Looks like we have a few rope fibres under his fingernails, Carl. Green nylon, by the look of it.'

'Do you think a slender young woman could have pulled that rope?'

'Guess it would depend on the element of surprise. If she'd

been able to sneak up behind him, especially if he'd been sitting on a rock, I suppose so. But he's no lightweight, is he? It's more than likely he was pulled down onto his knees or even pushed into the sand. There's plenty of sand up his nose but that could've got there after he was dead. Who knows how long he'd been in the surf before his wife found him?'

'Or called it in,' said Harry.

'Did they find his mobile phone?' asked Carl.

'It was in his pocket, along with his wallet and credit cards when I got there,' said Mike. 'I'm pretty sure Dean's people bagged all that stuff.'

'So, doesn't look like a robbery gone wrong, does it?' said Harry.

'No. I'd say someone wanted our Mr Walker dead, Harry,' said Mike.

'Well, I guess we'd better go find out who,' said Carl. 'Let us know if you find anybody else's skin under his fingernails, Mike.'

CHAPTER 27

Monica Webb led Carl and Harry into the front room of her seaside apartment, located on the Esplanade at Bayside.

'I certainly wasn't expecting this, Inspector. The poor man had only just retired.'

'Yes, so his wife told us.'

'How is she? Not too distraught, I hope.'

'It's never easy for a wife in these circumstances, Miss Webb. Her mother was with her.'

'That's good. At least she's not on her own. Now, what do you want to know? I assume you haven't called to simply pass on your condolences, Inspector.'

Carl looked at her. She must be at least sixty, he thought, if she had been wife number one. 'When was the last time you saw him?'

'At that horrible board meeting we had in December, when he announced he'd sold out to bloody Mario and that he was retiring.'

'I take it you weren't happy with that development?'

'I had no problem with Peter retiring. He'd worked hard for years. Even a bastard like Peter deserved some time in the sun before dropping dead. But he should have passed the company to Dustin, our grandson, but he talked Dustin into selling his shares to Mario as well.'

Carl wondered whether Dustin Walker simply hadn't been interested in his grandmother's plans for him. He certainly wasn't the first young man to walk away from a family business to pursue his own interests that Carl was aware of.

'I understand you own shares in the company.'

'Not any more. Once Warren confirmed he'd sold to Mario as well, what was the point?'

'Who's Warren?'

'Warren Hunter. He and Peter go way back. They were at school together. Peter had the dreams and Warren was the one that organised the financial backers and did the books. He'd already retired from working in the business but he had a fifteen percent stake, so he was still on the board.' Monica shook her head. 'Poor Warren, he lost the plot when his wife died. Rumour has it he lost a lot of money at the casino too, which probably explains why he sold.'

'So, this Mario now owns the business?'

'He made us a generous offer and, besides, half the fun was in goading Peter. It's not like I needed the money.'

'Who exactly is Mario?'

'Mario Imbroglio. Have you met him?'

Carl shook his head.

'Funny thing is, he stepped in to save the company when the banks lost their nerve during the global financial crisis. James introduced him to Peter, and then I found out his sister was married to Warren's son, Trevor. Small world, isn't it?'

Carl filed that bit of information for later analysis. It sounded like there might be more to this Mario Imbroglio.

'What was Peter like?' said Carl.

'I thought he was charming when I first met him.' Monica flashed Carl a smile. 'I didn't find out what sort of a bastard he was until after I'd given him his son and heir. Man couldn't keep his dick in his pants. He was having an affair with Rachel even while I was expecting James. And, she wasn't the only one. He had a string of them, and even with his current bimbo, you'd think she'd be more than enough for a man his age, but I hear he's been seen with other young women.'

Carl wondered who her information sources might be.

'What about in his business dealings? Did he make enemies?'

'Peter was ruthless. It was his way or no way. He was always fighting with someone over money, and he prided himself with always getting the best deal, even if that meant driving some poor contractor to the wall. So, yes, I'd say he had plenty of enemies.' She looked at Harry, who was taking notes. 'You'd think if someone he'd screwed during one of his big projects had wanted to kill him, they would have done it well before now, wouldn't you?'

'Yes, I'm inclined to think his death is more likely connected to something more recent,' said Carl. 'What was the company working on when Peter decided to sell and retire?'

'James, that's our son, wanted to go into the casino business. We'd even purchased a site but that all got put on hold when James had his accident. Hit a rock skiing down some mountain in Austria.' Monica paused and then shook her head. 'Peter sort of lost interest after James' death, so it was the shopping malls and the cleaning business that were keeping the company afloat. I'm certain Mario will go ahead with the casino, he and James were together on that project.'

'Was Peter in any financial trouble? Do you think that may be why he sold out?'

Monica smoothed the folds in her skirt. 'Peter was never good with money, Inspector. He spent like there was no tomorrow. Look at his fancy penthouse, and that place he built at Carrick.' She shook her head from side to side. 'He even had a private jet parked out at the airport until just before he retired. God only knows how he paid for that, and Rachel and I both took him to the cleaners.' She chuckled. 'We only ended up with shares in the company because he didn't have the cash to pay us out. Mind you, I did very nicely out of that arrangement and now that Mario has bought me out, I've got nothing to complain about.'

Rachel Foley lived in a two bedroom apartment in Walker Tower, ten floors below the penthouse suite she had shared with Peter Walker until their divorce. Her maid opened the door and led Carl and Harry through to the lounge, where they enjoyed the view across the city to the coast until Rachel joined them.

Carl decided she looked several years younger than the Mrs Walker she had replaced, and that she was old enough to be the mother of the one that had replaced her.

'Sorry to trouble you, Miss Foley, but I need to ask you a few questions about your former husband,' said Carl, as he took the seat opposite Rachel.

'It's all still a bit of a shock, actually, Inspector. I know Peter was difficult to get along with at times but I never thought anybody would murder him. Heaven knows I wanted to kill him myself enough times but I never thought, not even in my wildest dreams, that anybody would actually kill him.'

'When was the last time you saw him?'

'Friday. He dropped in to tell me that he and Hayley were going down to Carrick for the weekend.'

'Was that usual?'

'What, them going for the weekend or him telling me?'

'Both.'

'He always told me where he was going. It's something he'd been doing for more than thirty years, Inspector, but as for was it usual for them to be going there, I can tell you that Peter had been spending quite a lot of time at Carrick since he retired. In fact, I'd say he'd been doing that ever since James was killed.'

'Did he happen to mention why he was going to Carrick for the weekend?'

'They were attending some fundraising dinner for Richard Nelson at the golf club.'

'This would be the Honourable Richard Nelson, I presume?'

'Yes. Peter was one of his backers. They go way back. Went to the same school and all that sort of stuff. They were always doing things together. There's three of them, actually. Warren Hunter's the other musketeer. He worked for Peter until a few years ago. Poor man hasn't been the same since his wife died.'

'Peter ever mention anything about receiving death threats?'

'Not to me, and I'm pretty sure he would have if he'd received any.'

'Any possibility he was being blackmailed?'

'I guess that's possible. His biggest weakness was young women. I lost count of the number of affairs he had while we were married but I don't recall any of them trying to blackmail him. It was common knowledge that he was a bit of a playboy.'

'Is that why you divorced him?'

Rachel smiled. 'That might have been why Monica divorced him, Inspector. She was very naive when she married him, but I knew what I was getting myself into by becoming Mrs Walker, and I made it work for me. No. I didn't divorce Peter. He traded me in for a younger model. I take it you've met Hayley. She's quite a stunner, isn't she?'

Carl smiled but refrained from answering her question. 'Do you think she'd be capable of killing him?'

'Hayley? Think you're barking up the wrong tree there, Inspector. She's such a sweetie. I can't imagine her doing anything to hurt Peter, let alone murdering him.'

'She'd have a good reason.'

'The money? Nah, Hayley's folks are loaded. I'd say Hayley was worth a lot more than Peter. In fact, I accused him of marrying her for her money, but life's funny, isn't it? I used Peter to get what I wanted but I'm pretty sure Hayley actually loved him.'

Carl wondered what else might be in the pre-nuptial agreement Hayley had mentioned to them. Maybe the pre-nuptial had been drawn up to protect her interests more than Walker's.

'Any idea who else might have wanted Peter dead?'

'I think you should talk to Mario Imbroglio. I've never trusted that man.'

'Oh, why's that?'

'I've never been able to work out where Mario gets his money from. He's only ever told us that he represents a group of private investors, and he showed up with deep pockets when nobody else, not even the banks, wanted to back us.'

Harry parked the car in the street outside 12 Seaweed Lane, Bayside, a modest courtyard home with a tiny front garden that was within walking distance of the beach.

A white haired man with a ruddy complexion opened the door to them.

Carl showed him his badge. 'Mr Hunter?'

'Call me Warren.'

He led them into a front room furnished with antiques. 'Take a seat. Don't worry, they won't collapse on you. My wife was an antique dealer. She had all this stuff restored before we moved in.'

'How long have you been here?'

'Bit over seven years. Mary wanted to retire by the beach but she didn't get to enjoy it for very long. Breast cancer. Knocked her down in six months. She's been gone for five years now.' Warren shook his head. 'But, I guess that's not what you boys are here to talk about.'

'No, as I mentioned when I called, we're looking into the death of Peter Walker. When was the last time you saw him?'

'That would have to be a couple of weeks ago. Hayley dragged me out to some charity event with them.' He chuckled. 'She said I needed to get out more but I think she wanted me to keep an eye on Peter while she worked the floor. She's something that girl. I've never seen anybody get people to part with their money like she does.' Warren shook his head. 'Don't know how Peter ever talked her into marrying him? And, now he's gone. I hope she'll be alright.'

Carl paused to allow Mr Hunter time to collect himself. 'I understand that you and Peter worked together for years. What was he like to do business with? Was he the sort that made enemies?'

Warren stroked his chin. 'Peter liked things done his way, Inspector, and on his terms. Sometimes he was bloody unreasonable. Expected people to do things for nothing. Didn't care if he put people out of business as long as we made a profit. He'd have had a lot more enemies if I hadn't been there to step in and renegotiate things.'

'Anybody ever threaten to kill him?'

'Just about every major contractor we worked with, at one time or another. It's just as well we made plenty of money on our projects to pay Peter and everybody else, otherwise we'd never have been able to start another one.'

'So, was money an issue for Peter?'

'He was a dreamer, not a money manager, which is why I managed the firm's finances. I couldn't stop him spending like he did but I did at least stop him from sending the firm bankrupt to pay for his lifestyle.'

'Do you know if he might have been in financial difficulty?'

'Even if he was, what Mario paid him for his share of the company should have set him right, and besides, Hayley's got plenty of money. I don't think he would have owed anyone enough to justify killing him for non-payment, if that's what you mean.'

'What can you tell me about Mario Imbroglio?'

Mr Hunter poured himself a whisky. 'Can I offer you one, boys?'

'You can offer, Warren, but we'll have to refuse,' said Carl, thinking he wouldn't mind a Glenfiddich, if he hadn't made that promise to Nina and wasn't on the job.

'I met Mario at a wedding about twenty years ago. My son Trevor is married to his sister, Angela. They've given me three beautiful grandkids.' Warren smiled and pointed to the photographs on the mantlepiece above the gas fireplace.

'Mario was in the restaurant business in those days. Then he went overseas for a few years. When he came back he was running an investment firm for private investors, venture capitalists I suppose you'd call them. Apparently, they only invest in private companies, like ours. Makes it easier to get an ownership stake, especially if the company is in financial difficulty, like we were.'

Warren smiled to himself.

'Anyway, I only ever saw him at family functions, you know, like when Trevor's kids were christened or had birthdays, and things like that. It was at one of those birthday parties that I mentioned we were having trouble with the banks. That was when we were building Walker Tower. Bastards lost their nerve during the global financial crisis. Mario said he might be able to help, so I put him in touch with James. There was no point putting him in touch with Peter. James had a much better head for finance than Peter ever did.'

Warren took a sip of his whisky.

'Guess things would have worked out differently if James hadn't been into skiing. I'd handed over control of the finances to James by then. Lost interest in the whole thing when Mary died.' He paused for a moment and then looked at Carl. 'Peter seemed to lose interest after James was killed, and that gave Mario the opening to buy us all out.'

'Would Mario have had any reason to want Peter out of the way?'

'I wouldn't think so. I guess now that he has control of the firm he'll go ahead with the casino that he and James wanted to build. Peter wasn't keen on it but I understand he introduced Mario to Richard Nelson, you know, the minister.'

Carl nodded to indicate he knew who he was talking about.

'I expect everyone, including the government, will make a killing out of that. I'd say Mario was more likely to be grateful to Peter than anything else, Inspector.'

The head office of the Walker Group was located on the top floor of a building Peter Walker had built on East Terrace at the turn of the century. The entrance foyer was an expanse of pink granite walls and shiny black floor tiles. Carl and Harry took the elevator to the fifteenth floor.

The doors of the elevator opened onto a sea of grey carpet in front of a reception desk backed by a wall of black marble.

'Inspector West to see Mr Imbroglio,' said Carl.

'Please take a seat, Inspector. I'll let Mr Imbroglio know you're here.'

At least the chairs are firm, thought Carl, as he sat to wait. He hated being offered a seat in a lounge chair that swallowed him whole. He heard his iPhone ping. A message from DC Beard popped up.

'Looks like young Whitaker missed his flight back from Bali.'

'Wonder what that means.'

'Guess we'd better look into it when we finish here. That's a loose end we need to tie down.'

The glass door in the southern wall of the reception area opened, and a short man with dark hair, wearing an Armani suit that Carl could only dream of owning on his salary, walked across the carpet towards them and extended his hand.

'Mario Imbroglio, Inspector. Sorry to have to meet you under these circumstances.'

Mario led them into his office and they sat around the circular table he used for entertaining visitors. Carl wondered how anyone would be able to work in a room with a view like the one he could see through the window opposite the table.

Mario poured them each an espresso from the percolator his receptionist had placed on the table.

'Peter's death is a bit of a shock, Inspector, especially coming so soon after the death of his son last year. And, to hear he was murdered. I don't know what to think.'

'How long had you known him?' said Carl.

'I joined the board in 2009, towards the end of the financial crisis. They were having a bit of a crisis themselves. I bailed them out, otherwise they would have gone under.'

'Are you aware of any strained relationships Mr Walker may have had?'

'Let's be honest, Inspector. Peter was a pain in the arse to work with. He was always getting his project partners offside.'

'So, why did you bail him out?'

'I was introduced to the group through his son, James. Now James was a gentleman. He was easy to work with and we had some big plans for the group. Have you spoken to Warren Hunter?'

'Yes.'

'He knew how to keep Peter under control, and he worked closely with James and I on rebuilding the group after I joined the board. We'd basically managed to talk Peter into semi-retirement before Warren's wife died and he became less involved in the business, and then James went and got himself killed skiing in Europe.'

'Did that upset your plans?'

Mario placed his empty cup in the saucer on the table. 'Just a bit, Inspector. You see, James and I had started down the road towards getting government approval to build and operate a boutique casino inside our next hotel development. Peter got cold feet. The project went nowhere for nearly a year. In the end, he asked me if I was interested in buying him out.'

'Would that delay have put anybody out?'

'Hard to say, Inspector. We've only just got approval. By the way, that's not public knowledge yet. We have to wait for the minister to make the announcement. Should be any day now.'

'That would be, Minister Nelson, I take it?'

'Yes. He was a friend of Peter's. I gather they went to school together. Actually, Peter's decision to sell made it easier to get approval. No conflict of interest problems for the minister, you see. But, to answer your question, as far as any potential partners go there really wasn't any delay. We didn't discuss the project with any of our builders until we put together the final submission.'

'Anyone who might have had a historic grudge against Peter Walker?'

'As I said, Inspector, Peter was a hard man to deal with. I guess there would be a long list of people in the industry he'd upset but, as far as I know, he'd never received any death threats. To be honest, I'm not sure I can help you there.'

'Before we go, Mr Imbroglio, perhaps you could tell me who runs the cleaning side of your business?'

Mario sat upright and looked at Carl. 'Why would you want to know that?'

'One of my other cases. Are you aware of the death of a public servant by the name of John Drake?'

'Saw something about it on the news.'

'Mr Drake managed the payment of several cleaning contracts you have with the government. I may want to speak to whoever he dealt with.'

'You don't think one of my people killed him, do you?'

'I have no idea who killed him, Mr Imbroglio, but, like we're doing here today, I'd like to speak to anybody he dealt with to see if they can shed any light on his death.'

'Give me a minute, Inspector.' Mario picked up the telephone on his desk. 'Trevor, can you come to my office for a moment? I have the police with me.' He turned back to Carl. 'Trevor looks after the cleaning side of the business.'

The door opened and a man, who looked like a younger version of Warren Hunter to Carl, walked into the office to join them.

'This is Trevor Hunter, Inspector.'

Mario waited while Carl shook hands with Trevor and introduced him to Harry.

'Trevor, the inspector wants to know who deals with the government department that pays for our cleaning services.'

'That would be me.'

'Did you deal with John Drake, at all?' said Carl.

'No, all my dealings are with Pam Watson. I understand Drake worked for her. I send all the accounts through to Pam by email. If they have any questions, she calls me. Can't say I had any direct dealings with Drake, Inspector.'

CHAPTER 28

CARL AND HARRY walked back to Police Headquarters after leaving Mario Imbroglio's office.

'What do you think, Harry?'

'Interesting response when you said you might want to talk to whoever had dealt with Drake.'

'Yes. A bit like seeing a rabbit caught in your headlights. He obviously wasn't expecting that question. Anyway, seems none of them talked to Drake if Hunter is telling the truth. What did you make of Imbroglio's portrayal of Walker?'

'Matches with the others. Can't say we learnt anything that'll help us work out who killed him. Sounds like half the people in the state would have a motive.'

They stood at the intersection and waited for the lights to change.

'Maybe it's got nothing to do with his business dealings,' said Carl.

'That puts us back with the wife.'

'What did you find out about her?'

'Her father is Speld Software Solutions. He's one of the richest guys in the country. She's his only child and works as one of his software developers. Based on what's in the public domain, she could have bought Walker out several times over. If she killed him, it wasn't for the money.'

'You have to wonder what a smart young woman like that was doing with an old fart like Walker.'

'He must have had something that you and I haven't got, Boss.'

'Oh, I don't know. You seem to be doing pretty good for yourself.' Carl nudged him in the side. 'Jessika still keeping your bed warm?'

Harry pulled out his smartphone, opened the Photos app, selected an image and showed it to Carl. 'The ring. Picked it up last night.'

'Sure you can afford something like that on your pay?'

'Jessika has a friend who's a jeweller. She's given us a good price.' Harry put his phone back into his pocket.

Carl wrapped his arm around Harry's shoulders and squeezed him. 'Congratulations! When's the big event?'

'We're announcing it at a family dinner Saturday night. Thought we'd wait until Nina pops out young West before going public. Wouldn't want you to miss out on joining us for a drink. By the way, how's she doing?'

'Can't wait to get it over with and, to be honest, I can't wait either.'

'Yeah, well, if what my mum says is right, your real nightmare is about to begin.' Harry laughed.

'Think I remember Charlie Head telling me something like that. Can only hope it gets better. Anyway, too late to worry about it now. What's Jessika say about having kids?'

'If she has her way I'll be a father before I'm thirty-five.'

'Might not be a bad idea, Harry. Mike's always saying he wished he'd had his kids earlier.'

'Hope I don't have to put up with you saying that for the next twenty years.'

DC Beard was waiting for Carl when he and Harry arrived back at Police Headquarters.

'So, what's the score, Nigel?'

'Whitaker's been arrested in Bali.'

'What for?' said Carl.

'Possession.'

'How'd you find out?'

'The Consulate called his mother this morning. I went to see her after Ryan didn't show. She's a mess, which is not surprising given how the Indonesians treat drug users, especially foreigners. They're saying he had more than five grams of heroin on him when he was arrested. That means he could be facing the death penalty.'

'Shit! That's not going to help us much.'

'Perhaps we can get someone from the Consulate to interview him, Boss.'

'Get anything out of the girlfriend, Nigel?'

'Not so sure she's his girlfriend, Inspector. She told me he'd only asked her to go with him the day before they left. Spun her some story about Georgina pulling out at the last moment and that he'd already paid for the trip. She couldn't resist the offer of an all expenses paid holiday in Bali. Claims she only found out he wasn't coming home with her last night.'

'Hang on a minute,' said Harry, as he scrolled through his notes. 'Here it is. Helen Daniels told us that she wasn't aware that Whitaker and Brock had split up. In fact, she told us they'd gone to Bali together, and' he scrolled further back, 'and Whitaker's neighbour told us they'd had a fight the last time Brock had visited him at his apartment.'

'What are you trying to say, Harry?' said Carl.

'I think Nigel is right. This Samantha isn't his girlfriend. I think Brock was still his girlfriend, despite what his mother told us. I reckon this Samantha was a cover.'

'Did you get her contact details, Nigel?'

'Yes, and would you believe her name is Samantha Paulus.'

'We need her story right from when she first met Ryan. I can't imagine she'd go off to Bali with someone she didn't know, even if he was paying. Bring her in. She might be a little more forthcoming if she thinks she could be in trouble. And, find out how she's connected to Finestra. That might be the missing link. Get Lisa to sit in on the interview with you.' Carl turned to Harry. 'Think we'd better go and talk to Mrs Whitaker and then take a look at Ryan's place.'

'Do you want me to call Forensics?'

'Yeah, do that while I update the chief and arrange a search warrant. Tell them we'll see if we can get a key from his mum, otherwise we'll need to contact his landlord.'

There were three cars in the driveway when Carl and Harry arrived at the Whitaker residence in Morton Sands. The door was opened by a young woman in a business suit, who introduced herself as Ryan's sister, Kylie.

Ryan's parents, Jack and Maureen, were sitting in front of their home computer when Kylie escorted Carl and Harry into the house.

'The police are here,' said Kylie.

'Be with you in a minute,' said Mr Whitaker.

'They're booking a flight to Bali,' said Kylie. 'They don't know what else to do.'

'Are you going?' said Carl.

'No. I'll be holding the fort this end.'

Mrs Whitaker came into the sitting room. 'Oh, hello,' she said to Harry. 'Who's your friend?'

'Inspector West,' said Carl, showing her his badge. 'I'd like to clear up a few things with you before you leave for Bali.'

Mr Whitaker came into the room. 'What brings you boys here?'

'We're investigating the death of Georgina Brock.'

'George?' said Mr Whitaker.

Carl nodded.

'What's that got to do with us?' He looked at his wife. 'I thought you told me you'd already told the police all you knew about her?'

'I spoke to that one,' said Mrs Whitaker, pointing to Harry, and there was another detective that came to see me earlier when Ryan didn't turn up at the airport. I gave them a copy of his flight details.'

'Yes, you've been most helpful, Mrs Whitaker,' said Carl, 'but I'm not sure you've been completely honest with us.'

'What do you mean? I told you everything I know.'

'You told us Ryan hadn't seen George for months and that he had a new girlfriend, this girl Samantha that went to Bali with him. That's what he told you to tell us, isn't it?'

'Mum, how could you be so bloody stupid?' said Kylie. She turned to face Carl. 'He's been pulling the wool over her eyes ever since he could talk. What did he say this time?'

Mrs Whitaker bit her bottom lip and looked at her husband. 'He said that if anyone asked I was to say that he'd broken up with George after Christmas and taken up with the girl he was taking to Bali.'

'Why is this of any relevance?' said Mr Whitaker.

'It's possible your son may have killed Georgina Brock, Mr Whitaker. I suspect that's why he's been arrested in Bali.'

Mr Whitaker sat down next to his wife. 'I know he's no saint but why would he kill George? He told me he wanted to marry her.'

'Are you aware that she was working for an escort agency?'

'What?' said Kylie. 'I can't imagine George doing that.'

'Did you know that she and Ryan have been accused of selling drugs on campus?'

Mr Whitaker looked Carl in the eye. 'You're serious, aren't you?'

'I'm afraid so, Mr Whitaker. For a student, he seems to have had access to a lot of money. Any idea how he earned it?'

'He worked part-time for some guy with a fancy Italian name.'

'Doing what?' said Carl.

'Debt collecting. He gets a percentage of whatever he collects.'

'Can you remember the name?'

'Imbroglio,' said Kylie. 'I work for his brother, Mario. He's taken over the firm I work for. Ryan works for Gianni Imbroglio. He owns Spy and Fry. They chase up credit card and store accounts I think.'

Carl checked to confirm that Harry had captured the details. 'So, you work for the Walker Group?'

'Yes. I do the accounts in the cleaning division.'

'Does that mean you work for Trevor Hunter?' said Carl.

'You seem to know a lot about us, Inspector.'

'I'm also investigating who killed your former boss, Peter Walker.'

'Probably someone who'd had enough of his sexual harassment,' said Kylie. 'The man was a sleaze.'

'Like to elaborate?'

'He was a bloody nuisance. Every time you went into his office he couldn't keep his hands to himself, and he wasn't one of those guys who just wanted to touch you on the arm. He'd squeeze your butt or try and run his hand up your skirt.'

'Why didn't you report him or change jobs?' said Carl.

'They pay really well and, besides,' her face opened into a grin, 'we girls turned it into a game to see who could tease him the most. You know, short skirts and that kind of stuff. We drew up a score card and rated his performance every time we went into his office. The girl with the highest score got free drinks after work on Friday.'

'How many of you were playing this little game?'

'Oh, there's been three or four of us since I joined the firm, but I'd hate to imagine how many he'd harassed over the years, and I doubt they all saw it like we do. None of us took it seriously, but I know some of the others did. The girl I replaced, for example, was paid out after she'd made a complaint.'

'Who was that?'

'Do you have a card? I can send you her details when I'm back at work.'

Carl handed her one of his business cards.

'I really had no idea that was going on where you work,' said Mrs Whitaker. 'Are you sure you want to stay there?'

'It's all different now. The new boss is very nice.'

Mr Whitaker looked at his wife and daughter, and shrugged his shoulders. 'So, what do we do now?'

'Do you have the keys to Ryan's apartment?'

'They'd be on his keyring I suppose. Where's that, Maureen?'

'He left it in his room.'

'He still has a room here?' said Carl.

'The room he's always had, Inspector,' said Mrs Whitaker.

'When was the last time he used it?'

'The night before he went to Bali.'

'Do you mind if we take a look?'

'Kylie, can you show them Ryan's room?'

Carl and Harry stood.

'Has anyone driven his car since he went to Bali?' said Carl.

'Only me,' said Mrs Whitaker. 'I drove it back from the airport the day he left.'

'Has it been cleaned since then?'

'Who has time to wash a car these days?'

Ryan's room looked like it belonged to a sports mad teenager.

'What sports did your brother play, Kylie?' said Harry.

'Rugby in the winter and cricket in the summer, right through school. But he stopped when he started uni. He only goes to the gym as far as I know. Too busy earning money is what he says whenever I tease him about it.'

'Play sport yourself?'

'Basketball. Playing div one for Morton Sands.'

'Sounds pretty impressive,' said Carl.

'I've always been good at it and, besides, it keeps me fit. Are you looking for anything in particular? It doesn't look like this room has changed much since he left home.'

'Are these his keys?' said Harry.

'Yeah. Are you going to search his car?'

'Forensics will when they arrive,' said Harry. 'They'll probably take it away.'

Carl looked inside the wardrobe. It was empty, apart from an assortment of rugby and cricket clothing pushed to one end. The desk was crammed with what looked like the detritus of Ryan's last year of high school.

'When did your brother move out?'

'At the start of his third year at uni. He'd been working for a couple of years by then. Reckoned he needed to get away from Mum. Can't say I blame him. She's always spoilt him rotten but he didn't see it that way. He thought of it as being suffocated. She always wanted to do everything for him. Guess he just wanted to be treated as a grown up and not a little kid.'

'Yeah, mothers can be like that,' said Harry.

Carl's phone pinged.

'Forensics are outside,' said Carl.

They went back into the sitting room, where Carl informed Ryan's parents that they'd be searching his car and his apartment.

'When will you be leaving for Bali?' asked Carl.

'We're booked for Friday,' said Mr Whitaker.

'It'll be tough,' said Carl, 'and it could be a long time before he goes to court. I'm sure the Consulate will do what they can to help you get a handle on the situation.'

'And what will you do, Inspector, if you think Ryan killed George?' said Mr Whitaker.

'We will apply for extradition but we may have to await the outcome of his trial. It's not straight forward in cases where a person has already been arrested for something serious. If he's convicted in Indonesia, he will probably have to serve his time before they'll release him to us.'

'That's if they release him,' said Kylie.

Mrs Whitaker slumped into a chair and burst into tears.

Carl couldn't help but feel sorry for her. Even if she'd told them the truth sooner, there was no way things would have worked out any differently. It wasn't like the extradition process happened overnight and, given Indonesia's recent treatment of Australian drug users, Carl thought Ryan would probably be coming home in a box.

CHAPTER 29

THIS PLACE IS STARTING to resemble a picture gallery, thought Carl, as he stood in front of the section of the whiteboard with Peter Walker's photo attached to it.

'If you've read this morning's paper, you'll know the media are having a field day with this one. They seem to know as much about Peter Walker as we do. Someone's told them about his predatory sexual behaviour in the workplace. They even have a picture of the woman that made a complaint against him and then settled out of court.' Carl paused. 'And, they're painting us as the latest version of the Keystone Cops, so, as you can imagine, the Commissioner wants this case shut down with a conviction ASAP.'

'We need to find someone who was in Carrick on Saturday afternoon, Boss.'

'Sure it wasn't the wife, Inspector? She was there,' said DC Paterson.

'What would be her motive, Wayne? We know she doesn't need the money.'

'Maybe she found out he'd been cheating on her. He's got form.'

'Have you seen her, Wayne?' said Carl.

'I'm just saying that a leopard doesn't change his spots, that's all. Let's face it. He's been married three times and his first wife was a looker in her day, but that didn't stop him having God knows how many affairs. Personally, I can't understand why Hayley Speld married him in the first place. Maybe she's nuts. You don't need a motive when you're nuts. You just do it.'

'She's a pretty successful nut, if that's the case.'

'But that doesn't make her psychologically stable though, does it? She married him after all.'

'Lisa, see what you can find out about Hayley Speld. Talk to her friends.'

Carl turned his attention to the part of the whiteboard with the images of Georgina Brock.

'Got anything from Forensics yet, Harry?'

DS Fuller opened his iPad. 'Traces of blood in the front of Whitaker's Toyota near the pedals. Looks like he may have carried it out on his shoes. We've also got a shirt and a pair of jeans with traces of blood on them, found in the dryer in Whitaker's apartment, and another stash of heroin, like the one we found at Brock's. Forensics are running tests to see if the blood's Brock's, and they've collected enough material from his bathroom to get his DNA profile. And, it looks like he forgot to put his trash out. There was an empty plastic wrap box in his bin, with thirty metres stamped on the side.'

'Sounds like our boy might have been in a bit of a panic,' said DC Beard.

'Okay, keep me posted with what they come up with. We need to know whether that's Brock's blood.'

Carl moved to the section of the whiteboard nearest the window. 'We've finally got some good news on this one. Forensics have matched the blood on Drake's shirt to Finestra, and one of the hairs from the back seat of Finestra's car to Drake. Dean's also matched the footprint from the warehouse where the body was found to the sneakers Finestra was wearing when he was arrested.' Carl looked up from his notes. 'It might still be circumstantial as far as Long Street is concerned, but I think we have the links we need to charge him for Drake.'

'Any luck with testing those hairs with Hendri?' said DC Beard.

Carl looked at the report he had received from Dean Lang. 'Another match.'

'So, I wonder who the other guy in the car is,' said Harry.

DC Paterson's mobile rang. He stepped out of the room to take the call.

'That's something we still need to follow up. How did you get on with those credit card numbers Hendri gave us, Harry?'

'Just let me open their email.'

DC Paterson walked back into the room. 'Inspector, that was Crime Stoppers. They've just had a call from a bloke who wouldn't leave his name, claiming that he saw Drake being dragged into a car, a black SUV, on Seaview Street around eleven on the Monday night we think he was killed.'

'Don't suppose he got the rego? Be nice to have a witness confirming what we know.'

'Nah, said it was too dark and that the car's lights were out, but Crime Stoppers traced the number he was calling from. Turns out it was that public phone outside Morton Sands Post Office, the one used to threaten Hendri.'

'Check and see if the Post Office has replaced their security camera, Lisa?' While DC Templar called the Morton Sands Post Office, Carl turned his attention back to Harry.

'How'd we go with those credit card numbers, Harry?'

They waited while Harry searched through his emails. 'Here it is. This could be interesting, Boss. One of them belongs to Peter Walker.'

Carl watched the evening news with Nina after they'd finished eating.

The lead item in the local news segment covered the release of plans for redeveloping the derelict buildings on the corner of Long and William Streets into a hotel and casino. They watched in silence as the Minister for Recreation and Sport congratulated the chairman of the Walker Group for gaining development approval for their plan.

'Isn't that where those homeless men were found dead?' said Nina.

'Sure is. I wonder where they'll go now.'

'Doesn't the government have some plan for a new shelter attached to the bus station?'

'The government's always got some plan. What I'd like to see is some action to get them off the street.'

Carl's mobile phone rang. He looked at the caller ID: Todd Hendri. He took the call.

'You watching the news, Inspector?'

'Are you psychic or something, Mr Hendri?' Carl could hear the sounds of people talking in the background, and guessed Hendri was at the Bayside Hotel eating his evening meal.

'Did you see that bloke that's going to build some hotel in Long Street?'

'That's Mario Imbroglio. He's the chairman of the Walker Group.'

'He looks like the fellow who offered me protection.'

'You sure?'

'Look, I know it was dark and I only got a brief look at him in the light of the laptop, and I could be way off target, but there's something about the way he holds himself and the hair. Made me think of the guy in the back of the car.'

'You could be right. We got a match with your DNA and a hair found in Finestra's car, and he works for Mario Imbroglio's brother, Gianni.'

'Name doesn't mean anythings to me, Inspector.'

'By the way, Mr Hendri, it doesn't look like Finestra torched your office, so keep your wits about you. There's obviously some-body else out there intent on destroying your business.'

CHAPTER 30

Carl took DC Wayne Paterson and SC Charlie Head with him to the offices of Spy and Fry, located on the second floor of the Walker Building in East Terrace, while Harry and DC Beard and two uniformed officers raided Gianni Imbroglio's house in the suburbs.

When Harry's text message arrived, confirming he was in place, Carl opened the door into the offices of Spy and Fry and the raid was on.

Gianni Imbroglio appeared startled by the arrival of three policemen, one obviously armed. 'What's going on?'

Carl noted the expensive suit, the gold rings on his fingers and the flash of gold beneath his sleeve where his watch was fastened to his wrist. 'We're here to search your office.' Carl pulled the search warrant out of his inside coat pocket and handed it to Gianni.

'I'm calling my lawyer.'

'You do that.' Carl signalled to Wayne and Charlie to begin the search.

'Your wife's on line one, Gianni. She sounds upset,' said the woman at the desk outside Gianni's office.

'You'd better take the call,' said Carl.

Gianni Imbroglio took the receiver from his receptionist. Carl watched as Imbroglio listened to his wife, imagining her distress at being raided by the police.

Gianni slammed down the phone. 'Why the fuck are you threatening my wife and kids?'

'I'm not threatening anyone, Mr Imbroglio. I'm looking for something I have reason to believe is in your possession.'

'What?'

'I understand this man works for you?' Carl showed him a photograph of Dario Finestra.

'Dario. Yes, he works for me. I hear he's in hospital because he's been shot by your lot.'

'Well, he did do a runner from a breath testing unit down at the Bay and try to run over one of the officers that intercepted him. However, I understand his injuries are not life threatening.'

'I must admit, Inspector, that's not the sort of behaviour I'd expected from him. He's normally very sober.'

'That was the puzzling part. He was sober at the time.'

Gianni looked at Carl. 'Then why did he run?'

Carl thought that sounded like a genuine question driven by curiosity. 'How well would you say you knew him?'

'He's worked for me for about five years. One of my better operators, actually. Does a lot of training of the students that work for us.'

'Do any socialising with him?'

'I have lunch with him every now and then, sort of informal management meetings, if you know what I mean.'

'Any idea what he does after hours?'

'He's one of the quiet ones. Likes his own company.'

'Seen any indications that he might be a heroin user?'

Gianni shrugged his shoulders. 'I'd be surprised if he was a user, Inspector. You must know his history. From what he's told me, he's never been a user, despite being caught up in the game when he was a youngster.'

Gianni's eyes followed Wayne and Charlie as they searched the three rooms that made up his office.

'Any chance he could have gone back to his old ways?'

'What, dealing? I wouldn't think so. I don't think he enjoyed his time inside.'

'Well, when we searched his vehicle we discovered why he'd done a runner. He had a sizeable stash of heroin on him, and considerably more was found in his apartment.'

'Heroin?' Gianni shook his head. 'Are you sure?'

'I've got four bodies in the morgue full of heroin, Mr Imbroglio, all found in places visited by Dario. It looks like he's been using heroin to kill people.'

'Are you saying Dario has been killing people with heroin?'

'Looks that way.'

'I pay him to collect debts, Inspector, not to kill people.'

This guy is a damn good actor or Finestra's been freelancing on the side, thought Carl, as he watched the disbelief on Gianni's face.

'Do you know this man?' Carl showed Gianni a photograph of John Drake, and watched his eyes.

Gianni Imbroglio shook his head. 'Isn't that the fellow found dead down at the Bay?'

'Yes, this is John Drake. Not only is his body full of heroin but his shirt is stained with Dario's blood.'

'What?'

'And Dario's phone records put him in the location where the body was found at about the time we think he was killed.'

Gianni sank into a chair. 'You mean Dario killed him? I don't believe it.'

'He's been charged with four counts of murder.'

'What's he's said?'

'He hasn't said anything. It's as if he's taken a vow of silence.' Carl noted the tiny smile that flitted around the edges of Gianni's mouth and eyes.

Carl waited while Wayne searched the office they were in.

'What are you looking for?'

'Drake's laptop.'

'You're wasting your time and mine, Inspector.'

'Your car parked downstairs, Mr Imbroglio?' said Wayne.

'Yes.'

'The keys?' Wayne held out his hand.

Gianni handed over his car keys. 'The Alfa in bay 2A.'

Carl noticed that Charlie Head was standing outside the office chatting with the receptionist. Obviously, they hadn't found the laptop.

'I understand this man works for you as well.' Carl showed him a photograph of Ryan Whitaker.

'Ryan. His sister dropped in the other day to tell me he'd been arrested in Bali.' Gianni shook his head. 'Silly boy. He's been working for me since he started uni. Another good operator, trained by Dario, in fact. I can't understand why he'd get mixed up with drugs in Bali. He had such a great future in front of him as an engineer.'

'Do you know this young woman?' Carl showed him a photograph of Georgina Brock.

'Ryan's girlfriend. I've met her once or twice. Think she goes by a boy's name. George, I think.'

'Her name's Georgina Brock, and you're right about her calling herself George. We think Ryan may have killed her before he went to Bali.'

Gianni's eyes opened wide. 'Why would he do that?'

194

'Might have had something to do with her working as an escort.'

'Didn't seem the type to me.'

Carl didn't doubt that Gianni would know what type of girl worked as an escort. His mobile phone pinged. He looked at the message from Harry and did his best not to smile.

Carl scrolled through his photographs until he found Todd Hendri.

'Do you know this man?'

'Don't think so.'

'His name is Todd Hendri. He and Drake were the owners of the escort agency Georgina worked for.'

Gianni shrugged his shoulders but Carl noticed a nervous tick in his left cheek.

'Someone torched his office the Monday night before last, about half an hour after Dario had visited him. Sure you don't know him?'

'I employ Dario, Inspector. I don't own him. What he does after hours is not on my account.'

'Well, this is where we have a problem, Mr Imbroglio. Hendri claims you were with Dario that night, and offered him protection in return for Drake's share of the profits from the escort business.'

'What? The man's clearly delusional, Inspector. We're a debt collection agency, not standover merchants.'

'Would you say you resemble your brother, Mr Imbroglio?' Carl stepped back and looked him up and down. 'I would.'

'What's that supposed to mean?'

'There was an item on the news the other night about your brother's company gaining approval to include a casino in its new hotel on Long Street, with shots of Mario and the minister. Did you see it?'

Gianni nodded.

'Well, Mr Hendri called me right after that story aired. He's made a statement about you having Drake's laptop.' Carl paused and waved his mobile phone in front of him. 'And, my colleague has confirmed that he's found the laptop in your house.'

'I want to call my lawyer.'

'That might be wise, Mr Imbroglio, but you can do that from the station. I'm arresting you for racketeering, and for being an accessory to the murder of John Drake.' Carl stepped over to the doorway. 'Charlie! Read Mr Imbroglio his rights.'

Lisa studied Samantha Paulus as Nigel went through the standard protocol for setting up a formal interview. The perspiration forming on Samantha's brow, despite the chill in the room, confirmed for Lisa that this was the first time Samantha had been interviewed formally by police.

'Samantha, we're investigating the death of Georgina Brock, and we have reason to believe she may have been killed by Ryan before you went to Bali with him. We're trying to get an understanding of where you fit into the picture,' said Lisa.

'Okay,' said Samantha.

'How about you start by telling us how you met Ryan?' said Lisa.

'He was a year ahead of me at high school. He was one of the hunks in the rugby team. I was in the cheer squad.' She smiled. 'All the girls in the cheer squad had a crush on him.'

'And did you have a crush on him?' said Lisa.

'I wanted so much to be his girlfriend but he was only interested in Helen, and she wasn't even in the cheer squad.'

'Would that be Helen Daniels?'

'Yes.'

'Is she a friend of yours?'

'I wouldn't say we were friends. I just know who she is. She's doing law, I think.'

'And what are you studying, Samantha?' said Lisa.

'Commerce.'

'Did you know Georgina Brock?'

'Not really but I'd seen her a few times with Ryan. He treated her like a princess. I thought she was a bitch.'

'Oh, why's that?' said Lisa.

'Hard to say exactly. There was just something about her I didn't like.'

'You weren't jealous of her, were you?' said Lisa.

'Nah. Ryan and I aren't going anywhere. We're just mates.'

'So do you spend much time with Ryan on campus?'

'There's a Morton Sands group that meets for lunch most Fridays. I generally catch up with him there. Helen comes sometimes, but George isn't invited. She didn't go to Morton Sands. He's always a lot more fun when George isn't around.'

'What do you mean?' said Lisa.

'You know, he flirts with all the girls, and he's always telling jokes.'

'Were you surprised when he asked you to go to Bali?'

'I certainly wasn't expecting it. I thought George was going with him, in fact, he'd told me she was the previous Friday.'

'Why do you think he asked you?'

'Well, he knew I had a passport. We'd talked about a group tour over lunch the previous Friday and someone had asked if we all had passports, seeing we were discussing going to Europe for the mid-year break. And, I suppose I'm someone he feels comfortable with.'

'What made you decide to go? It was pretty short notice, wasn't it?' said Nigel.

'It's not every day someone offers you an all expenses paid holiday in the sun with no strings attached, is it?'

'What about your studies?' said Nigel.

'It's all online. You can catch up on anything you've missed or go over the lectures if you want to. I could do that just as easily in Bali. I didn't need to be here.'

'Were you surprised that Georgina had changed her mind about going with him?'

'To be honest, nothing that girl did surprised me.'

'Did you know she was working as an escort?' said Nigel.

Samantha's eyes widened. 'An escort? You mean like a prostitute?'

'Yes.'

'Can't say I expected that.'

Nigel slid a photograph of John Drake across the table to her. 'Did you ever see this man on campus?'

'He's a friend of Helen's. I saw him with her a few times at the Merlin. She's got a thing for older men.'

'He was one of the owners of the escort agency that Georgina worked for,' said Nigel.

'Are you telling me Helen works for him, too?'

'We're not at liberty to disclose that sort of information.'

'Would certainly explain where she gets her money, if she is. Her father's a real tight-arse. Wouldn't even pay her for working in the coffee shop.' Samantha looked at the photograph again. 'So, who is this guy?'

'His name was John Drake. He was murdered around the same time as Georgina,' said Nigel.

'And you think Ryan killed him as well?'

'We're pretty sure we know who killed Mr Drake, and it wasn't Ryan,' said Nigel, sliding her a photograph of Dario Finestra. 'Do you know this man?'

'No.'

Nigel slid her a sheet of paper. 'This is a listing of the call log from his phone.' He pointed to one number with his pen. 'Recognise this number?'

Samantha leant forward and studied the number. 'That's my number. What's his name?'

'Dario Finestra.'

Samantha relaxed back into her chair. 'Ryan works with him. He used my phone to call him the day we went to Bali. He dropped his when we were going through security. Whole thing disintegrated.' She spread her hands apart. 'He had to put it into a plastic bag. I thought it was really funny.' She grinned. 'First time I'd ever seen Ryan embarrassed in my life.'

'So what happened in Bali?' said Lisa.

'I had a great time. It's really nice being treated like a princess.'

'What was Ryan like while you were there?'

'He was like there was never going to be a tomorrow. We did everything there was to do; he took me all over the island, and then he said he wasn't coming home. Said he'd decided to go to Europe instead.'

'Do you know if he tried to contact Georgina while you were in Bali?'

'Now that I think of it, I don't think he mentioned her once. It was like she didn't exist.'

'Do you know if he contacted his parents?'

'Told me he'd sent his mother an email to tell her he was going to Europe.'

'Did you know that he'd told his mother to say that you were his girlfriend?' said Nigel.

Samantha blushed. 'I was while we were in Bali but I knew it wasn't going to last.'

'When was the last time you saw him?'

'Tuesday night. He was gone when I woke up Wednesday

morning. He'd left a note saying he was catching an early flight to Singapore.' She stopped and looked at Nigel. 'I can't believe he's been arrested for doing drugs or that he'd kill anyone.'

'I'm afraid all the evidence is pointing to him being Georgina's killer,' said Nigel. 'Thanks for coming in.'

CHAPTER 31

LATE IN THE afternoon of the last Friday in May, Steven Wilmington sat in his office with Paul Murphy, who was leading the special audit of the Office of State Supply's contract approval process.

'Drake was on to something, Steve, but he must have had a lot of time on his hands to figure it out though.'

'Oh. What have you uncovered?'

'We did all the standard checks and, on the surface, it looks like they've followed the sanctioned procedures. Nothing appears out of the ordinary. Everything's documented down to the last full stop and linked to an appropriate policy or procedure.'

'So, what's the problem?'

'All that documentation. It's too comprehensive. I've never seen anything like it in all my years in the game. It's as if they've constructed a defensive wall around the entire process, and it's only when you start peeling back the layers that you realise it's not all it seems.'

Steven didn't like the sound of what he was hearing. He was fond of Sonya. She'd been his lover for the last two years, and it was starting to sound like she'd been screwing him in more ways than one.

'So, it's entirely possible Elena didn't peel back enough layers?'

'It looks like she's been fooled by the defensive wall they've constructed.'

'What's the damage?'

'Drake was right. They've approved the Walker contracts with a fifteen percent premium over comparable tenders.'

'Who do you think is in on it?'

'I'd say the whole committee, including Pam Watson. She's done most of the documentation, and she attends all their meetings.'

Steven stared out the window of his office but saw little of the view bathed in the fading light of the sinking sun. 'Fuck! I'm screwed.'

'What do you mean, Steve?'

'The Corruption Commissioner's going to accuse me of turning a blind eye.'

'Be reasonable, Steve. You make your assessment based on what Chris and Elena report to you after each audit.'

'Well, apart from the fact that he'll accuse me of hiring incompetent staff, which will be bad enough, he'll be accusing me of a conflict of interest I haven't declared.'

'You sure you want to tell me this, Steve?'

'If I have to tell someone, Paul, it may as well be someone I trust.' Steven walked over to his cabinet and poured two glasses of Scotch before returning to his seat opposite Paul. 'I've been having an affair with Sonya Curtis for the last couple of years.'

'Shit, Steve. Why didn't you say something sooner?'

'I didn't mean for it to happen. It simply got out of hand after Mary had her stroke, and then I didn't know what to do about ending it.'

'I think you better tell him before he finds out, and before I present my report.'

Steven walked over to his desk and rang the Corruption Commissioner. 'Patrick, got a minute? Can you come past my office on your way home. I've got Paul Murphy with me. There's a couple of things we need to discuss.'

He turned to Paul. 'He'll be right down.'

Steven poured a glass of Scotch for Corruption Commissioner Patrick Flynn when he arrived.

'Paul's just been telling me Drake was correct. They've been giving preferential treatment to the Walker Group.'

'You're sure about this, Paul?' said Patrick.

'As sure as I can be. I can have a written report for you early next week,' said Paul.

'This is not looking good for you, Steve,' said Patrick, sipping his Scotch.

'It gets worse, Patrick. It's going to look like I've been deliberately turning a blind eye.' He paused and swallowed his pride. 'I've been having an affair with Sonya Curtis for the last couple of years.'

Patrick smiled. 'I'm glad you finally told me, Steve, but it would have been better if you'd declared it earlier, though I understand why you might not have wanted to, seeing Mary's still officially your wife, even if she is in a coma.'

Steven looked at him as the penny dropped. 'You mean you knew?'

Patrick took another sip of his Scotch and relaxed back into his chair. 'Steve, I worked in military intelligence before embarking on the legal career that took me to the bench and, eventually, to this role. One thing I've always remembered from my military training is to have multiple sources of information before deciding on the value of any intelligence. I've got eyes and ears all over the city, all through the public service and beyond. I know all about your meetings with Sonya downstairs in the back corner of the coffee shop, and about your trysts down on the South Coast. I don't think you'd make much of a spy, Steve. You're too bloody open.'

Steven felt a weight lift from his shoulders.

'So, what do we do now? I'm meeting Sonya for dinner in an hour or so. I don't want to tip her off that we're on to them, and she's sure to ask about the audit.'

'You're going to have to play it cool, Steve, and tell her a little white lie. If she asks, tell her that Paul is giving you his update next week and hasn't told you anything to date. Think you can do that?'

'I should be able to do that. It's not like it will be the first lie I've ever told, Patrick. Thankfully, she's going to her daughter's place for the weekend to see her new grand-daughter after dinner tonight, and I'm committed to golf with some friends from Church this weekend. We're going down to Carrick for a tournament tomorrow morning.'

Patrick smiled and swilled his remaining Scotch. 'Paul, I think you had better get something to me first thing Monday morning, sooner if possible.'

'I should be able to get something to you by Sunday. I've got kids' sport most of tomorrow. Hopefully, I can pull something together Sunday morning, before they get up. Might have to come into the office.'

'Do that.'

CHAPTER 32

MONDAY NIGHT WAS Reg's night for playing cards or for going to the casino with his mates. On the nights he went to the casino he left home early and treated himself to a meal in Players Steak-house, before joining his mates at the tables. This Monday night, he'd told his wife they were going to the casino and left home just before six, in time to be at the casino by six-thirty. But instead of heading for the casino in the city, he headed to Bayside. By six-fifteen he was sitting in his van, parked two houses up from the building that housed Hendri Accounting Services, waiting for Hendri to leave, and wondering what was keeping him. Hendri was usually gone by six, according to the information he'd paid for.

A black SUV exited Hendri's car park and disappeared down the street towards the Bayside Hotel, where Reg knew Hendri went for his evening meal. Obviously, Hendri had had a late appointment. Ten minutes later, Hendri's black BMW appeared beneath the dim street light outside the entrance of his car park and Reg watched as its tail lights moved away from him towards the Bayside Hotel.

He waited five minutes, and then drove his van into Hendri's car park and parked it close to the back entrance, where he knew

Hendri parked his BMW. He got out of the van and slipped his overalls over his suit, and then changed into his old sneakers, carefully placing his dress shoes on the seat inside the van. He looked around him in the dark. The houses either side of Hendri's office were in darkness. They were offices like Hendri's, and their occupants had gone home for the night. He knew the back of the building was not visible to the residents living in the houses across the street from the row of offices.

He took the can of paint thinners and the bag of twigs he'd gathered from the back garden out of the van, picked up his torch, and checked that he had his matches. Then he stepped onto the porch and inspected the door. It looked solid enough but when he gave it a push the whole thing moved in the frame. Two swift kicks later, it swung open, leaving a gash where the lock had parted from the doorframe.

The backroom of the office looked like a closed-in verandah, and for a moment he wondered whether the door leading into the house proper would be locked as well but, when he tried it, it was open. He stepped through the door and switched on the torch. The room the backdoor opened into looked like a storeroom. It was full of paper stacked on wooden shelving, broken furniture and waste paper inside two large plastic bags.

He emptied the waste paper onto the floor next to the shelving, and then tipped his bag of dry twigs onto the waste paper. He picked up two broken wooden chairs and placed them over the pile. Then he carefully poured the paint thinners onto the twigs and the waste paper, taking care not to splash it onto his clothing or sneakers. He didn't want to set himself alight.

He picked up two packets of paper and placed them on top of the empty can next to the door. Then he walked back to the shelving, struck a match and dropped it onto the pile of paper and twigs, which ignited with a whoosh. He watched for a moment to make sure it didn't go out. Then he picked up the paper and the can, pushed the door with his foot so that it was wide open and retraced his steps to the outside door, where he dropped the two packets of paper onto the floor and used his foot to push them up against the door, so that it would stay open and allow a free flow of air into the building to give life to the fire.

Less than ten minutes after entering the car park, Reg drove back out into the street and headed towards the Bayside Hotel, where he turned onto the Esplanade, before joining the flow of traffic heading into the city. When he arrived at the casino, he dropped the empty can into a trash container inside the car park, and walked to the elevator that would take him up to Players Steakhouse.

CHAPTER 33

CARL WAS FIXING Nina a cold drink in the kitchen, listening to the evening news on the TV, when the story broke that four public servants working for the Office of State Supply, including Sonya Curtis, the head of the agency, had been suspended on full pay pending the outcome of an inquiry by the Corruption Commissioner, and that Auditor General Steven Wilmington had tendered his resignation to the Premier.

He stopped what he was doing to ponder the implications, and decided that Drake must have been onto something after all.

'Carl!'

He rushed into the bedroom, taking care not to spill Nina's drink. She was on the bed with her hands on her swollen belly. Her face was red and covered in perspiration.

'They're getting really strong.'

'How often are they coming?' He handed her the drink she had requested.

'Every few minutes.'

'Aren't we supposed to wait until it's been like that for about an hour?'

'They've been coming and going all day. I think it's time to go. Ring the hospital.'

Carl pulled out his mobile phone, called the number the hospital had given them, and explained the situation. The person on the other end told him to bring his wife in. He collected the bag Nina had prepared and waited while she went to the loo for the fifth time since he'd arrived home from work. Then he helped her into the car and set out for the hospital.

'Can't you go any faster?'

'There's a speed limit, honey.'

'I don't want to give birth in the bloody car!'

'Breathe, sweetheart.'

'I'll give you breathe! Get me to the bloody hospital!'

Fortunately, most of the traffic was heading out of the city, so it only took Carl ten minutes to drive to City Hospital, where he pulled into the driveway of the maternity wing. As soon as he stopped the car, a nurse appeared with a wheelchair, and helped Nina out of the car.

'How are you doing, dear? How frequent are the contractions?'

'Every couple of minutes.'

'Okay. You're in the best place now. Try and relax.'

By the time Carl had parked the car Nina was in the labor ward. Carl spotted Dr Merry, Nina's obstetrician, going into a room off the corridor as he was getting out of the elevator.

'Mr West?' said the nurse at the desk in front of the elevators.

'Yes.'

'You'd better get a move on. Here. Slip this over your clothes and I'll take you down.'

She handed him a green gown. Carl thought it was ironic that he had to wear the same uniform to the birth of his daughter that he wore to a post mortem. He quickly put it on and followed her instructions to wash his hands with a clear liquid that smelt like disinfectant.

'Come on, Mr West, or you'll miss it!'

Carl followed her down the corridor to the room he'd seen Dr Merry enter, and walked into what looked like organised chaos.

'Make yourself useful, Carl, and hold Nina's hand,' said Dr Merry. 'You're just in time. That's it Nina, push.'

A small head covered in wet black hair appeared, and then a small red body slid into the room, attached to a cord that led back into the womb she had just exited.

Carl watched in amazement as his daughter made her entrance and took her first breaths. Nine months of waiting had come to an end, and here she was, making herself heard at the top of her lungs. Carl wondered where she got the energy, there was so little of her. She was tiny. He'd never seen anything so beautiful in his life, and felt a wave of love for this tiny new person wash through him. He was a father. He could hardly believe it.

Dr Merry cut the umbilical cord and checked her vital signs before gently placing her in Nina's arms. 'Say hello to your mother.'

'She's beautiful,' said Nina, looking at the baby, and then at Carl.

Carl reached out his hand and gently touched his daughter. She was soft and warm, and not much bigger than his hand.

'Just like her mother.'

'Have you decided on a name?' said Dr Merry.

'Sophie,' said Nina. 'Sophie Alice West.'

While Nina and Sophie were transferred to the nursery ward, Carl telephoned DCI Rankin, who'd been like a father to him ever since he'd been a young detective.

'Chief, I'm at the hospital. I'm the proud father of a beautiful baby girl.'

'Congratulations! How's Nina? No complications, I hope.'

'She's fine. It was all pretty quick. I nearly missed the birth parking the car.'

He heard the chief laughing and relaying the message to his wife.

'Evelyn wants to know if this little darling has a name?'

'Sophie Alice West.'

'Sophie. Wasn't that your mother's name, Carl?'

'Yes, we decided to call her after both of her grandmothers.'

'Give Nina our love, Carl.'

He called Robert and Nancy Strong, Nina's uncle and aunt, and told them where they'd be able to find the newest member of the family. Nancy was so excited he thought he'd never get her off the phone.

He called Frank Mulligan, who'd become a close friend and frequent visitor to the West house since he'd agreed to officiate at their wedding, and told him the news. Frank asked after Nina and promised that he'd call in to see her and meet Sophie.

He called his cousin, Daryl, and told him the news, and had to speak to each of Daryl's kids, who wanted to hear about their new cousin from Carl himself.

When Daryl's kids let him go, he called Mike Jonas, who welcomed him to the club of older fathers and reminded him that the fun was only just beginning.

Then he called Harry, and arranged to meet him and Jessika for a celebratory drink on his way home from the hospital.

After sharing his news, he went to see how Nina and Sophie were settling in, and to take some photographs of his daughter in preparation for the inevitable questions he knew he'd be getting in the days ahead.

Nina was tired but wanted to know who he had called. He went through the list.

'Aren't you going to call Charlie, and Jane? She won't forgive you if she hears about if from someone else.'

Carl searched through his contacts for Jane Priest and called her number. She was excited with their news and wanted to talk to Nina. Carl handed Nina the phone and listened, while his wife went over the details and laughed about him almost missing the birth with his former lover.

When she handed him back the phone, he called Charlie Head and told him where he was meeting Harry to celebrate Sophie's birth.

'Don't go overboard with those celebratory drinks, honey,' said Nina, 'remember, you still have to go to work tomorrow.'

Carl smiled. 'I'll only have a couple. Jessika will be there.'

'Are you going to give Sophie a cuddle before you go?'

'Do you think that's wise?'

'You'll be fine. Just be gentle.'

Sophie lay wrapped in a blanket in the bedside cradle. Carl reached into the cradle and gently lifted the tiny bundle, and cuddled his daughter. He thought she was the most precious thing on earth, even though her eyes were tightly closed, and wondered why he'd ever been afraid of becoming a father.

Nina took a photograph of the proud father holding his daughter, then Carl put Sophie back into her cradle and took several shots of her with his iPhone.

It was close to ten by the time Carl walked into the front bar of the Royal Oak. The crowd was a little bigger than he had expected. Harry had called in the team.

Jessika hugged him and kissed him on the cheek. Harry shook his hand and slapped him on the back. Charlie handed him a beer and wished him luck. Lisa wanted to see a picture of Sophie. Nigel and Lily crowded in to look at his photos. Even Wayne was excited.

The atmosphere in the room felt like a different world to Carl. These were the same people he worked with every day, but tonight they were not the same. No-one was talking about work. Everybody was happy for him. Everybody was wishing him well, and saying what a great father he would be.

Swept up in the emotion of the moment, Carl ordered drinks for everyone and relaxed, knowing he was with friends.

CHAPTER 34

CARL STOOD in front of the team in the Incident Room on Tuesday morning, the day after Sophie's birth. The intimate atmosphere of the previous night's celebrations had given way to the reality of his working world.

Forensics had sent him an update on the Brock case, so he decided to start the briefing with their findings.

'Forensics have matched the blood found on Whitaker's clothing and in his car with Brock. They've also matched the DNA profile from the semen sample taken from her body with the profile extracted from the material in Whitaker's bathroom.' He scanned the page and located the line Dean Lang had highlighted. 'Several of the pubic hairs found in Drake's bedding appear to be Brock's, so it looks like she was sharing his bed.'

'Looks like you were right about the jealous boyfriend, Sergeant,' said DC Paterson.

'At least we have a motive, even if we can't get our hands on Whitaker,' said Carl.

'Anything come of our extradition request, Inspector?' said DC Beard.

'As I told his parents, Nigel, we're in the queue. I don't expect we'll get access to Whitaker until after his trial in Indonesia, and that might be all we get if he gets the death penalty.'

'So, where does that leave us, sir?' said DC Templar.

'We need to make sure there are no loose ends, nothing we've overlooked, and then write this one up so that whoever is available at the time can take it to the next level, if and when Whitaker is released to us. We'll also need to make sure the forensic evidence is stored and safe from contamination. Otherwise, we're done on this one for the time being.'

Carl walked past the section of the board holding the Drake case and stood in front of the images from the Hendri arson case.

'The fire investigators have identified the storeroom at the back of the premises as the ignition point. Looks like the arsonist set fire to a pile of trash next to the shelving, and the fire spread to the ceiling from the shelving. They've also determined that the arsonist left the back doors open to fan the flames.'

'Sounds like someone who knew what he was doing,' said DC Paterson.

'Do you think it was Finestra?' said DC Beard.

'Who knows? He's not talking, but his phone puts him in the city near Spy and Fry's offices around the time the fire was reported. He'd have had to use a delayed action incendiary device, and there's no evidence one was used. The fire investigators reckon our arsonist used paint thinners and a match.'

'What about Imbroglio?' said DC Templar.

'Not his style,' said DC Paterson. 'I'm actually surprised he called on Hendri in the first place, but I'd say torching Hendri's office wouldn't have been part of his game plan, if he was interested in getting money out of him from his escort business.'

'That means someone else has to be after Hendri,' said Carl, 'perhaps the same person who threatened him. Any luck with the Morton Sands Post Office, Nigel?'

'They've got their camera fixed now, not that that's of much help for the calls we wanted to follow up.'

'I wonder if the same person made both calls,' said Carl.

'Why would someone threaten Hendri and then report seeing someone else abduct Drake?' said DC Templar. 'Doesn't make sense to me.'

'What if he'd been after Drake the same way he's after Hendri?' said Harry. 'Maybe that's why he saw the abduction? It's not like he called it in when it happened. It was weeks after. In fact, it was after the fire at Hendri's office.'

'You think he was trying to steer attention away from himself, Harry?' said Carl.

'It's a possibility.'

'If it's not the mob, who is it?' said DC Paterson.

Carl looked at the whiteboards. 'Who else would want to kill these guys?'

'If we've got an angry boyfriend, who's killed his girlfriend because she was mixed up in their agency, could we have an angry parent?' said Harry.

'We've got an angry parent in Morton Sands,' said DC Beard. 'Reg Daniels.'

Carl made a note on the whiteboard. 'See what you can find out about his movements, Harry.'

He walked over to the Walker case. 'I've got the Commissioner breathing down my neck on this one. Any fresh leads?'

'I asked Hendri to run a query on his database against Walker's credit card number,' said Harry. 'He got two hits, and one of them could be very interesting, in light of our discussion about Daniels. Walker was a frequent user of Helen Daniels. It looks like he'd only booked Brock once but he'd been hiring Daniels at least once a month for the last six months.'

'How would her father know that?' said DC Templar.

'Who was the friend that told him about the agency?' said Carl.

'He didn't say,' said Harry.

'Maybe it's time to find out.'

Carl listened as Harry explained the formal interview protocols to Helen Daniels before activating the tape and starting the interview.

'Miss Daniels, we're investigating the death of Peter Walker.' Carl placed a photograph of Peter Walker on the table in front of him, and turned it so she could see it. 'I understand he was one of your clients.'

'Yes, he was one of my regulars. Always gave me a big tip.'

'Where did you meet with him?'

'His penthouse, you know, at the top of Walker Tower.'

'And, what level of service did you provide to Mr Walker?'

'For an old man he was always horny. He only ever wanted sex, Inspector. He certainly wasn't interested in my skills as an intelligent conversationalist.' She smiled.

Carl noticed she hadn't even blushed while answering his question, and guessed having sex with older men was simply a business transaction from her perspective.

'Who else knew he was one of your clients, apart from Drake and Hendri?'

'Henry knew. He knows who all my clients are. That's how it works.'

Carl looked at Harry.

'Walk us through how you got into Mr Walker's penthouse,' said Harry.

Helen looked at the ceiling for a moment. 'Henry always dropped me at the front entrance, and then I'd introduce myself to the concierge and tell him Mr Walker was expecting me. He'd check his list and open Mr Walker's private elevator for me, and up I'd go. Great view from that penthouse, mind you. He never closed the curtains.'

'And when you left?'

'I'd call Henry when I was leaving and he'd be waiting for me where he'd dropped me off.'

'How many concierges do you remember?'

'Just the one. A man with grey hair and silver rimmed glasses. He was always very polite but I think he knew what I was there for. Mr Walker had quite a reputation, after all, didn't he?'

'Does that mean you always went at the same time?' asked Carl.

'It was usually around nine in the evening, Inspector, on a night his wife was interstate on business.'

'I understand your father isn't very happy about your work as an escort, Miss Daniels. Has he ever threatened you over it?'

Helen laughed. 'Dad's been threatening to do stuff to me ever since I was little, Inspector, and he was always threatening to cut me out of his will when he didn't like my boyfriends, but he's all talk no action. It's just the way he is.'

'What did he think of Ryan Whitaker when he was your boyfriend?' asked Harry.

'Dad thought he was a brainless jock; good at rugby and not much else.'

'Is that why you broke up with him?'

'Not really. I would've stayed with Ryan just to piss Dad off, but when we got to uni there were so many more people to play with. He ended up with George. I met John and he introduced me to a whole new way of playing, if you know what I mean, and it gave me a way to leave home.'

'Things that bad at home?' said Carl.

'Look, don't get me wrong. My folks are nice people but

they've got pretty narrow views when it comes to how people should behave. Like, I was expected to work in the shop out of love, so they could get a bit of free time. Ten years of slave labour was enough. I took the first opportunity that came along to get myself out of there.'

'Does your father have any interests besides his business?'

Helen relaxed back into her chair. 'He works long hours. He has to get up early every morning to bake but he plays cards with his mates on Monday nights, and he always goes to the football on Saturdays. He's a member of the Bayside Football Club. I don't think he's missed a Bay's game since my brother and I were old enough to help Mum out in the shop.'

'When was the last time you saw your parents?'

'I went to see them a couple of days ago, actually. I miss my Mum. Dad tried to talk me into giving up work. Said they were really worried about my safety after what happened to John and George. I told them the agency had shut down and didn't know if I'd go back. Dad even offered to pay my rent if I stopped. I'm thinking about it. I know they love me.'

Carl wondered if Reg Daniels loved his little girl enough to do anything to save her. He knew he would for Sophie, and she'd only just arrived in his life.

'Miss Daniels, do you have any idea who told your father you were working as an escort?'

Helen sat up straight. 'I'd assumed he found out by accident. He's always on the internet.'

'No, he told us a friend had told him, and sent him a link to the agency's website.'

'I've no idea. You'll have to ask him.'

After interviewing Helen Daniels, Carl wondered whether the concierge that worked the evening shift at Walker Tower was the person who had told Reg Daniels his daughter was working as an escort.

Walker Tower was a five minute drive from Police Headquarters. When they arrived, Harry parked the car in the street outside the front entrance that Helen Daniels had described to them. The front doors of the building opened automatically as they approached, and they walked up to the concierge desk, where a grey haired man wearing silver rimmed glasses was taking delivery of several parcels. They waited until he'd signed the delivery docket and turned his attention to them.

'Can I help you, gentlemen?'

Carl took out his badge. 'Inspector West, City Police. 'We're investigating the death of Peter Walker. I'd like to ask you a few questions about people's movements into and out of this building.'

The concierge scratched his head. 'Why? He wasn't killed here.'

'That doesn't mean his killer hadn't visited him at home,' said Carl.

'Oh, I see what you mean.'

'How many people work as concierge on this desk?' said Carl.

'There's six of us. We're here twenty-four-seven but we don't work on the desk all the time. We have other duties as well.'

'What about yourself, do you always work during the day or do you work nights as well?'

'I usually work the four to midnight shift but Phil's on holidays, so we've had to change the roster this month.'

Carl scrolled through the photos on his iPhone until he found the one of Helen Daniels he wanted. 'Do you recognise this young woman?'

'Yeah, she was one of Walker's tarts. She was here every night his missus was out of town.'

'Do you know who she is?'

'She always said her name was Alexis but I knew that was a lie. She's the spitting image of her mother, when she was younger. Her real name's Helen Daniels.'

'How do you know that?'

'Long story. I was keen on her mother before she met Reg. She probably doesn't remember me. She was a little girl the last time I visited their place. She sat on my lap and pulled my moustache.' He smiled. 'I've been interstate for the last ten years. Came back when my wife died a couple of years ago. I caught up with Reg and Maggie down at Morton Sands last summer. Helen had moved out by then. Reg said she was studying law, so I was surprised when she turned up here as a call girl, I can tell you.'

'Did you happen to mention anything about that to her parents?' said Carl.

'Is that a crime?'

'No. That's not a crime.'

Carl showed the concierge a photograph of Dario Finestra. 'Has this guy ever been here?'

'Not to my knowledge.'

'What about this guy?' Carl showed him a photograph of John Drake.

'That's John Drake. I went to school with him. I haven't seen him for years, not since we left school, actually. Sad that he got killed like that, but he's never been here while I've been on duty.'

'Did you know he was one of the owners of the escort agency that Helen Daniels works for?'

The concierge's eyes opened wide. 'John? You're kidding me, aren't you?'

'Afraid not. It's probably why he got killed.'

'Shit, didn't think that would be a dangerous business.'

'What about this guy? Has he ever been in?' Carl showed him a photograph of Ryan Whitaker.

The concierge studied the photograph. 'He's here quite a bit, actually, but I haven't seen him for a few weeks.'

'Who does he come to see?'

'What's his first name?'

'Ryan.'

'He comes to see the woman in 10C.'

'Who's that?'

'Her name's Pam Watson. She's one of those public servants that was on the news the other night, something about corruption.'

'Is she home?'

The concierge checked his monitor. 'Yes.'

Carl found his photograph of Todd Hendri. 'What about this guy? Has he been here?'

The concierge smiled. 'That's Mr Hendri. His mother lives in 16A. He's here most Sundays. Takes his mother out for dinner.'

'Can you give Ms Watson a call, and let her know we'd like to speak to her.'

CHAPTER 35

Pam Watson opened the door to her apartment when Carl pressed the buzzer but made no move to let them in.

'What do you want? I'm not sure I should be speaking to you without a lawyer?'

'We're not here to talk about that, Ms Watson.' Carl showed her his photograph of Ryan Whitaker. 'The concierge downstairs told us Ryan was a frequent visitor. We're looking into his background as part of a murder inquiry. Mind telling us how you know him?'

'You'd better come in.' She stepped back and allowed them to enter the apartment.

10C had a view over the hills, which Carl imagined would provide access to some spectacular sunrises for anyone up that early. He glanced around the open plan apartment as they walked into the family area, and noticed several photographs of a young boy and a girl, who appeared to be in her late teens or early twenties.

'My kids,' said Pam, when she noticed Carl looking at the photographs. 'Shelley and Brian.'

'Nice looking kids,' said Carl. 'Bit of an age gap?'

'Well, things happen. Do you have any children?'

'Yes, a daughter. She was born last night.' He showed her his photograph of Sophie.

'Oh, she's cute. You know your troubles have only just begun, don't you, Inspector? They're beautiful when they're young but things change when they grow up. That's why we know Ryan.'

'Oh?'

'Shelley has a habit. I had to find a way to keep her out of those places in the city where the young ones go to buy drugs. You know, like that place in Long Street you people raided the other week.'

'What's she on?'

'She was on heroin. I've managed to get her into rehab. I hope it works this time.'

'Where does Ryan fit in?'

'He was her supplier.'

'And, you were paying him?'

Pam hung her head. 'It was the only way I could keep her off the streets.'

'Guess that wasn't cheap,' said Carl.

'No, and neither is the rehab.'

'When did you get her into rehab?'

'That Monday I told you I was home looking after Brian. I didn't want to tell you then.'

Carl nodded to show he understood.

'Do you own this place, Ms Watson?'

'Heavens no! I could never afford to buy a place like this.'

'Is it expensive to rent?'

'I suppose it is but I don't really know, actually. Brian's father pays the rent.'

'Oh, and who's that?'

'Not many people know who Brian's father is, Inspector. He's married to someone else but I guess it will come out during the inquiry. His name is Trevor Hunter.'

'Is this the Trevor Hunter that works for the Walker Group?'

'Yes.'

Carl looked at the photographs of Brian and the resemblance became obvious now that he knew what to look for.

'Obvious when you know, isn't it? He looks like his father.'

'When was the last time you saw Ryan?'

'He helped me take Shelley to rehab. He was just as keen to get her off the stuff as I was.'

'Bit unusual for a dealer,' said Carl.

'He might have been a dealer but he wasn't a user, at least that's what he told us.'

'Must have been a bit of a shock to hear he'd been arrested in Bali for possession?'

'I can't imagine what his poor mother must be going through. At least I have a chance of getting Shelley back.' Pam looked out at the view. 'Did you say you were asking about Ryan in relation to a murder inquiry?'

'Yes. It looks like he killed his girlfriend before going to Bali.'

'I saw where she'd been killed. Shelley took that pretty hard. She and George were school friends. In fact, she's the one that introduced her to Ryan. God, she'll be devastated when she hears that.'

Carl wondered how she'd feel when she found out her mother had been arrested for corruption but decided to leave that conversation for another day.

After the meeting with Pam Watson, Carl and Harry went back to Police Headquarters.

'Let's go for a coffee, Harry. We've got some stuff to process,' said Carl, as Harry parked the car.

They walked around to Lena's and ordered.

'What did you make of that?' said Carl.

'Guess it explains the bags of heroin found in Whitaker's apartment, and confirms what the Brocks told us,' said Harry. 'Might also explain why she's on the take if Drake was right. Can't be cheap supporting a daughter's habit.'

Carl took a sip of his coffee and looked around to see who was within earshot. Nearly everyone in the shop was in Uniform.

'I'm intrigued by her confession that Trevor Hunter is the father of her son, and that he's paying her rent.'

'One way of doing child support, I suppose,' said Harry, sampling his coffee to see whether it was cool enough to drink. 'Guess that's something we can pass on to the Corruption Commissioner.'

'What about what the concierge told us about Daniels?' said Carl.

'Sounds like her father knew she was servicing Walker. The question is did he do anything about it?'

'I think he'd have motive. I'd hate to think some old fart was screwing my daughter,' said Carl.

'You've become paternal pretty quickly, Boss. She was only born the other night.'

'It's not only that, Harry. I've met too many people whose daughters have been abused or worse.'

They drank their coffees in silence.

'What are we going to do, Boss? We don't have anything connecting Daniels to Walker's death.'

'Let's see if we can place him at the scene of the crime.'

'How are we going to do that?'

'Walker was killed some time between one thirty and four thirty on the twenty-first of May, a Saturday afternoon. If what Helen told us is right, Reg should have been at the footy. Check the program. Did the Bays play at home that weekend?'

Harry pulled out his iPad and checked online. 'Yes. They played the Eagles at the Bay.'

'Get on to the Bayside Football Club, find out his membership number, and get them to run a check on his ticket. They should be able to tell us when he swiped it at the turnstile on the way in.'

Harry finished his coffee. 'What about the wife, Boss? What if she'd found out he'd been seeing call girls while she was away on business? I don't think Jessika would take too kindly to me doing that.'

'I don't know, Harry. Anyone marrying Walker would have known what he was like, and been prepared to take the risk I'd imagine.'

'But we don't know that for sure, do we?'

'You chase up Daniels. I'll have a word with Mrs Walker. Might be interesting to have our hotshot pursuit driver take me for a ride.' Carl looked at his watch. 'Guess they must be on their way to Morton Sands by now.'

Lisa arrived in the square in front of the Morton Sands Post Office at fifteen minutes to four. She parked the car, pulled on her windproof jacket and woollen hat, and walked along the Esplanade to the Hot Sands Bakery Coffee Shop. She noted that the winter opening hours were from seven thirty in the morning to four in the afternoon. It was five minutes to four. She pushed open the door. There was one customer nursing a coffee at a table next to the window, and Reg Daniels was behind the counter, obviously getting ready to close up shop.

'Hope I'm not too late for a coffee,' said Lisa.

'No, the machine's still on, Luv. What will you have?'

She purchased a takeaway latte and walked back to the

square, where she sat on the bench facing the Post Office in the weak winter sunshine. She sipped her drink and watched the waves splash up against the breakwater. When she'd finished her coffee, she pulled out her iPad and pretended to read while she waited.

At four fifteen, Reg Daniels walked past her and made his way to the Post Office. Lisa snapped a shot of him climbing the three steps into the foyer where the post boxes and the public phone were located, and another of him leaving the building a couple of minutes later with mail in his hand. Then she pointed the iPad at the ocean and took another photograph, to make it look like she was simply taking pictures of the square and the beach.

Reg ignored her when he walked past reading the mail on his way back to the shop.

Five minutes after Reg had disappeared inside the coffee shop, Nigel walked out from behind the bakery, with a camera dangling from a black strap around his neck and walked over to the beach, as if he was just another tourist snapping photographs of the dunes that gave Morton Sands its name.

At four forty, Nigel joined Lisa in the car and they compared notes and photographs.

'There are two cars around the back. A white van and a white sedan; both with Hot Sands Bakery signage.' He showed Lisa his images.

'And, it looks like he goes to the Post Office after he shuts up shop for the day. Right about the time those calls were made.'

Carl signed out early and headed for the hospital. He was keen to see Sophie and find out how Nina was doing. As he drove to the hospital, he hoped they'd solve the Walker case sooner rather than later, so he could take a few days off to be with Nina and Sophie when they were discharged from the hospital.

Frank Mulligan was sitting with Nina when Carl arrived in the nursery ward. Her room was decked out with flowers and cards that had not been there the night before, and there was a large teddy bear propped up in a corner amongst a pile of boxes wrapped in baby pink paper.

Frank stood and shook Carl's hand. 'How's it feel to be a father, Carl?'

'Surprisingly good, actually, Frank.'

Frank turned and looked at Sophie, asleep in the crib next to the bed. 'She's beautiful, isn't she?'

'Luckily she looks more like Nina than me,' said Carl.

'Let's hope it stays that way,' said Frank, winking at Nina. 'I'd better get going so you two can have some time together.'

'Thanks for dropping in, Frank. I'll keep what you said in mind,' said Nina.

Carl sat down on the chair vacated by the priest and pulled it closer to the bed so that he could lean over and kiss Nina.

He held her hand between his on top of the sheets. 'How are you feeling?'

'I'm exhausted. I've had non-stop visitors since ten o'clock this morning. Look at all this stuff.' She waved her arm to take in the room. 'You'll have to take some of it home with you otherwise there will be nowhere for anyone to stand.'

Carl looked at the presents and mentally calculated how many he'd be able to take with him. 'Might have to get a bag.' He turned back towards Nina. 'Have Nancy and Robert been in?'

'Who do you think bought her the teddy bear? You'd think they were the grandparents, they're so excited.'

'Well, I guess this is the closest they are going to get, seeing they don't have any kids of their own.'

'That could work to our advantage, honey, especially when

she's older.'

'Think they might get some competition from the chief and Evelyn,' said Carl, thinking that his daughter wouldn't have any shortage of people to choose from for grandparents.

Sophie stirred and opened her eyes, and then started to cry.

'Can you hand her to me, and then shut the door.'

Carl placed his left hand under his daughter and gently lifted her out of the crib. Her crying intensified. He quickly passed her to Nina and stood to walk over and shut the door. Before he had taken two steps a nurse appeared in the doorway, with a chart in her hand.

'Everything okay, Mrs West?'

'I think she wants a feed.'

'Okay, let's see if we can get her to suckle.'

Carl stood out of the way, while the nurse helped Nina arrange herself and Sophie into a feeding position and waited to see whether Sophie would attach herself to a nipple successfully.

'That's good. She's latched on. Remember to keep her awake while she's feeding, Mrs West, and you'll be fine. I'll drop back in and see how you're doing a bit later.'

The nurse left the room.

'I thought this would be easy,' said Nina, 'but it's not. It's bloody frustrating.'

'I'm sure it will get easier when you've both had more practice.'

'I bloody hope so, otherwise she'll be on a bottle before she get's home.'

'Seems to be doing fine to me,' said Carl.

'And, what would you know about breast feeding?'

'I've had a lot of practice sucking tits, yours especially, and she seems to have my technique.'

Nina laughed. 'Go and find a bag for those presents while I do this. You're making me nervous.'

CHAPTER 36

THE TEAM STOOD around the whiteboard displaying their thoughts and findings on the Walker case.

'How did you go at Morton Sands, Lisa?' asked Carl.

'Daniels went to the post office around four-fifteen to collect his mail,' said Lisa.

'I wonder why he doesn't go earlier in the day,' said Wayne.

'Maybe he does his paperwork last thing,' said Harry.

Carl shrugged his shoulders. 'What did you find out, Nigel?'

'Looks like the bakery has two vehicles. A Mitsubishi van and a Kia sedan. Both white, with Hot Sands Bakery signage on them.'

'No sign of any other vehicles?'

'Not that I could see. I guess it's possible they have a private car.'

'Run a check with Registrations. If they don't, and if Daniels is our killer, someone might have seen a Hot Sands vehicle around Carrick.'

Carl looked at his notes. 'Now, according to his daughter, Daniels is a member of the Bayside Football Club and never misses a game. If he is our killer, he couldn't have been at Carrick and the football at the same time, and it takes at least an hour to drive from Carrick to the Bay. If what Mrs Walker told us is correct, Walker didn't go on his walk until one-thirty, and it took Harry and I a good half hour to walk from Walker's house to where his body was found. If Daniel's killed him, there's no way he could have been at the Bay Oval in time for the start of the main game at two-thirty.'

'How are we going to prove that?' said Wayne.

'When was the last time you went to the football, Wayne?' said Carl.

'Wrong code, Inspector. I like the round ball game,' said Wayne.

'Well, you have to swipe your ticket in the turnstile these days.'

'So how does that help?'

'If Daniels is a member, he'll have a numbered ticket he uses every time he goes to a game, and God only knows how much data they're collecting on their members for marketing purposes. So, there's a chance they'll have a record of when he entered the stadium, right down to the precise second.'

'Ah, I keep forgetting we live in a digital world.'

'Why don't you go with DS Fuller and find out how much data they're capturing?'

'Okay. I'll do that, Inspector.'

'Now, Harry and I spoke to one of the concierges at Walker Tower yesterday. Turns out he's an old boyfriend of Mrs Daniels, and he'd recognised Helen when she was visiting Walker. He's the one that told Daniels his daughter was working as an escort and sent him the link, so Daniels knew Walker was having sex with his daughter. That might be our motive.'

'We need a few of these dots to join up, Inspector, otherwise this is all speculation, isn't it?' said Lisa.

'You're not wrong there, Lisa, so while Harry and Wayne are down at the Bay, you and I are going to have another chat with

Mrs Walker. We need to see her reaction to the news that her husband was entertaining a call girl while she was interstate on business. At this point, she's still in the picture, especially if she's the jealous type.'

'That's not what her friends are saying, sir,' said Lisa. 'They're saying she's a pretty cold fish. Calculating and determined to get her own way are the words they used. In fact, one of them told me she thought Hayley had teamed up with Walker purely for business reasons. She claimed Hayley wanted access to his contacts to get donations for her family's charitable foundation, and that Peter wasn't the first Walker she'd used her sexual charms on. Apparently, she had an affair with James Walker before marrying his father.'

Hayley Walker worked from an office in her penthouse in Walker Tower, and had agreed to an eleven o'clock appointment. Lisa drove Carl through the morning traffic and parked their car across the street from the front entrance to Walker Tower.

Carl introduced himself to the young man on the desk inside the foyer, who checked his screen before ushering them into the elevator that serviced the penthouse. It was a quick ride to the top floor of the building. Obviously, Walker hadn't liked the idea of stopping for the convenience of other residents, thought Carl, as they exited the elevator onto a secure landing outside the door to the penthouse.

The door was opened by Mrs Walker's personal assistant, a young woman dressed in a smart business suit. 'Mrs Walker will be with you in a moment, Inspector. Please take a seat.'

Carl took in the view, and imagined Helen Daniels doing the same on her first visit to the apartment. He glanced over at Lisa, who was also looking out across the city.

'Quite a view, hey?'

'Bit different from the one from our front window.'

'Oh, what can you see?'

'Woolies car park.'

'Must be convenient when you need to go shopping.'

'That's not much consolation. It wasn't there when we bought the house, now we can't sell it.'

'How long's it been on the market?'

'Six months. Looks like we'll either have to give it away or build a bloody big fence.'

The click of a door closing ended their conversation, as Hayley Walker joined them. She was dressed in a business suit similar to the one worn by her personal assistant.

'Are you making any progress on finding Peter's killer, Inspector?'

'We're pursuing a couple of leads, which is why we're here.'

Hayley Walker sat opposite Carl at the table in the centre of the room. 'Go on.'

'Mrs Walker, I discovered something about your husband, quite by accident, while investigating the death of a girl named Georgina Brock.'

'Oh. Who was she?'

'She was a student working as an escort for an agency called Discreet City Escorts.'

'I suppose you're going to tell me Peter was one of her clients.'

'The agency's records show that he'd used her once in the month prior to her death but they also show that he was making regular use of another girl who went by the name of...'

'Alexis,' said Hayley.

Carl looked at her. 'You knew?'

'Who do you think organised them? Surely not Peter?' She laughed. 'He couldn't use a computer to save himself let alone book an appointment online. Don't look so surprised, Inspector. It's not like we were a couple in that sense. Organising a girl for him while I was away was one way of keeping him happy and at home, where he couldn't get himself into too much trouble or make a fool of himself in the public eye.'

Carl glanced at Lisa and caught the fading signs of a smirk leaving her face He recalled the words she'd told him Hayley Walker's friend had used to describe her, and wondered whether Hayley was calculating enough to have disposed of Peter Walker when he'd reached his use-by-date in her plans for him.

'The lead I'm following is connected to that girl. Appears one of the guys working on the desk downstairs recognised her and told her father what she was doing. Her father wasn't very happy about it, and it's possible he may have killed your husband out of a sense of enraged family pride.'

'Does this man have a name?'

'I'm not at liberty to divulge that at present, Mrs Walker, but I'll let you know if what I believe may have happened turns out to be correct.'

'This is a long shot, don't you think, Sarge?' said Wayne, as he parked the car outside the Bayside Oval.

'Let's say it's a theory, Wayne, and we're here to test it,' said Harry. 'We'll either put a spotlight on Daniels or eliminate him as a suspect.'

They walked over to the club's administration office and went inside, where a woman was working behind a large wooden desk.

'DS Fuller to see Howard Brown,' said Harry.

'Through that door, Luv.' She pointed to a door to her right.

They entered the manager's office and found Howard Brown reading the morning's paper.

'Ah, Detective Sergeant, must say your call was a bit of a surprise. Can't say anybody's asked me to do this before. What's going on.'

'We're checking an alibi and thought you may be able to help. Are we correct in assuming that your turnstiles record members' passes being used when they attend home games?'

'Yes, they sure do.'

'If you don't mind me asking,' said Wayne, 'why do you do that?'

'Every ticket is swiped at the turnstiles. That's how we count attendance and it also helps us keep track of which members attend games or not. All helpful for marketing.'

'So, do you have a Reg Daniels from Morton Sands on your membership list, Mr Brown?'

'Do you have a search warrant, Detective Sergeant?'

Harry produced the search warrant Carl had organised for him and showed it to Mr Brown.

'Thanks. Got to protect me backside, you know, in case people start asking questions.'

'No problem. I understand,' said Harry.

'Now let's have a look.'

Harry glanced at Wayne, who was looking at the trophies in the cabinet on the manager's wall.

'Here we are. Member number 156783.'

'Can you find out if he attended the game on the twenty-first of May?'

Mr Brown ran a query on the turnstile database. 'He was here. Ticket was swiped at one-fifteen.'

'Do people swipe on their way out?'

'No.'

'What about if they leave early and then come back in?'

'They'd have to swipe again coming in.'

'Did he only come in the one time?'

'Looks like it.'

'Well, that only means someone used his ticket,' said Wayne.

'Do your members have allocated seats, Mr Brown?'

'They sure do.'

'So, Mr Daniels would be sitting with the same people each home game?'

'He sits between member 156782 and 156784.'

'Were they here that day?'

They waited while Mr Brown ran his query.

'156784 was.'

'Who's that?'

'Someone called Robert Reid.'

'Can I have his contact details?'

'I'll just print them off for you, Sergeant.'

Harry looked at the page Mr Brown handed him and smiled, as he recognised the address of the recently retired DI Reid.

When they were outside the building, Harry called Bob Reid.

'Bob, did you go to the Bays game on the twenty-first of May? It was the one where they thrashed the Eagles.'

'Yeah, it was a great game. Why do you want to know that, Harry?'

'I'm checking an alibi. Do you remember who was sitting next to you?'

'The usual people. Reg on one side and Wally on the other.'

'Did they stay the whole game?'

'Yeah, we had drinks in the bar after. Best game in years.'

The team gathered in the Incident Room for an end of day debrief.

'What did you find out from the football club, Harry?' said Carl.

'Daniels was at the footy when Walker was killed. His ticket was swiped at one-fifteen and DI Reid, who's also a Bayside member, has confirmed he was there for the whole game.'

'Bob Reid? How did you know to ask him?'

'Sits next to Daniels at every home game.'

'Okay, looks like we can cross Daniels off as a suspect in the Walker case, then. That puts us back on square one.'

'I still think we should focus on the wife, Boss. She was there. She had opportunity. She even has a motive, if what she told us about his will is correct.'

'She's certainly a person of interest, Harry, and an interesting one at that. She knew about the call girls. In fact, she told us she was the one who made the appointments for Walker so she could keep him out of the public eye when she wasn't in town.'

'Didn't his first wife tell us she'd heard rumours of Walker being seen around town with young women, Boss?' Harry opened the Notes app on his iPad and scrolled through his interview notes. 'Yeah, here it is.'

'Maybe she found out that he'd been playing outside their agreed rules?' said DC Paterson.

'I think their so-called marriage was some sort of business arrangement,' said DC Templar. 'Maybe she was using him as a way of getting to his contacts for their money, as her friend claimed.'

'What would have been in it for Walker?' said Harry.

'If they've been married for a couple of years, that would mean he married her before his son was killed, and before Imbroglio bought him out. Maybe she was his retirement plan, and for a guy with an ego like his, she'd be quite a catch to brag about, wouldn't she?' said DC Paterson, 'even if she wasn't giving him any sex.'

'The question is whether she's calculating enough to have killed him, once she'd milked all of his contacts to feed her foundation,' said Carl.

'God, we're never going to find any hard evidence, are we?' said DC Beard. 'If I'd killed my husband on the beach with a rope, I would have dropped the rope into the sea and let it wash away.'

'Maybe, Nigel, but you're thinking rationally.'

'Someone who's planned a murder thinks rationally, Inspector. It's only those that act on impulse that don't,' said DC Beard.

'Not necessarily, Nigel. Think about Finestra. I'd say the way he killed those homeless guys was definitely planned. Just look at the equipment he had. But, we wouldn't have him if he hadn't been impulsive,' said Carl. 'I reckon we only got him on camera because he got cocky or careless. But, the other night down at the Bay, you'd have to agree he made a very rash decision?'

DC Beard nodded. 'So, I guess there's always the chance she'll do something that will give her away, then. It's not like she's a professional assassin, like Finestra, is it?'

'She's a bloody professional something, though, Nigel. She's back at work, and she's only just buried him.' Carl paused to collect his thoughts. 'I think we need to probe a little deeper into the Walker family set up. His wife might not be the only one with a reason to kill him.'

'Haven't you interviewed them already?' said DC Templar.

'We haven't spoken to the grandson, Dustin, or his mother. Think we should do that while Dustin is still here.'

CHAPTER 37

CARL HAD ASSUMED that James Walker's widow still lived in the palatial house in the eastern suburbs that she'd shared with her husband, and was surprised when he discovered that she was now living in one of the less affluent areas of Bayside. He didn't know what to expect as they drove to Bayside to interview her and her son, as areas of the suburb were undergoing what town planners referred to as urban renewal, and many of the older dwellings had been demolished and replaced with modern townhouses and condominiums. When Lisa stopped the car in front of the address she had given him, he realised that the woman he'd thought of as a rich widow was living in a dated, semi-detached townhouse in a Bayside backstreet.

He let Lisa ring the bell and admired the small neat garden that separated the house from the street. The door was opened by a young man with blonde hair, who resembled the photos of Peter Walker they had on the Incident Board.

'You must be Dustin,' said Carl, offering his hand. 'Inspector West, City Police. This is my colleague, DC Templar.'

Dustin showed them into the front room and went to get his mother from the kitchen at the rear of the house.

A few moments later, Dustin returned with a tall, athletic looking woman wearing a tracksuit and running shoes.

'Excuse my appearance, Inspector. I've just got back from my run. Please, take a seat.'

'Thank you for agreeing to see us, Mrs Walker. As I mentioned on the phone, we're trying to get a better picture of your late father-in-law that might help us understand who may have wanted to kill him, so anything you can tell us about him could be helpful.'

'Where do you want to start, Inspector?'

'Perhaps you could tell me about your relationship with your father-in-law?'

Marion looked at her son and smiled. 'Peter never liked me, Inspector. As far as he was concerned, I was the tart that got her hooks into his little darling. He never forgave James for marrying me. At best, he tolerated me as the mother of his grandson.'

'That must have been tough. How did your husband cope with his father's disapproval?'

'James knew how to get around him, but there were a lot of things Peter never understood about James.'

Carl got the feeling she'd been loved by her husband and suspected he'd shielded her from his father.

'And, how were things between you and your father-in-law after James' death?'

'Peter got rid of me as soon as he could. Fortunately, James had taken out a life insurance policy in my name, so I was able to buy myself somewhere to live.'

Carl wondered why she'd needed to find somewhere to live. 'What happened to the house you were living in with James?'

'That house was never ours, Inspector. It belonged to the Walker Family Trust. One way Peter made sure James did as he was told, especially after getting me pregnant and then marrying me. The man was a control freak. He sold it, and evicted me, almost immediately after we'd buried James.'

'Didn't your husband have any other assets?'

'Everything was tied up in the firm. The plan was for James to take over when Peter retired.' She paused and looked at the photographs on the wall behind Carl. 'If that had happened, Inspector, we would have been set but nothing belonged to James. It all belonged to Peter or the firm. After James died and Peter decided he'd had enough, he transferred the shares he'd earmarked for James to Dustin, on the condition that Dustin did as Peter directed him at board meetings.'

Carl turned to Dustin. 'Is that why you sold your shares to Mario, Dustin?'

'Partly. I wasn't really all that interested in the business but I wanted to look after Mum.'

That sounded interesting to Carl. 'How did you get on with your grandfather?'

'I'm a twenty-five year old spoilt brat, Inspector. My grandfather indulged me and did his best to turn me against my mother, but the man was a hypocrite. Surely you know of his reputation when it comes to women? My father was nothing like him, in that regard. I can't say I liked my grandfather, Inspector, but Dad always encouraged me to take advantage of his largesse, and,' he smiled, 'I always listened to my father.'

'And, did that work in your favour as far as the will was concerned?'

'I suppose you could say that, Inspector, since he left most of his estate to me. I got most of the cash, his cars and the house at Carrick. He left the penthouse and a couple hundred grand to Hayley, not that she'd need it.'

'Did you know he was going to do that?'

'Yes, he told me about his will when we were discussing selling the firm to Mario. He knew I wasn't interested in the business, and told me I'd be able to set myself up in whatever it was that I decided to do with my life.'

'So, you're fairly well set for whatever that is, then?'

'Yes, and I can look after Mum.'

Another one with a motive thought Carl, but one that would have had to arrange an assassin, since he was in the United States at the time of his grandfather's murder. Carl turned back to Marion.

'Did you know about the will?'

'Dustin told me about it as soon as his grandfather had told him that was his intention. He didn't keep anything secret from me, even if he was told not to tell me.'

Carl decided to change tack. 'How did you get on with his wives?'

'Monica and Rachel made life tolerable for me, at least. They insisted I was included in family gatherings, even if Peter would hardly say anything to me. We did a lot of things together that Peter never knew about, like meeting up in town during the week, or they'd drop by the house without him. Monica, especially, doted on Dustin almost as much as Peter did.'

'What about Hayley?'

Marion looked at her immaculately manicured fingernails. 'Did you know that people have accused her of having an affair with James, Inspector?'

Carl looked at Lisa, who was noting every word spoken. 'We'd heard a rumour.'

'Well, it's not true.' Marion looked him in the eyes. 'Carmel Speld, that's Hayley's mother, well she and I have been friends since we were kids. Carmel and Hayley run the Speld Foundation, which does a lot of work raising money to help the homeless, especially homeless women and children. About three years ago, she asked James to introduce Hayley to some of his friends, so she could talk to them about the work of their foundation. Hayley is very good at soliciting donations. James went to a few functions with her, that's where the stories come from.'

'Were you surprised when she married Peter?'

'Shocked, to be honest. I couldn't believe an intelligent girl like Hayley would fall for Peter's charm. It's not like she didn't know what he was like.'

'Do you think she'd be capable of killing him?'

Marion considered the backs of her hands.

'Who knows what any one of us is capable of, Inspector?'

'Have you ever been to Carrick, Mrs Walker?'

'Many times, Inspector. Most of the family functions, you know, things like birthdays and Christmas, happened at Carrick, and we used it as a beach house most years when Dustin was little. Despite our differences, we usually enjoyed ourselves down there even when Peter was there.'

'Good place to run on the beach, I'd imagine.'

'Yes. Not crowded like the beaches around here.'

'When was the last time you saw Peter alive, Mrs Walker.'

'At James' funeral. The bastard didn't have the decency to evict me himself. I got a letter from his lawyers.'

'I trust you'll understand that I have to ask you this question, but where were you the afternoon he was murdered?'

'Here, Inspector. On my own, seeing that Dustin was overseas.'

Carl climbed into the car and waited for DC Templar to shut her door and slip the key into the ignition.

'What did you make of that, Lisa?'

'I'd say that was a woman with a good reason for killing Walker, Inspector.'

'Certainly hard done by, if what she told us is true.'

'Ironic that Walker left his money to Dustin, who's obviously devoted to his mother, don't you think, sir?'

'Some might call that poetic justice but my problem is she knew that was Peter's plan.'

'Do you think she'd be capable of killing him?'

'Who knows? But it's interesting that she doesn't have an alibi for the day of the murder.'

'Yes, I noted that.'

'We'll need to see if anyone can corroborate her story of being home on the day. Perhaps I'll get Nigel to discreetly ask her neighbours after we've spoken with Monica and Rachel.'

As soon as Monica Webb opened the door of her apartment, Carl got the impression she wasn't pleased at seeing him again.

'I thought you would have had this solved by now, Inspector.'

'Sometimes solving a murder is like looking for a needle in a haystack, Miss Webb. You know it's there, but you just can't see it.'

'Somebody must have seen something, Inspector. The poor man was killed on a public beach in full view of a golf course, in broad daylight. Surely someone must have been playing golf at that time of day? It was a bloody Saturday afternoon, after all.'

'Unfortunately, no-one has come forward, which means I need to ask you some more questions.'

'Well, you'd better come in then. Can't have the neighbours listening, can we?' She stepped back from the doorway and allowed them to enter her apartment. 'Would you like a cup of tea?'

Carl looked at Lisa, who nodded. 'Yes, thank you.'

'Make yourselves comfortable. I'll just put the kettle on.'

Carl looked around the sitting room. Every flat surface held a picture frame with a family photograph. On closer inspection, he realised the photographs were of James and Marion, posing with Dustin at various stages of his life from toddler through to graduation.

Monica came back into the room with a tray holding three cups of tea and a plate of biscuits, which she placed on the table in front of Lisa. She smiled as Lisa passed a cup to Carl and then took out her notebook and pen.

'You must be very proud of Dustin,' said Carl, pointing at Dustin's graduation photograph.

'Not hard when you only have the one grandchild, Inspector, and he's a bright boy. Pity he's not interested in the business.'

'What is he doing with himself?'

'Medical research at some university in America. He did tell me what it was called but my memory's not what it used be. He's here at the moment. Came home for Peter's funeral. I think he'll be here for a few weeks. He has to do something with Peter's estate. Have you met him, Inspector?'

'Yes. We spoke to him and his mother earlier today. Seems like a nice young man.'

'You know, Peter did his best to turn him against his mother. Just goes to show how little the man knew about women and kids.'

'Any particular reason why he wanted to do that?'

'Peter always called Marion a gold-digging harlot. Poor James. He loved his father but he was hopelessly besotted with Marion; and what young man wouldn't have been? You saw what she looks like. Imagine what she looked like twenty-five years ago.' Monica got up and walked over to the mantelpiece above the gas heater and picked up a photograph, and handed it to Carl. 'That was taken at their engagement.'

Carl looked at the photograph. 'He's lucky I didn't meet her first.'

'He was lucky Peter didn't meet her first, and I think that was the real reason for the way Peter treated her. He was jealous. James had something he couldn't have, and I've no doubt he tried. In fact, Marion told me as much herself after he'd divorced me.'

'Obviously, you kept in touch with her going by all these photographs.'

'James was my son as much as he was Peter's, Inspector. Peter may have tried to buy his loyalty with the way he had things set up but he also kept him on a very short leash. The boy worked for peanuts and a dream, but he never forgot his mother. Besides, Marion and I get on quite well, and who do you think did all the babysitting when they were out and about?'

'Do you still keep in contact with Marion?'

'Oh, yes. We catch up every week or so.'

'How do you think she handled James' death?'

'They were a very close couple, Inspector. Nothing like Peter and I had been. She was devastated, of course. Did you know she was on the slopes with him when it happened?'

'No, I wasn't aware of that.'

'They were both crazy about skiing. It was the only reason they ever went on holidays. Even Dustin is a good skier.' Monica paused and then looked at Carl. 'Marion hasn't gone skiing once since James' accident.'

'Marion told us that Peter evicted her after James' funeral.'

'That was dreadful. I told him he was being heartless. He just laughed and told me to mind my own business. Poor girl had to move in with her parents until James' insurance money came through. Can you imagine?'

'Bit ironic that Dustin's using his inheritance to look after his mother, don't you think?'

'It might be ironic, Inspector, but it's exactly what I'd expect him to do. Peter never understood how much that boy loved his mother.'

'Do you think either of them could have killed him?'

'Well, Dustin's definitely out of the picture, Inspector, he was in California. But, as to whether Marion could have killed him?' She paused and looked at the cup in front of her. 'She'd have every reason to hate him enough to kill him, Inspector, but somehow I don't think so.'

'And, where were you on the day Peter was killed, Miss Webb?'

'Oh, I thought you'd never get around to asking me, Inspector.' She smiled. 'I was here watching the Bays thrash the Eagles on the TV.'

'On your own?'

'Who else do you think an old lady would be watching the footy with, Inspector? Of course, I was on my own!'

'Get the impression we might have taken two steps forward and two steps back, Lisa?'

Carl opened his door and slid into the car while Lisa did the same.

'We're still left with a suspect with a good reason to kill him, though, sir. Perhaps even a better reason than his wife might have had to kill him.'

'Can't argue with that, but do you really think she'd be capable of strangling him? Killing someone, even someone you hate, with your bare hands is not all that easy, and there's not much of her, is there?'

'Guess it would be pretty hard to creep up on someone on an open beach, but what if she'd planned to meet him?'

'She'd still have to overpower him, and you've seen the photos. He wasn't exactly a lightweight, was he?'

Lisa steered the car into traffic and headed south along The

Esplanade, until they reached the intersection with Jetty Road, where she turned East, and joined the stream of cars going towards the city.

'What if she didn't kill him herself but hired someone to do it for her?'

Carl smiled. 'How would a suburban housewife go about doing that, Lisa?'

Lisa shrugged her shoulders. 'I guess it's not like you can look one up on the internet, is it?'

'You want to try searching for hiring a hit man or an assassin online. You might be surprised.'

Lisa looked at him. 'You're kidding me, aren't you?'

'Lisa, there are parts of the internet most people don't go. It's called the dark net and, if you're prepared to take the risk, you can find people offering all sorts of what we'd call illegal services.'

'How would we track if she'd done something like that?'

'We'd have to seize her computer, assuming she has one, or get clearance to access her online record from her internet service provider.'

'If she was going to those lengths, wouldn't you think she'd use an internet cafe? I would.'

'Of course there could be an easier way, I suppose. No-one does that sort of stuff for free. We could access her bank account to see if she's made any unusual payments or withdrawn a large amount of cash around the time Walker was killed. In fact, why don't you look into that when we get back to the office? Might give us the evidence we need to get access to her internet records.'

'Do you think it might be worthwhile looking into her background? You never know who she might know right here in town.'

'Sounds like a good idea to me. Ask Nigel to give you a hand after he's spoken to her neighbours, and let me know what you find out.'

CHAPTER 38

ON FRIDAY MORNING, Carl received an email from Crime Stoppers with a link to an mp4 file on their server. He clicked on the link and watched the video that played. It was a recording of a street scene, captured by a dash mounted video camera, and appeared to have been taken at night.

Carl didn't immediately recognise the street and was wondering why they'd sent him the recording, when he noticed a van pulling out of a driveway and moving away from the camera. He watched as the car holding the camera followed the tail lights of the van, and gradually closed in on the back of the van as it slowed to turn left. Carl recognised the intersection when a sign for the Bayside Hotel appeared on the right of the screen. Then he saw the three words on the back of the van: Hot Sands Bakery.

He looked closely at the text of the email and located the mobile phone number the caller had given Crime Stoppers.

'Is that Scott Peters?'

'Yes, who's this?'

'Inspector West, City Police. I'm calling about the video you sent to Crime Stoppers.'

'Is it useful?'

'Where did you get it?'

'I made it.'

'Any reason why you only sent it in now?'

'I didn't know I had it. Let me explain.'

'Go ahead.'

'I turn the camera on every time I'm in the car, you know, just in case. Anyway, I made that recording on the sixteenth of May, on my way to the airport. I left my car in the long-term car park. I only got back yesterday. I thought it might be useful when my mother told me the fire that burnt that office down was on the night I left to go to the Gold Coast.'

'Scott, where are you now?'

'I'm at work. I work at Rileys in William Street.'

'Can you come into Police Headquarters today and make a statement?'

'Sure.'

Carl called Harry into his office.

'Take a look at this.'

Carl showed him Scott Peters' video, and then repeated what Scott had told him.

'Unless someone else was driving that van, Boss, that just about nails him, doesn't it?'

'Get Dean's people to see if they can enhance this video, and then find Nigel and take him down to the Bay and shoot a video along that stretch of Bay Street in daylight. I don't want there to be any doubt that this was taken in the street where Hendri's office is located. We need to pick up the same landmarks. See that mailbox and that pole with the white stripes on it just before the van comes out of the driveway?' Carl jabbed his finger on his monitor. 'We need to know exactly where they are in relation to Hendri's office.'

Carl placed a call to Operations and arranged for a Uniform Patrol to meet him at Morton Sands. Then he summoned DC Paterson into his office. 'Wayne, get your coat. We need to go for a drive to Morton Sands and pick up Reg Daniels.'

It took them just under half an hour to drive to Morton Sands. They parked in front of the Post Office, where Carl had arranged to meet the officers from Uniform. Carl outlined his plan with the constables, and then he and Wayne walked the short distance to the Hot Sands Bakery. Wayne went around behind the building to where the vehicles were parked. Uniform parked their patrol car in the street between the bakery and the bike shop, out of sight of anyone looking through the front window of the coffee shop.

Carl pushed open the door of the coffee shop and was surprised to see Helen Daniels standing behind the counter.

'Hello, Inspector. Can I get you a coffee?'

'Not today, thanks, Helen. Is your father here?'

Helen poked her head through the doorway leading to the room behind the shop. 'Dad! Inspector West is here to see you.'

Reg Daniels came through the doorway wiping his hands on his apron. 'What do you want to see me about?'

'This may seem like an odd question, Mr Daniels, but who drives the bakery's van?'

Reg looked at Carl. 'I'm the only one that drives it. Michael doesn't have a licence and the wife has her own car. Is there a problem?'

'So, you would have been driving the van on the night of Monday, the sixteenth of May?'

'Yeah. I went to the casino with the boys.'

'Didn't go past Todd Hendri's office by any chance?'

Reg shook his head. 'Who's he?'

'John Drake's partner.'

'Didn't know the bastard had a partner.' He glared at Helen, standing behind the coffee machine. 'I'm hoping she'll give it away now that Drake's dead. I've even offered to pay her rent.'

Helen looked away as the door to the coffee shop opened and two uniformed constables walked in and stood behind Carl.

'Better get your coat, Mr Daniels. You need to come with us.'

Reg stood to his full height and crossed his arms on his chest. 'What the hell for?'

'I'm arresting you for setting fire to Hendri's office.'

'You've got to be fucking joking!'

'Arson is not something I joke about, Mr Daniels. Do you have a lawyer?'

CHAPTER 39

MAX WALSH WAS the duty lawyer on the day Carl arrested Reg Daniels, and sat in on the interview with him.

'Mr Daniels, this is a formal interview, so we will be recording what is said and may use it as evidence,' said Carl

'Suit yourself.'

Carl waited while Wayne walked Reg Daniels through the protocol and then asked everyone participating in the interview to state their name for the recording.

'Mr Daniels, would you say you were happy with your daughter's decision to work as an escort?'

Reg's eyes widened slightly and he sat up straight in his chair. 'What father could be happy about that?'

'I understand from what you told DS Fuller that you knew John Drake had recruited her into the business. Is that correct.'

'Yeah, she told us.'

'When did you actually find out she was an escort? Before or after she told you?'

'Before. One of Maggie's old boyfriends works at Walker Tower. He recognised Helen and told us about her visits to that pervert, Walker. Before that we thought she'd moved in with

Drake. Another bloody pervert who couldn't keep his hands off her.'

'Did you ever want to get even?'

'Get even? I wanted to kill the bastard!' Reg slammed his palm onto the table, and then leant back into his chair and grinned. 'Fortunately, some other prick beat me to it.'

Carl took out his mobile phone and located the voice recording from Crime Stoppers. He looked at Max Walsh. 'This is a recording of a call made to the Crime Stoppers Hotline.' He tapped the play arrow.

They listened to a man's voice describing the late-night abduction of John Drake.

'Was that you, Mr Daniels?'

Reg looked at Max Walsh and hung his head.

'You realise I can have a voice analysis run on that recording against your voice on the recording we're making now, don't you?' said Carl.

'Yeah, that was me.'

'What were you doing out at that time of night?'

'I wanted to confront Drake.'

'And, do what?'

'Beat the living shit out of him! Okay?'

Carl paused to let the tension in the room dissipate.

'You know Drake had a partner, don't you?'

Reg crossed his arms on his chest. 'Did he? I didn't know that.'

'I'm not sure I believe you, Mr Daniels.'

'Why not? How is anybody supposed to know who owns the bloody agency? There's nothing on their website. I've looked.'

'Are you sure that's all you did? You didn't happen to go to his partner's office on the evening of Monday, the sixteenth of May, and start a fire by any chance?'

'How could I do that if I don't know who this partner is?'

'So, where were you that night?'

'Like I told you this afternoon. At the casino.'

'What time would you say that you arrived at the casino?'

'We went to the steakhouse first. I would have arrived between six-thirty and seven.'

'Anybody who can verify that?'

'I play with the same group of mates every Monday night. Sometimes we play at home. Sometimes we meet in the casino. Okay?'

Carl pulled out his notebook and a pen, and pushed them across the table to Reg. 'Names and contact details, Mr Daniels.'

When Reg handed back the notebook Carl made a show of reading through the details. 'Can you put your mobile number on the bottom of this list?'

Carl watched while Reg added his mobile number to the list and then asked Wayne to activate the flat screen monitor on the wall.

'When would you say you left home that night?'

'Around six.'

'Anyone who can verify that?'

'My wife, I guess.'

'This is a recording taken by a member of the public in Bay Street, Bayside, on the evening of Monday, the sixteenth of May, this year. You'll see the time stamp in the lower left of the picture.'

Wayne hit the play button and they watched the video captured by Scott Peter's dashcam up to the point where the registration number and the lettering on the rear of the van in front of Scott's car came into view.

'I have confirmed with Registrations that the van on screen is registered to Hot Sands Bakery Pty Ltd, and we all know that the van has not been reported stolen at any time,' said Carl.

Reg looked at Max Walsh. 'Do I have to say anything here?'

'You can choose to remain silent, if you wish, Mr Daniels,' said Max.

'I have another witness that says she saw a van come out of Hendri's car park less than ten minutes before she noticed the fire that destroyed his office on the evening of the sixteenth of May. I've had my officers double check the location of the mailbox and that pole with the white stripes on it that appears just as the van comes out of the driveway, and we have confirmed that driveway is the exit from Hendri's car park.'

Reg crossed his arms.

'You have a motive, Mr Daniels, as you so eloquently told us when we discussed John Drake, and this recording puts you at the scene of the crime.'

'So I went to see him and he wasn't in his office. So what?'

'I thought you didn't know who he was.'

Reg looked at the floor. 'Helen told me about him.'

'Your problem, Mr Daniels, beside the fact that you've lied to me, is the next thing that happened after you visited Hendri's office was that it burnt down. And, I have a report here from a fire investigator confirming that the fire was started by an arsonist.' Carl looked at Reg. 'All the evidence points to you being that arsonist.'

Reg lifted his head. 'I wanted the bastard to suffer like we had.'

CHAPTER 40

DC BEARD KNOCKED on the door of the house opposite Marion Walker's, and showed his badge to the elderly lady that answered his knock.

'I was wondering if you were home on Saturday the twenty-first of May, the day the Bays thrashed the Eagles?'

'Only until mid-day, Luv, then we went to the game. We never miss a game when they play at home.'

'Do you know the lady that lives across the road in number eleven by any chance?'

'Well, I've met her, but she keeps pretty much to herself. Why do you want to know?'

'I need to confirm her whereabouts on that day. Did you happen to notice whether she went out before you went to the football?'

'Just a minute, young man. I'll ask my husband. He's in the garden every Saturday morning. If anyone had seen her, it would be Bill.'

Nigel surveyed the manicured garden as he waited on the front veranda. A picture of his father down on his hands and knees weeding the front lawn popped into his mind. He didn't think he'd ever be seen doing that and was thankful the apartment he shared with Lily was on the third floor, a long way from the closest patch of lawn in the park opposite the building. He didn't mind looking at grass but he hated cutting it, thanks to all those weekends he'd spent behind the lawn mower before he'd managed to escape from home.

'Detective, this is my husband, Bill.'

Nigel shook hands with the white haired man that stepped out onto the veranda.

'Understand you want to know if the woman over there went out the day the Bays played the Eagles, a couple of weeks back?'

'That's right.'

'As the wife probably told you, I work out here in the garden every Saturday morning, unless it's raining of course.'

'I'm pretty sure it didn't rain that Saturday,' said Nigel.

'No, and that's probably why the Bays played so well. Did you see the game?'

'Only the highlights on the telly. Had to work that weekend. So, did you notice whether she went out or not?'

'She drives one of those little Mazdas. A blue one. I reckon she went out about eleven thirty. Got no idea what time she came back, though. Her car was in the driveway when we got home from the footy, around six.'

Nigel took a formal statement over a cup of tea in the front room of the house before knocking on the door of the next house, and discovering that the little blue car had been seen returning to number eleven around four in the afternoon on the twenty-first.

While he was walking back to his car, a blue Mazda 323 turned into the driveway of number eleven. He wrote the registration number into his notebook and waited for the woman driving the car to go inside the house. Then he pulled out his iPhone and snapped a photograph of the rear of the car.

When he got back to Police Headquarters, he arranged access to the recordings from the traffic cameras on the Southern

Expressway, the road that carried traffic from the metropolitan area to the southern suburbs and the towns, like Carrick, on the South Coast.

DC Templar read the copy of James Walker's marriage certificate that the Registrar of Births, Deaths and Marriages had sent her. Then, she researched Marion Amber Stormer and discovered she'd been a successful model before marrying James and giving birth to Dustin. A review of the City Times archives provided a string of stories from the social pages, showing the young Walker couple entertaining and being seen about town, and a collection of more recent pieces written at the time of James Walker's death. There was no further mention of Marion following a story reporting on James' funeral. It was like she had ceased to exist once he'd been buried.

She was about to request a warrant to search Marion's bank accounts when Nigel called her and told her what he'd found out, and asked her to join him in reviewing the recordings from the cameras on the Southern Expressway.

When Carl and Wayne returned from interviewing and charging Reg Daniels, they discovered Harry, Nigel, and Lisa in a huddle around the largest monitor in the Incident Room looking at traffic recordings.

'What are you lot up to?' said Carl.

'Mrs Walker lied to us,' said Lisa.

'Which Mrs Walker?'

'Marion,' said Lisa.

'There,' said Nigel. 'That's the turnoff for Carrick, and there she goes.'

Harry hit the pause button and then the key to print the screen. 'Boss, we have her driving towards Carrick at 12:34 on the twenty-first of May, and coming back onto the Expressway from Carrick at 15:17. Looks like she was in Carrick when Walker was being murdered.'

'Circumstantial,' said Wayne. 'You've only got her heading towards and coming from Carrick at specific times on that date. There are lots of other places she could have been between those times besides Carrick. For all we know, she could have visited Spring Gulley or Mount Compass, or any of the other little towns between the expressway and Carrick.'

'Maybe,' said Carl, 'but she also told me that she was at home that afternoon.'

'Now that we know what we're looking for, Boss, why don't we see if anybody remembers seeing that car in Carrick?' said Harry.

'How can we do that without alerting her?' said Lisa.

'I've been thinking about the crime scene,' said Carl, sitting on the table under the whiteboards, 'and how Monica Webb described it as being in full view of the golf course. Well, it's not, is it? There's a row of bloody sand dunes between the golf course and the beach where the body was found. When Harry and I visited the scene, we thought that the killer probably left his car on the road between the golf course and the sand dunes. In fact, there was an indistinct set of footprints leading from the beach up through the sand dunes to that road. But that road is in full view of the golf course. There's a green almost on the fence line. Would someone have parked there while they were committing a murder?'

'Not likely,' said Wayne.

'Harry, bring up the crime scene on Google Earth.'

They waited while Harry played with Google Earth, and then zoomed in on the address for Peter Walker's villa at the southern edge of Carrick.

'Okay, move along the beach to where he was killed,' said Carl.

'That looks like the spot,' said Harry.

'Pan over the sand dunes towards the golf course,' said Carl.

Harry zoomed in and slowly moved along the fence line separating the golf course from the road. 'There. Look! That looks like a gate.'

'Zoom out again, Harry. Find the clubhouse. I reckon that's where the car park is.'

They watched as the scene receded, and a row of trees traced a pathway from the gate in the fence to the clubhouse car park, about two hundred metres inside the fence line from the road.

'She could have parked there and walked over to the beach and back, and nobody would have taken any notice,' said Carl.

'How would she know he'd be on that stretch of beach?' said Wayne.

'She probably only had to know he was in Carrick,' said Carl. 'If Walker was anything like the rest of us, he'd have been a creature of habit. She'd have known his routine if she'd ever spent any time at Carrick or asked his wife.'

'What do you want to do, Boss?' said Harry.

'Ring the golf club and see if they keep records of who uses their car park.'

Harry went to his desk to make the call.

'What got this going?' said Carl.

'One of her neighbours told me she'd left home around eleven thirty in the morning, and another that he'd seen her car come back around four on the day the Bays thrashed the Eagles,' said Nigel, 'so I figured that if she'd gone to Carrick she would have used the expressway, which is monitored twenty-four-seven.'

'Good work, Nigel.'

Carl smiled, as Nigel blushed and the others slapped him on the back.

Harry rejoined them. 'Members park for free but non-members have to use a credit card to open the entrance. They're sending through the list of credit cards used on the twenty-first.'

When the list arrived from the Carrick Golf Club it contained thirty-five credit card numbers, each date stamped with the time the card had been used to open the gate to get into and to exit the car park. Harry ignored the numbers used in the morning and sent the others to his contact at B&A Bank before going home.

CHAPTER 41

CARL ARRIVED at City Hospital right on nine-fifty and made his way up to the nursery ward with the baby capsule. Nina was sitting in the chair beside the bed, all packed and ready to go when he walked into her room, with Sophie asleep in her arms. Carl placed the capsule on the bed and bent over and gave Nina a kiss.

Nina gently placed Sophie into the capsule. 'I've signed the forms, honey. We're clear to go. Come on. I can't wait to get out of here so I can sleep in my own bed, and not have someone waking me up every minute to see if I'm still alive.'

'I thought you liked it here?'

'It's a hospital, sweetheart, not a bloody five-star hotel with room service. Everything happens according to their timetable. It's enough with madam here wanting to be fed every three or four hours, without some nurse coming in between feeds and wanting to poke something into me as well.'

'Okay. Let's get you home, then.'

Carl picked up the capsule with one hand and Nina's bag with the other, and they walked slowly towards the elevators to start their journey home.

Despite all the times he'd practiced, it still took Carl several attempts to lock the baby capsule in place on the back seat of the car. 'These things are definitely childproof. You can't get them in or out without reading the bloody instructions.'

'I'm sure you'll get the hang of it.'

'I bloody hope so, or Sophie's going to be spending a lot of time at home.'

Nina laughed. 'Come on. You worked out how the remote worked on the TV, didn't you?'

When they got home, Carl set about reversing all the work he'd done to secure Sophie for her ride home, in order to get her out of the car and take her inside.

'You do some cleaning or something?' said Nina, on noticing the tidiness of the apartment.

'Had Marisa give the place a once over yesterday.'

'Thought we were going to let her go.'

'Thought you might appreciate a bit of help while you get on your feet. It's not like she costs a fortune.'

Nina kissed him on the cheek. 'Thank you for doing that.'

'Where do you want me to put Sophie?'

'Put the capsule on the table. I'll make up her cot and we can put her in there.'

'I've already done that. It's next to our bed.'

Nina looked at him. 'Next to our bed? How you'd know I'd want it there?'

'Lisa told me that was the best place to put it. Said you wouldn't want to be running all over the house at all hours of the night.'

'Did you do that shopping I asked you to do, honey?'

'It's in the kitchen. I did it before I came to the hospital. Do you want a coffee or something?'

'Coffee would be nice.'

Carl checked on Sophie asleep in the capsule on the table and hoped she'd wake up so he could cuddle her. He was tempted to tickle her but decided that would be a mistake, especially if instead of smiling at him she started crying. He went into the kitchen and started on the coffees as Nina came in and transferred Sophie to the cot in their bedroom.

'Let's make the most of these few minutes, honey, before she wants to be fed.'

As he handed Nina her coffee, Carl wondered how long it would be before this new life took on a sense of the routine, and recalled that Charlie Head had warned him it wouldn't be any time soon.

CHAPTER 42

AT TEN-THIRTY ON TUESDAY MORNING, the bank responded to Harry's request for account holder details of the credit cards used to access the Carrick Golf Club car park on the afternoon of the twenty-first of May.

Harry looked at the list of account holders. Marion Walker's name was not on the list. He turned to DC Templar. 'Lisa, what did you say Marion Walker's maiden name was?'

'Stormer, Sarge.'

Harry picked up his phone and called Carl.

'Boss, just got the credit card details from the bank. Mrs Walker isn't on the list but there's a Malcom Stormer on the list. Stormer is her maiden name.'

Carl looked over the side fence into Marion Walker's backyard while Harry knocked on her front door.

'Be with you in a minute!'

Carl heard several doors being closed and then the sound of someone walking in heels towards the front door.

'Oh, I was expecting someone else,' said Marion.

'We have a few questions, Mrs Walker. Do you mind if we come in?'

Marion looked at her watch. 'Will you be long? I'm going out.'

'Should only take a few minutes,' said Carl.

'Okay, otherwise I could meet with you later,' said Marion.

'I think now would be best, Mrs Walker.'

Marion opened the door fully and let them in.

'What is it you want to know?'

'Mrs Walker, you told me you were here, at home, on the afternoon that your father-in-law was killed.'

'That's right, I was.'

'Do you know how many traffic cameras there are on the Southern Expressway, Mrs Walker?'

'Quite a few I'd imagine. Why is that important?'

Carl turned to Harry. 'Show her the pictures.'

Harry opened his iPad and located the images he'd captured from the expressway cameras, and then handed it to Marion. 'Scroll through those to the right, Mrs Walker.'

'That's my car,' said Marion.

'See those figures at bottom right?'

'Yes.'

'They're the timestamp. They tell us when the picture was taken.'

Marion's eyes widen. 'It says the twenty-first of May. Oh, now I get it. You think I went to Carrick that day.' She handed the iPad back to Harry. 'I didn't. I was here, except for when I drove over to my brother's. He borrowed my car, but I had no idea he'd gone down the Southern Expressway.'

'Is your brother's name Malcolm by any chance?' said Carl.

Marion sat down. 'Yes.'

'Why was he driving your car?'

'His was in for repairs and he needed to finish a job out at Northfield. I wasn't using mine, so I lent it to him for a few hours so that he wouldn't have to use a taxi.'

'Does he play golf?'

'Golf? You've got to be kidding. Malcolm couldn't hit the side of a barn with a basketball, let alone hit a golf ball.'

'What does he do?'

'He's an electrician.' She looked at Carl.

He watched as realisation spread across her face.

'Oh my God! What has he done? I never thought he do that. I thought he was only joking when he said he'd...' She put her hands over her mouth.

'Do what?' said Carl.

'Kill Peter,' she whispered. 'I thought he was just bullshitting like he always does; besides, it was months ago when I was staying with Mum and Dad after Peter had me evicted.'

'Did he know about the terms of the will?'

'Yes.'

'We will need a formal statement, Mrs Walker.'

Marion was signing the statement when there was a knock on the front door.

'I'll get it,' said Carl.

He opened the door to find Hayley Walker, dressed for her luncheon date with Marion, standing on the porch.

'Hello, Inspector. What are you doing here?'

Carl smiled. 'Come in Mrs Walker. Marion won't be long, we're just about finished.'

Carl stepped outside and took out his mobile phone, while Hayley went in to find Marion.

'Wayne, pick up Stormer. And, Wayne, treat him as dangerous.'

Carl watched Malcolm Stormer, who was sitting in interview room three, through the two-way mirror. He was staring at the ceiling. He didn't look anything like his sister. He was dressed in dirty grey work overalls, with his hair buzz-cut short. Carl decided he looked a little overweight, and then looked at his watch and wondered what was keeping Stormer's lawyer.

Ten minutes later, Bernard Hemmings, from Knight and Freeman, was escorted down the corridor to interview room three.

'Sorry to keep you waiting, Inspector. Had a bit of trouble getting away from my last client. What's Mr Stormer being charged with?'

'Homicide,' said Carl.

'That's not my usual brief, Inspector. I usually defend claims of criminal negligence.'

'Do you want to call in someone else from your firm?'

'Let's do the initial interview and let me decide. Okay?'

Carl ushered the lawyer into the room and they waited while Harry stepped Malcom Stormer through the protocols.

'Do you have a credit card, Mr Stormer?' said Carl.

'Yeah.'

'Got it on you?'

Malcolm reached inside his overalls, pulled out his wallet and extracted his credit card, which he placed on the table in front of him.

'Have you ever reported it lost or stolen?'

'No.'

'Where are we going with this, Inspector?' said Bernard.

'That will become clear in a moment, Mr Hemmings,' said Carl

Carl pushed a sheet of paper across the table to Malcolm. 'Mr Stormer, this is a list of the credit cards that were used to access the car park at the Carrick Golf Club on the twenty-first of May this year. Take a look and tell me if you can see your credit card on the list.'

Malcolm crossed his arms and stared at Carl without looking at the sheet of paper.

'For the record, Mr Stormer's credit card is listed as being used to enter the car park of the Carrick Golf Club at one thirteen pm and to exit the same car park at two fifty-eight pm on the twenty-first of May.'

'So, I went to a golf club. So, what?'

'Tell me about your sister, Mr Stormer? Why were you driving her car on that day?'

'Who says I was driving her car?'

'She does. In fact, she told us she lent it to you so you could complete a job at Northfield. That's a long way from Carrick, Mr Stormer.'

Malcolm turned to his lawyer. 'Do I have to put up with this shit?'

'You don't have to answer any of his questions but we can't stop him asking them.'

'Do you get on with your sister, Mr Stormer?'

'She's my sister. What do you think? Course I get on with her.'

'Would you describe your relationship as close?'

'Pretty close. There's only the two of us. I've been looking out for her ever since she was a kid.'

'Would you do anything to protect her?'

'Wouldn't you for your little sister?'

'What did you think of her marriage to James Walker?

'Jim was alright. We got on pretty well. It was his prick of a father that was the problem. Do you know the bastard kicked Marion out of her house with fuck all, right after Jim died? What sort of a father-in-law is that?'

'And, you did something about that, didn't you?'

'Too fucking right I did!'

'You went to Carrick and sorted out Walker, didn't you?'

'You don't have to answer that,' said Bernard.

'Yeah,' said Malcolm, leaning back in his chair. 'I sorted him out alright.'

Carl thought he could see a big weight lifting as Malcolm relaxed his shoulders and let out a deep breath.

'How did you know where to find him?'

'Marion told us all about their flash holiday house. I used to listen to her stories and wish I had a place like that. She even invited me down once, when the old man was overseas and Dustin was little. One of his birthdays I think. When I saw it, I have to admit I was jealous. Then the bastard took it away from her. Kicked her out like she wasn't family. Well, she's got it back now, hasn't she?'

'I take it you knew about the will?'

'Yeah. She told me about that after he'd kicked her out of her house.'

'How did you know Walker would be at Carrick on that particular weekend?'

'I did a job for a lady in Walker Tower on the Friday before. I overheard Walker telling her he was going down to Carrick for the weekend.'

'How did you kill him?'

'Strangled him with a bit of rope. It was too easy. He didn't even hear me walking up to him. Silly prick was meditating or something.'

'Just out of interest, Mr Stormer, why did you take your sister's car?'

'Mine's got my name all over it.'

Carl turned to Bernard Hemmings. 'I'll send you a copy of the transcript. The Magistrate's hearing should be first thing in the morning.'

THE SUSPENDED members of the Office of State Supply Contracts Approval Committee convened for an informal meeting over coffee in Sonya Curtis' apartment to prepare themselves, in direct contravention of the order issued by the Corruption Commissioner banning them from meeting prior to the start of his inquiry.

Helen Stein had picked up Mary Grant and Pam Watson in her son's car, and driven them into the underground car park, before they'd entered the building through its rear entrance after buzzing Sonya to let them in.

'How are we going to handle this?' said Helen, as Sonya served hot carrot cake and coffee.

'I've given this some thought,' said Sonya, sitting at the table with them. 'He needs a money trail or a trail of gifts or other perks provided to us to prove corruption. He needs to show that we got something in exchange for renewing the contracts. Otherwise all he can argue is that we didn't follow due process or that we're incompetent.'

'Well, we did get paid,' said Mary.

'I know that, Mary, and you know that, but how's he going to find out unless one of us tells him? It's all offshore. In fact, we need to be offshore to access it.'

'Can't they track that these days?' said Helen.

'Only if the money going into those accounts leaves Australia or if we're silly enough to try and access those accounts from here. I hope you all realise that,' said Sonya.

'What if he gets a search warrant?' said Pam.

'Look, the accounts aren't even in our names,' said Sonya.

'Yes, but we've all got cards to access our accounts when we're in Europe. What if he finds them?' said Pam.

'It's up to us to make sure that doesn't happen. Hide your card somewhere away from where you live, if you have to,' said Sonya. 'This won't go on forever. Just remember where you put it.'

'Are we certain Trevor's honoured his end of the bargain and only used offshore money to pay us?' said Mary.

'He's not stupid, Mary,' said Pam. 'Do you think he'd want a trail leading back to him?'

'So, how are we going to explain awarding the contracts to Walker when there were other tenders at more competitive prices?' said Helen.

'Same as we always have, Helen. It's all in our charter. We aren't charged with getting services at the cheapest price, despite what most people think. We're charged with ensuring the government gets value for money, and Walkers have always provided top service. We don't get any complaints about their cleaners, not like we get from most of the others, and let's remember that they clean two of our most sensitive buildings: City Hospital and Police Headquarters. We can justify the price we pay on the basis of what it costs to get security clearances for people to work in those buildings, and Walkers have saved the government heaps there with their low staff turnover.'

Mario Imbroglio sat in his office sipping coffee while he waited for Trevor Hunter to join him.

The family was not happy that Gianni had been caught up in the execution of John Drake and the extortion of Todd Hendri. At least he'd been told that Gianni would live to tell the tale, but it was likely that Dario Finestra would meet with an accident in prison before he was tried for the murder of Drake and three homeless men. The family did not forgive freelance acts of senseless violence on innocent victims by any of its members, no matter how talented.

Trevor arrived to discuss how they were going to handle the Corruption Commissioner's probe into their business dealings with the Office of State Supply.

'The family is not happy about this, Trevor. We don't need to do these types of deals anymore.'

'Well, things were different when this started. Walker was desperate for the cash flow.'

'I don't think anyone is going to believe that, and besides, I'm sure they'd argue we were taking advantage of the fact that he's dead and can't defend himself, if we go down that path.'

'Well, he never dealt with State Supply in any case. It was always me. He just expected that I'd make it happen and turned a blind eye to how I did it.'

Mario smiled. Peter Walker had been much like his own father in that regard.

'If it comes to the crunch, Trevor, you're going to have to take a hit for the family on this one.'

Trevor poured himself a coffee. 'How are we going to make it look like it was all my doing?'

Mario rubbed his hands together. 'I've had a look at the way Walker set up your remuneration. You always got a bonus if you managed to get those contracts renewed at a premium. That's our solution. You did it without management knowledge to ensure your bonus. Pretty straight forward, wouldn't you say?'

'What if they don't buy it?'

'Mate, I don't want this little fiasco threatening the casino deal, so it's up to you to make sure they understand you were responsible for all aspects of the negotiations for getting those contracts renewed. That's precisely what I'll be telling them if I'm called to testify.'

Trevor took a sip of his coffee. 'But there's no way they can show I paid them anything.'

'Then you'll come out of this looking like a smart operator that got the best deal for your boss. And, when that happens there will be no more payments for getting those contracts renewed. Once the casino is built we'll no longer need the business.' Mario stood to indicate the meeting was over. 'You'd better start reading up on casino operations, Trevor, otherwise I'll have to let you go.'

Trevor shrugged. 'Casino operations? What part do you want me to look into?'

'Internal security. I need someone we can trust to keep an eye on the employees working the tables. Of course, if things don't work out with this inquiry, Trevor, you'll be facing early retirement.'

'Yeah, right, Mario. Think I'll go read up on casinos.

Corruption Commissioner Patrick Flynn met with Liam Winter, who was leading the investigation into the members of The Office of State Supply's Contracts Approval Committee, for an update.

'Think we have something, Patrick,' said Liam, placing a

folder onto the table between them. 'I've been looking at their bank accounts.'

'Thought you said there was no sign of any payments into those accounts?' said Patrick.

'Sometimes it's what's not there that tells you what you want to know. Take a look at this.' He pushed a sheet of paper across the table to Patrick. 'This is a page from Curtis's credit card account. That transaction I've highlighted is payment for a trip to London that she booked in October last year and took in January this year. She was away for six weeks.'

Patrick raised an eyebrow. Liam presented him with another page.

'This shows all the transactions on her credit card between the date she flew out and when she returned. This transaction,' Liam pointed to a highlighted row of numbers, 'is payment for a book in the airport terminal the day she left. The next transaction is dated mid-February.'

Patrick looked at the page and then at Liam. 'So, how did she pay for her accommodation and meals while she was away?'

'She'd have several options.' Liam checked them off on his fingers. 'She could have taken foreign currency, travellers cheques, one of those prepaid travel cards or someone else paid for her.'

'Or, she has access to an overseas account,' said Patrick.

'Well, given that she'd have to take money out of one of her accounts to buy foreign currency or travellers cheques or to load up a prepaid card, and there's no evidence of any large cash withdrawals or transfers from any of her accounts, I think we're left with only two options. Either she has a patron or she has an undisclosed account somewhere, possibly in Europe.'

'What about the others?'

'Once I knew what I was looking for it was obvious. Stein and Grant are frequent overseas travellers as well, and their credit card accounts have a similar pattern. They purchase the tickets but pay for nothing else while they are away apart from some minor items in airports.'

'What about Watson?'

'She's the only one that hasn't been overseas in the last five years but Trevor Hunter from Walkers is paying her rent.'

Patrick opened his folder. 'I had an email from the police about that. Seems she told them that Hunter is the father of one of her children. Here it is.' He slid the print out across the table. 'You might want to confirm that before we ask her in public.'

Liam chuckled. 'Ironic, don't you think, Patrick? The only member of the committee we have a direct money trail to is the only non-decision maker on the committee. Watson's the secretary.'

'That may be so, Liam, but according to Paul Murphy, she's the one that documented the decisions and liaised with Walkers through Hunter. Be interesting to know how generous Hunter has been in supporting his child.'

Steven Wilmington sat next to his wife's bed in the hospice, holding her hand. It felt almost lifeless in his. There was no warmth and no movement. Her doctors had told him she was dying, and apart from the fact that her heart was still beating and she was breathing, it appeared to Steven that she was already dead. It had been five years since the stroke had sent her into a coma.

'I've been a fool, Mary. I let my pride get in the way of my duty. I suppose I should never have started the affair but I was lonely with you locked away inside your body out of reach. Now I've had to resign. I'm sorry. I know you'd be disappointed in me, but it would be so much better if you were still here to enjoy my retirement with me.'

He squeezed her hand gently. He knew she couldn't hear him or respond even if she could, but who else was there to pour his heart out to. Sonya had made it clear their relationship was over. Even he could see there was no way it would survive the scandal of the public scrutiny it was about to receive. As he watched the slight movement of Mary's chest that betrayed her living state, he wondered if there was any truth in Drake's allegations and if Sonya had been lying to him all along. He hoped not. He hoped the inquiry wouldn't be the end of her career like it had been for his.

He watched the monitor connected to Mary to track her vital signs. The line was still moving. He looked at her chest again. It was hardly moving at all. He'd agreed to them disconnecting the oxygen. He didn't see the point of prolonging her ordeal any longer than necessary.

They'd been married for nearly forty years; years that Steven mostly thought of as good years. He thought back to when they'd met during orientation week at the start of their first year at university. She'd been full of life then, dragging him away from his books to party in the city. He missed the Mary of those days, and the Mary that had become the mother of their daughter.

A shadow fell across the bed.

'Hello, Dad. I hope I'm not too late.'

Steven stood and embraced his daughter, who'd flown in from England after he'd called to tell her Mary was dying. She'd come straight from the airport and looked like she needed a sleep. To Steven, she looked just like her mother. He couldn't hold back his tears.

'It's alright, Dad. I'm here now. How is she?'

Steven sniffed and wiped his eyes with the back of his hand. 'She seems peaceful. She's stopped thrashing about in the bed.'

Beep! Beep! Beep!

Steven looked at the heart monitor. It was flat lining.

A nurse rushed into the room and felt for a pulse.

'I'm sorry, Steve. She's gone.' She switched off the machine and the beeping stopped.

'I guess it's for the best,' said Steven. 'She's free now, and I can get on with the rest of my life.'

CARL STOOD next to Sophie's cot and gazed down at his sleeping daughter. It seemed to him that she only did two things: sleep and feed. He corrected himself. No, she did three things. She also snuffled and snorted loudly enough to wake him up in the middle of the night.

He wondered when she'd be awake long enough for him to enjoy holding her. The only time he got to play with her was when it was his turn to give her a bath, and that was always tempered with his concern for holding her correctly so she wouldn't drown or hurt herself in any way. Whenever he undressed her for a bath, he was amazed at how tiny she was, and always wondered how she would ever grow into a woman like her mother.

Nina came in and stood beside him. 'Is this how you're going to spend your time off?'

'She's so beautiful. I could stand here all day.'

'How about spending some time with me? At least I'm awake, and I could use some adult company.'

'You've only been home a week. What are you going to be like after twelve months?'

'That's why you need to spend some quality time with me, so I don't go nuts.'

They went out into the kitchen where Carl made coffee.

'That bad? I thought you wanted to be a mother.'

Nina hit him in the shoulder with the palm of her hand. 'But I don't want to be a single mother. I've hardly seen you since I got home from the hospital, and you're asleep most of the time you're here.'

'Well, you've got my undivided attention for the next two weeks, sweetheart.'

'I doubt I'll ever have your undivided attention ever again, Carl West. Look at you. You're already a doting father. What are you going to be like by the time she's fifteen?'

'Not like Reg Daniels I hope.'

'What's that supposed to mean?'

'I don't want to turn into one of those possessive fathers that refuses to let his kids grow up and have a life of their own.'

Nina draped her arms around his neck. 'I don't think you'll have to worry about that, sweetheart, but I don't want you turning into one of those fathers that scares away her boyfriends either.'

'Boyfriends? She's going to have boyfriends?'

Nina tousled his hair.

'Come here and give me a cuddle.'

A NOTE FROM PETER

If you enjoyed **Whistleblower,** you can help other readers share your enjoyment by telling them about the book and writing a review.

Drop by at **www.petermulraney.com** and join my **Crime Readers Group** to download a free copy of **_Deadly Sands_** and be one of the first to know when my next book will be released.

ACKNOWLEDGMENTS

A book is a community project. I'd like to acknowledge the emotional support I received from Toni during the writing of this book, and the editorial assistance provided by Francesco during the massaging of the original manuscript into the final book. He was also looking over my shoulder when we designed the cover.

This book has also received assistance from the members of my Street Team, who act as beta readers and provide feedback that always improves the quality of the final product.

It's also great to have readers who write reviews and spread the work among their friends.

A big thank you to you all.

Everyday Business Skills

Everyday Project Management

Everyday Productivity

Everyday Money Management

Writings of the Mystic

Sharing the Journey: Reflections of a Reluctant Mystic.

A Question of Perspective

My Life is My Responsibility: Insights for Conscious Living

I Am Affirmations: The Power of Words

Beyond the Words: Reflections on I Am Affirmations

Mystical Journey: A Handbook for Modern Mystics

Sharing the Journey Coloring Books

Mandalas

Mandalas by 3

Sharing the Journey Coloring Journals

Sharing the Journey Coloring Journal

Discovery

Reflection